FAMILY SECRETS

A Whispering Pines Mystery

Shawn McGuire

OTHER BOOKS BY SHAWN MCGUIRE

WHISPERING PINES Series
Missing & Gone, prequel short story
Family Secrets, book 1

THE WISH MAKERS Series
Sticks and Stones, book 1
Break My Bones, book 2
Never Hurt Me, book 3
Had a Great Fall, book 4
Back Together Again, book 5

Gemi Kittredge mystery novellas
One of Her Own
Out of Her League
Over Her Head

Short Stories
The Door
Escaping the Veil in Off Beat: Nine Spins on Song

FAMILY SECRETS

A Whispering Pines Mystery

Shawn McGuire

Brown Bag Books

Copyright © 2017 Shawn McGuire
Published by Brown Bag Books
ISBN-13: 9781546719892
ISBN-10: 154671989X

For information visit:
www.Shawn-McGuire.com

Cover Design by Steven Novak
www.novakillustration.com

First Edition/First Printing July 2017

For Rachael.
Thanks for luring me to the dark side.

psithurism

(n.) The sound of the wind in the trees and rustling of leaves.

Chapter 1

"I'M LOSING IT, MEEKA."

My West Highland White Terrier sneezed in response. Most likely she was agreeing with me, but she was also mad, so I couldn't be sure. She loved car rides, which to her meant around town, getting out often to meet people. Five hours crated in the cargo area of my ten-year-old Jeep Cherokee made for one angry pup.

Had we gone fifteen miles yet? I forgot to check my odometer against that last sign. It had probably only been five. All I knew for sure was that I'd been driving on the two-lane country road through Wisconsin's Northwoods for so long, a funhouse effect had settled in. The never-ending tunnel of pines, oaks, maples, birches, and other species I couldn't identify was not my normal. I was used to row after row of houses crammed close together. Row after row of trees, not so much.

After another couple of minutes, we passed a sign so small I almost missed it: *Whispering Pines 5 miles.*

"We're almost there, girl. Less than ten minutes and you'll be running your little legs off."

My phone rang, and my mom's face gazed at me from the phone in the holder clamped to the air vent. I reached a finger toward the answer button but froze before touching it. I told her I'd call when I got to Gran's. Guess she thought I should be there by now. I was twenty-six years old. When was she going to stop micromanaging my life?

The phone rang for a fourth time then went quiet. I clenched my hand into a fist and waited for her inevitable re-call. After a minute and no ringing, I relaxed and silently vowed to call her once I got to the house.

Up ahead on the right, the sign indicating the beginning of the village limits appeared. I slowed, checked that there was no one behind me, then pulled to a stop. The impressive wooden marker had to be at least ten feet wide and eight feet tall, the logs on either side were a good foot-and-a-half or two in diameter. It appeared to have been hand-carved by an artisan rather than machine-lathed.

Welcome to Whispering Pines
Est. 1966

A symbol was etched into the wood below the date—a circle with a pentacle in the center and a crescent moon flanking either side. When I was little, I thought the symbol represented the sun, moon, and stars. Now I knew that it was the Triple Moon Goddess symbol and represented the Maiden, Mother, and Crone. Whispering Pines, Wisconsin had been founded by followers of the Wiccan religion and to my knowledge, Wiccans still made up half the population. A narrow four-foot by two-foot plaque hung from the bottom of the sign and read, *Blessed Be – Enjoy Your Visit.*

The welcome sign brought forth an unexpected flood of memories. I was ten years old the last time I'd been here, but I remembered that sign like I'd just seen it yesterday. Not only had it been a signal to me and my little sister Rosalyn that we were mere minutes from Gran's and Gramps' house, it made me feel good. I'd liked the idea of being blessed.

I continued down the road, remembering happier times

with my grandparents, and almost missed my turn.

"It's the first right past the welcome sign," my mother had reminded me numerous times, despite my assurance that my map app would get me there. "Be sure to stay on the left fork after you turn, Jayne, or you'll end up at that campground."

She'd said 'that campground' as though it was inhabited by a colony of lepers.

A quick glance as I passed showed that approximately half of the campsites were full. Whispering Pines' tourist season started in six days with Memorial Day weekend. Every spot would be full then. Every hotel room and rental cottage booked. My plan was to do what I could with the house and head back to Madison early Friday morning before the highways clogged with holiday traffic.

As the landscape changed from dense forest to a clearing, the edge of the lake house came into view. I stomped on the brakes and jerked to a stop, not quite ready to see it yet. I debated for a minute about whether I'd be able to do this then let the car creep forward. Most things from a person's childhood look smaller when seen as an adult, but in the sixteen years since I'd last been here, the house seemed to have grown. The seven-bedroom, nine-bathroom home had an enormous footprint, taking up almost half an acre. The steel-gray cedar siding and white trim were severely weather beaten. Winters in the Northwoods could be brutal, and the house looked like it had struggled to survive the last few.

"She hasn't done a thing to that house in years," Dad had warned in his email from . . . whichever Middle Eastern country he was currently searching for buried civilizations in. "We're not going to get anything for it. Empty it and do the bare minimum to get it on the market. The sooner we get rid of it, the better."

But as I stared at the house I hadn't seen in sixteen years, a sense of nostalgia flooded me. This was my grandparents' home. Despite my parents' refusal to remember, I had warm-n-fuzzy memories of being here.

"Don't worry, old girl," I told the house, dismissing my father's orders. "Nothing a few screws and a fresh coat of paint won't fix. I'll take care of you."

A sudden wind blew in off the lake, making the trees sway as though waving or bowing. Or nodding with approval?

Meeka barked from her backseat prison, snapping me fully into the present.

"Okay, okay."

I pulled forward and parked in front of the garage. As soon as the door on Meeka's crate was unlatched, she burst free from the SUV like a flare from a gun. She ran once around the car then raced in big circles around the perimeter of the near quarter acre of lawn, barking at invisible pursuers and burning off the energy built up from the five-hour drive.

As I watched her, laughing at her antics, another gentle breeze blew through. The air smelled earthy, like pine trees with a hint of fish, and the sun sparkled off the rippling water. I closed my eyes and faced the sun where it hung in the western sky, letting the rays soak in and warm me. An unexpected sense of serenity filled me and for the first time in months, I felt my shoulders relax and drop from their permanently hunched position.

I hadn't wanted to be the one to pack up the house, certain it would be too hard to be around Gran's things. Rosalyn had finals this week at UW Madison, and her summer job started next week. Mom was always too busy with the spa to take any time off. Dad was, well, he was out of the country like always. Since I'd been unemployed for the last six months, Mom and Rosalyn decided this task was mine. Now that I was here, with the fresh air and sun on my face, there was literally no place else in the world I'd rather be.

Next to the boathouse on my left, was the pier. Didn't it used to be much longer? Rosalyn and I used to run the length of it and, shrieking, jump into the lake. I had a sudden need to dangle my feet in the water. I'd taken three steps down the pathway of fieldstone pavers set into the grass when Meeka began to bark. Not her playful *hey, a squirrel bark*, but her red-alert *hey, something's wrong get over here quick* bark.

"What is it?" I snapped, as though expecting the little terrier to answer, and then sighed.

I hadn't gotten a good night's sleep in weeks and exhaustion had finally caught up to me, making me cranky. Now that I had started to relax, that's all I wanted to do.

Still, I turned toward the far right edge of the property. No, that wasn't accurate. The property spread out over ten acres. About two of those acres were taken up with house and lawn. The remaining eight or so were wooded with huge pines and a sprinkling of deciduous trees, currently covered with the bright green leaves that signaled the return of spring. Rebirth and renewal. That's where Meeka was having her fit, over by where the lawn met the tree line.

Concerned now, I jogged across the grass . . . which was in desperate need of fertilizing and weed control. I mentally added gardening to the list of chores that I suspected would be as long as my arm in a day or two.

As I got close to Meeka, she sat but still barked.

"This better be important."

Then I saw what she'd found. Definitely important. Five feet away from my dog lay a body.

Chapter 2

MEEKA WAS REALLY WORKED UP, partly from being in the car for so long, partly from her discovery. I had to calm her down so crouched in front of her, looked her square in the eye, and commanded her to be silent.

"Stay. Don't move or you're going back in the car."

She immediately dropped to her belly and rested her head on her paws.

The first thing I noticed was the victim's long, platinum blonde hair. My vision tunneled, and the earth seemed to tilt left and then right. That hair. It was the exact same color as Frisky's, my CI in Madison who had died because of me.

"Stop," I ordered myself. "You can't do this right now. Focus on what's in front of you."

I pressed my fingers to my eyelids until I saw stars and then released. By the time my vision cleared again, the memory had receded.

"Ma'am?" I called out, hoping the young woman was only unconscious. She hadn't moved, even after all the noise Meeka made, which told me she was likely deceased. "Miss, are you all right?"

Damn. No reaction. Not an eye flutter, not a finger twitch.

She was young, mid-twenties at best, and my guess—since she was in a semi-fetal position on her left side with her hands at her belly—put her at about five foot five. She had on short denim shorts and a bright yellow bikini top that revealed large breasts too round to be natural. Her partially-zipped white sweatshirt was stained with yellow-brown streaks and splotches that could be spilled food or maybe vomit. One of her red Converse sneakers had come untied.

The victim's cloudy blue eyes were partially open, staring out at the lake. A sprinkling of freckles across her nose and cheeks gave her a little girl appearance that contrasted starkly with the very womanly curves. An abrasion covered half of her right cheek, but there were no other visible bruises. How did she get the abrasion? Had she fallen here and scraped it on impact? Had someone hit her with something, a tree branch perhaps, and she fell? I glanced into the forest and noted fallen trees, large limbs, and clumps of dead but slowly re-growing weeds littering the floor. Had she tripped over something and scraped her face against a tree? Had she stumbled due to inebriation? Any number of scenarios were possible.

Areas of discoloration darkened the left sides of her legs, the sides against the ground. From the current position of the body, I couldn't be sure if it was simply a shadow or if it was lividity. Five years as a police officer taught me that the latter meant the victim had died a minimum of thirty minutes ago.

I needed to check for a pulse. I stepped closer and placed my index and middle fingers to her cold, rigid neck. No pulse and rigor had set in. That meant she'd died at least two hours ago.

I patted my back jeans pocket for my cell phone, but I'd left it in the car.

"Meeka, come." I jogged back to the Cherokee, grabbed my phone from the dashboard holder, and found . . . no bars. Damn. Mom had warned that cell reception in Whispering Pines was spotty on a good day.

My mind spun to formulate a plan. I needed to call the police and secure the scene. Which to do first? What if an animal wandered by and disturbed the body? What if the woman had been attacked and the assailant was still nearby? A quick glance at Meeka told me that no human or animal was in the area. If someone was close, her ears would be perked or she'd be standing at attention, looking in the direction of the intruder. She might be bitty, but Meeka was an excellent watchdog. The area appeared to be clear, so I'd call the police first.

Since my cell was useless, I'd have to use the house phone. From my backpack in the passenger's seat, I retrieved the keyring Mom had given me. It was the diameter of a softball and loaded with the keys for every item on the property that locked or required a key for power—the house, furniture, the boathouse, storage shed, garden tractor, motor boat, and a dozen others for as yet unknown items. As we hurried to the front door, I flipped through the ring until I found the one with the blue plastic disk around the head—the front door key. I was about to insert it into the lock when I noticed that one of the small panes of glass on the door was broken.

My cop instincts took over, screaming *crime scene, don't leave fingerprints!* I pulled my hand away, wrapped it with the hem of my T-shirt, and then grasped the handle. The door was closed, but unlocked. It hadn't even swung all the way open when it became clear I was going to be in Whispering Pines for much longer than a week.

"Meeka, sit." I pointed to a random spot at the side of the door. "You can't come in. Stay."

She sneezed, as if she understood, and crawled beneath one of four white wood rocking chairs on the porch to 'stay.' Quirky dog.

The house was a disaster, and not because Gran had let

the place 'go to hell during her last years' as my parents claimed. Someone had broken in and vandalized the place. At least what I could see from the entryway had been vandalized, which meant the hallway, dining room to the right, and sitting room to the left. Wary of contaminating the scene, I only took three or four steps inside.

In the dining room, the vandals clearly had a very good time destroying the possessions my grandparents had spent a lifetime acquiring. The crystal chandelier hanging over the polished walnut dining table had been smashed. The antique brass sconces mounted on either side of the once-gleaming china cabinet dangled from electrical wires. Deep green, Irish bone china plates I remembered eating a long-ago Thanksgiving dinner off of, lay in sharp shards on the hardwood floor. The dining chairs had been tossed about.

Numb, I turned away from the dining room and stood in the doorway of the sitting room. The vibrant blue damask upholstery on Gran's cherished antique sofa, where she used to read Rosalyn and me bedtime stories, was sliced open, bits of stuffing and an occasional spring poking out. An afghan Gran had spent one entire winter knitting lay unraveled on the floor. At least I assumed it was that afghan. The trio of brown, beige, and blue yarn looked familiar. Graffiti covered the ivory and beige striped wallpaper in both rooms. It was all symbols of some kind. Some resembled letters of the alphabet while others were more like crosses and arrows. They were more than just symbols, though. They seemed to form a message of some kind. But what?

Was the rest of the house in the same condition? I had to stay out and let the police and insurance folks walk through before I went any further. Speaking of the police, I picked up the extension on the table just inside the doorway of the sitting room and heard . . . nothing. No dial tone. I checked beneath the table, the line had been ripped from the wall.

"Are you kidding me?" I dropped my head back and let

out a groan of frustration. I'd just go get the police.

As I returned to my car, I was debating about covering the body when I spotted a man paddling past in a kayak twenty yards off shore. Perfect. Time to recruit.

"Sir!" I called as I ran closer to the water. "Sir, I need your help."

The man looked around, there were others farther out on the lake, and pointed to himself. "Me?"

"Yes, please. I've got a problem here."

He paddled over to the rocky shoreline and stepped out of the kayak when the boat touched bottom. He pulled it up onto the grass and dropped his paddle inside.

Approximate age late-twenties, five nine or ten, one hundred fifty pounds.

As though he had nowhere to be and no set time to be there, he hitched his dark-washed jeans up on his slim hips and sauntered over to me.

"Tripp Bennett." He held out a calloused hand.

"Excuse me?"

"That's my name." His reaction said he was used to responses like mine. "Tripper Bennett, but no one calls me Tripper."

"Nice to meet you, Mr. Bennett—"

"Tripp. And you are?"

"Jayne O'Shea. Look, Tripp, I've got a bit of a problem."

That's when Tripp looked past me toward the body at the edge of the lawn.

"I think I can guess what the problem is." He grimaced and respectfully removed his olive-green knit hat, releasing a mass of wavy, shoulder-length blonde hair. Casting a suspicious glance at me he asked, "What happened?"

"I don't know. My dog just found the body." I motioned toward the house. "I'm here to get the place ready to sell." I was blabbering, shaken up by both the dead woman and the scene inside the house. I needed to get control of myself in order to be in control of the situation. "My cell phone has no reception and the house phone isn't working. I need you to call the police while I secure the crime scene."

Tripp arched an eyebrow. "Secure the crime scene? Are you a cop?"

"Please." I slowly blew out a breath of frustration, the pressure in my chest releasing as I did. "Would you call the police for me?"

"I don't have a cell phone. Not that they work here anyway." Tripp pointed past the boathouse to the buildings on the far side of the bay, three or four football field lengths away. "Village is over there. It'll be faster for me to paddle than to go back to my campsite for my truck. I was on the way to return the kayak to the marina anyway. I'll get someone here as fast as I can."

"That's great," I said. "Thank you."

As Tripp paddled toward the village of Whispering Pines, I went into cop mode, scanning the area and taking in every detail. The lawn showed no signs of clues, at least nothing immediately visible. A careful grid search would need to be conducted.

I walked along the water's edge, getting the lay of the land . . . or the lake in this case. There was no beach to speak of, just a four-foot-wide rocky expanse—small stones, not boulders—that ran between the water's edge and the tree line. Did the victim walk along these stones to get here? Had she been with someone, a boyfriend maybe? Maybe they argued. Perhaps things got physical. Or maybe she'd been with a group. Had this woman been one of the vandals involved with the destruction of the house? Maybe she and her friends broke in to party or do drugs, or both, and things not only got out of control inside, they turned deadly outside.

It took all of my willpower to keep my curiosity in check and wait for the police to come and conduct an in-depth investigation. I felt helpless. I couldn't just stand there, I needed to do something. Pictures. I could photograph the scene while I waited without disturbing any evidence. Photos would be helpful for the police, too, although they'd surely take their own. Other than that, all I could do was stand guard and insure that nothing else happened to this young woman today. I took pictures with my phone—mostly of the body and the area immediately surrounding the body—and was back to standing guard when Meeka started barking.

Chapter 3

A WHITE SUV WITH A star insignia on the front quarter panel pulled in and parked next to my Cherokee. The words 'Sheriff' and 'Whispering Pines, Wisconsin' ran down the side in bold black and gold lettering. A middle-aged man— *five foot seven, slight paunch, salt-and-pepper hair cropped close*— got out of the truck. Instead of a full official uniform, he wore an official shirt with jeans. That would never happen in Madison. Clearly, things were more laid-back here.

He made his way slowly across the lawn. Not as though unconcerned, the sheriff had a limp. Had he been in an accident? Shot in the line of duty? Born with a disability? It wasn't just his physical issue, though. The sheriff's attitude was slow as well. He simply wasn't too concerned about the woman on my property. I could almost hear this man saying, "Body's not likely to get up and walk away now, is it?"

Meeka continued to bark, her intruder warning.

"Meeka," I called. "Friend."

She barked pointedly at the man once more and then lay down between two bushes next to the garage.

When the man got close, his eyes shot past me to the body in the woods. He frowned and looked down respectfully for a moment. Then he turned his attention to me.

"I'm Sheriff Karl Brighton. You must be the O'Shea girl."

I cringed at the word 'girl.' It was this damned new haircut. I thought the sleek, chin-length bob would make me appear sophisticated. Instead, it made me look sixteen rather than twenty-six. Being only five foot four didn't help.

It didn't help that lately I had been suffering from an almost paralyzing lack of self-confidence. It started with me not reporting my partner's personal problems, which resulted in Frisky's death. Then I quit my job without giving notice. I refused my boyfriend's proposal of marriage. I moved back in with my mother. What other horrible decisions could I add to the mix?

Then again, maybe his reaction had nothing to do with my appearance. Maybe the good sheriff was simply a misogynist.

"Yes, sir, I'm Jayne O'Shea. You knew I was coming?"

"We've been waiting for someone from your family to show up," Sheriff Brighton informed with disdain. "Your grandmother died three months ago. We figured one of you would have been here to take care of things before now."

He made it sound like Gran's body was still in the house waiting for someone to claim it. All of her things were in there, but I vividly remember the day her ashes were delivered to my parents' house. One of the worst days of my life. I wasn't going to let the sheriff's comment or his attitude get to me.

"We had to work out some details first." Tracking down my father in the middle of some godforsaken desert, for example, so we could ask what he wanted to do with the property. That was about as challenging a task as one would think. His was the only name on the will so we had to wait for his go-ahead. "I was inside the house earlier. Someone broke in and trashed the place. I'll need to file a report."

Sheriff Brighton gave me a blank look. "First things first, Miss O'Shea. Tripper Bennett tells me you've got some trouble out here as well." His gaze darted toward the victim again.

Great, now not only did he think we didn't care about the property, he thought I'd just ranked a vandalized house as more important than the death of a young woman. That wasn't the case at all. I knew things were about to get crazy and simply wanted to note the break-in before the sheriff got involved with his investigation.

He pulled a voice recorder from his pocket and clicked it on. I spent the next five minutes giving a statement, succinctly reporting everything I'd observed and done from the moment I arrived.

"I haven't touched anything except to see if she had a pulse. She didn't. Oh, I took pictures of the scene if you'd like them."

Sheriff Brighton nodded, seeming impressed with my report. "Good details. Appreciate that. I'm going to ask you to step aside now while I do my own investigating." He looked at the rapidly-setting sun. "If you would, I could use some light."

Lights. I glanced around, pausing on the boathouse thirty yards away. Specifically, the flood lights on the outside. Gramps had a habit of staying out on the lake for too long when the fishing was good. Rather than fret about him returning safely, Gran had lights installed and would turn them on if he wasn't back by the time dusk was becoming darkness.

"I'll go turn on the boathouse lights," I said. "I can also see if there are any portable lights on the property if that would be helpful."

"Flood lights are enough," the sheriff said, limping toward the body. "My deputy will be arriving shortly. We have all we need in the van."

After finding the right key for the boathouse door, I

quickly found the light switches. The floodlights lit up the backyard and lake area around the building nicely.

Fortunately, it didn't seem like the vandals had disturbed anything here. I glanced out at the water. The boathouse was visible from both the village across the bay and the lake itself, which almost always had a boater, jet skier, kayaker, wind surfer, or swimmer traffic. The chance of being seen was much greater here than at the secluded front door of the house, the apparent point of entry for the vandals.

Most of the ten-acre property was a thumb of land sticking out into the lake. The driveway entrance was marked with a 'Private – Do Not Enter' sign. Locals would know both of my grandparents had died now and would have no reason to come to the house. My understanding was that the majority of tourists stayed in the hotels and guest cottages on the far side of the village, unless they were staying at that campground. To me, the most likely vandal was one of the campers. I'd share that theory with the sheriff when the time came.

Meanwhile, the collection of water toys dredged up distant memories of Rosalyn and I spinning on inner tubes and searching for minnows with the goggles and snorkels. Gramps used to set up cots for us in the loft area above the boats so we could sleep out here. That was an option now, since I couldn't stay in the house until after the police and insurance folks checked it out. I could always try to get a room in the village for a few nights. But as long as the loft wasn't full of spiders or rats, I'd be fine there, especially for tonight. I was so tired I'd sleep in my car or on one of the lounge chairs on the patio if necessary.

Upstairs, I found that a lot had changed since Rosalyn and I slept out here. The unfinished loft was now a full studio apartment. A kitchenette with a small round table and two chairs and a small bathroom took up the center of the rectangular space. On the lake side was a living room with a sofa, end table, and a chair and ottoman set. On the yard side, a sleeping area with a queen bed, two bedside tables, a small dresser, and a freestanding clothes rack. This would be perfect.

I hauled all my stuff in from the car and set up Meeka's personalized doggie bed—monogrammed with her name surrounded by tiny dog bones. Rosalyn spoiled this dog so bad. I found some cleaning supplies beneath the kitchen sink and gave the place a quick cleanup. Must have been a long time since anyone had stayed here; it was quite dusty.

When I'd finished, I stood out on the sundeck and watched Sheriff Brighton and his deputy investigate. About fifteen minutes later, someone I assumed to be the medical examiner arrived. The ME checked over the body and supervised the placement of it into a body bag. Once the body was gone, it looked like they were wrapping things up, so I went downstairs and crossed the yard to the patio at the back of the house. There, Tripp was sitting in an Adirondack chair, somberly watching the process.

"You're still here," I said.

"The sheriff asked me to stick around in case he had any questions for me. Don't know why he would. I told him I never got closer to her than the pier."

A reasonable request. No witness should be disregarded. The most seemingly insignificant clue could crack a case.

"All done?" I asked the sheriff as he came closer. They must have checked the woods and done a grid search of the yard while I was cleaning the apartment. Half-an-hour didn't seem like enough time to do a thorough search, but if there was nothing to see, there was nothing to see.

"We are," Sheriff Brighton said. "I'll need you to come down to the station to make a formal statement."

"No problem." I'd expected that. "I'll be there first thing in the morning."

"It would be better if you came now," the sheriff

pushed. "Your memories are fresh now."

"I've already told you everything I know. I'd only be repeating myself."

Sheriff Brighton leveled a gaze on me that was clearly meant to intimidate and remind me he was the one in charge.

"Sir," I started respectfully, "I've had a really long day. I was on the road for nearly six hours, haven't had any dinner yet, and would like nothing more than to get some sleep. I assure you, I'll be at your office in the morning."

After a long moment, the sheriff nodded. "First thing in the morning, but only because I've already got an informal statement from you." He waggled the voice recorder in my face. "Remember, I know how to find you if you don't show up." He started for his SUV, stopped, and turned back. "Best place in town for dinner is The Inn."

Once the sheriff and his deputy had pulled away, I turned to Tripp. "Do you know where The Inn is?"

He pushed himself up from the patio chair. "I could eat. Can I catch a ride with you?"

"Sorry, I don't give rides to strangers. No harm in eating together, though. How about I follow you?"

Chapter 4

A CREEK STARTING FROM SOMEWHERE up north wound its way around the village of Whispering Pines, cut between Gran's property and the campground, and then emptied into the lake. The commercial part of the village lay south of the creek, north of it was the residential area and forest land. Just before the creek, as you drove in from the west on the two-lane highway, was a public parking lot.

The entrance to the lot passed beneath two large pine trees, a hand-carved wooden sign hanging between them alerted drivers that motorized vehicles weren't allowed in the main village. If you wanted to visit the shops and restaurants, you had to park and walk. That's where I met Tripp, in the lot, and we walked the quarter mile or so to The Inn.

Many things had changed in sixteen years, but the heart of the village, the area so many tourists flocked to, had not. A frozen-in-time feeling came over me the moment we passed by the Fortune Tellers' Triangle, a cozy area nestled between the road to Gran's house, the creek, and the highway. I felt like a kid again, or maybe a time traveler, when I saw the shadowy shapes of the wagons and tiny huts scattered around The Triangle. I wished it was daylight so I could see their bright colors and gingerbread trim. It was an attraction set up for the tourists, I understood that now, but as a kid I thought the fortune tellers, with their jangling jewelry, long flowing skirts, and crystal balls were magical. Visiting the exotic women had always been my favorite thing about coming to Whispering Pines. Other than seeing Gran and Gramps, of course.

Heavy shadows darkened the red brick pathways thanks to the villagers' preference to allow the night sky to remain as dark as possible. Small fixtures on the outside of cottages and a handful of pole lamps scattered randomly about cast only the dimmest light. When I was little, I was sure creatures of the night were hiding among the shadows, ready to pounce. I let myself think the same thing now and a thrill rushed through me.

A pentacle-shaped garden, the size of a city block, served as the heart of the village. This was the oldest section of town and had the appearance of a Renaissance Faire, or like it had just been plucked from some medieval English countryside and plopped down in northern Wisconsin. Some of the small cottages surrounding the garden were stained so dark brown they were nearly black. I used to imagine that witches might pop out of the cottages to steal Rosalyn and me and bake us into pies. Despite the dark, scary parts, it was all very charming. Easy to see why it had become a mecca for tourists.

The Inn, a crooked gothic-looking three-story building made of white stucco and dark brown timbers, sat between the pentacle garden and the lake. Tripp held the door open for me. The crooked outside appearance was echoed inside. We entered a cozy lobby where guests gathered by a floor-to-ceiling fieldstone fireplace or made inquiries at the front desk. A sign, propped in the arms of a suit of armor near the fireplace, indicated that the dining room was to our right.

When the hostess led us to a small round table in the center of the dining room, I pointed to an identical table in the far corner next to a much bigger version of the fireplace in the lobby.

"Could we have that one?"

"Oh." The request seemed to fluster her. "Sure."

Tripp held a chair out for me, but I'd already settled into the corner seat.

I squinted in the dark dining room light at the simple menu. There were six choices. Four traditional comfort-food dinners—Shepherd's pie, beef stew, clam chowder, and chicken pot pie—and as if to confirm that we were still in Wisconsin and not medieval England, bratwurst with sauerkraut or fish fry with coleslaw and deep-fried cheese curds. My stomach rumbled. It all sounded delicious.

The hostess was also our server. She had dark circles beneath tired blue eyes and wore an all-black uniform consisting of a short flouncy skirt, an off-the-shoulder peasant blouse, and knee-high black boots. She looked part Oktoberfest beer girl, part Wiccan high priestess.

"What can I get for you two?" she asked as she set two glasses of water on the table.

"Separate checks, please," I said. "I'll have the chicken pot pie, a side of curds, and I'd love some of the cherry cobbler afterwards."

"Pot roast and witch's brew for me," Tripp said.

"What's that?" I asked.

Tripp leaned in. "It's their homemade ale. They don't put it on the menu so you've got to know to ask for it."

"Is it good?"

He nodded. "Very."

I looked up at our server. "One of those for me, too, please."

Tripp turned to me as the priestess of beer walked away. "So, what do you think happened to the girl you found?"

"I can't tell for sure. Her clothing was relatively untouched, which tells me she hadn't been there very long.

Hard to know if it was natural causes or foul play. Won't know until the autopsy report comes in."

I hadn't detected a urine or feces odor. The bladder and bowel relax upon death and sometimes empty, so either that hadn't happened with her or there was nothing inside her to evacuate.

She could have died from exposure. The way she was dressed could have led to hypothermia, it still got chilly enough here at night for a jacket, but unless she'd been wandering the woods for many days, she should have been fine. Her clothes, other than those brownish-yellow stains on her sweatshirt, were clean, so my best guess was that she hadn't been wandering. There were coyotes and other scavengers in the area, so the fact that the body was untouched told me she had been there less than a day. The fact that the entire body had appeared quite stiff when they placed her in the body bag indicated she had been dead for at least twelve hours, but less than thirty-six when rigor starts to dissipate.

"Of course, I could be entirely wrong," I said as though I'd just spoken all those thoughts out loud. "Like I said, we'll have to wait for the autopsy results to come back to know for sure. What do you think happened to her?"

"Me? I have no clue."

"But you knew her," I said.

"No, I—"

"Oh, come on. The moment you saw the body you removed your hat. A sign of respect that could be made for anyone, but then you hung around."

"I told you," Tripp objected, "the sheriff asked me to stay in case he had questions for me."

"Right, that's what you told me. But your demeanor while the sheriff investigated the scene told me something different. You were sitting with your shoulders hunched forward, your hands folded in your lap. The look on your face was not *oh, what a shame, someone died* it was *wow, I'm shocked, what happened to her?"*

"Okay fine, I knew her," Tripp blurted. "Well, I didn't *know* her."

"What do you mean?" I sipped my water.

"You saw her." His hands were positioned in front of his own chest as though holding ample breasts. He dropped them into his lap. "Sorry. No disrespect intended. She's pretty. I notice pretty women. She showed up in the campground a week or so after me."

"As a tourist?"

"I'm not entirely sure what her story is. I heard from people at the campground that she was visiting an aunt who lives here. Guess they had a falling out or something. That's all secondhand. I never actually talked to her."

"But you noticed her?" I shook my head. Typical male.

He snorted. "Everyone noticed Yasmine Long. Men *and* women. Rumor was after her aunt kicked her out, she didn't have enough money to get back to wherever she came from so was trying to earn some."

A bad feeling crawled under my skin, and I thought of teen runaways who'd turned to prostitution to survive. An image of Frisky popped into my mind. She'd been busted a little more than a year ago on a solicitation and minor drug charge. In lieu of jail time, she vowed to get clean and then became an informant. Frisky, Mama Frisky to those in her neighborhood, saw everything—burglary, vandalism, girls who were heading for trouble. When she saw something going down, or about to, she'd call me. My partner and I would go and either break things up or haul away the offenders. The three of us were really making a difference.

I pushed the image away and returned my attention to Tripp. "I almost hate to ask, but how was she trying to earn money?"

"Washing cars."

"Excuse me?" Not the answer I expected.

Our server placed two big steins of beer and a board

with a loaf of rustic bread and cheese in front of us. "Your dinners will be up shortly."

"Thanks." My stomach growled embarrassingly loud. I knew I should have stopped in Wausau for lunch, but I just wanted to get here. Tripp was right, the witch's brew was good. Paired perfectly with the bread.

"Yasmine strutted around town," Tripp explained, "with a wash bucket, wearing nothing but a bikini and sandals, and offered to wash cars. Or motorcycles. Or bicycles. A woman at the campground helped her one time, but usually it was just her." He laughed. "Guess she even washed a dog once."

Numerous music videos featuring barely-clad women with sponges and hoses skittered through my mind. Soap *accidentally* ending up everywhere but on the item in need of washing. The women then rinsing off, the cold water causing erect nipples beneath see-through fabric. Men standing stupidly by with their mouths hanging open and crotches bulging as they watched the whole spectacle.

"It was pretty much what you're imagining," Tripp confirmed.

"How do you know what I'm imagining?"

"I know the look women get when they disapprove of another woman."

Was that what I was doing? Disapproving of a woman I didn't even know based on appearance and hearsay?

Tripp glanced cautiously at me, as though worried about causing further irritation. "Anyway, she was popular around the village, if you know what I mean."

"With men?"

He inhaled deeply. "Let's just say there's a reason the other residents of the campground asked her to move her tent to the farthest end. The noises coming out of it were —"

"I get it." I held up a hand. "Another source of income?"

"Couldn't say."

Popular girl, for the wrong reasons, attracts the

attention of men and entertains them in her tent. Maybe some of these men were here with wives or girlfriends who weren't too happy with Ms. Long's antics. Or maybe someone, man or woman, became jealous over the attention Yasmine gave to others. Or became jealous over the attention she got from others. Sounded like possible motive for murder to me. I'd have to ask around, starting with Yasmine's friend at the campground.

No. No I wouldn't. It wasn't my job.

"The friend who helped her with the washing that time," Tripp continued, "she's part of the group at the campground Yasmine latched on to. They're all in their twenties. All seem to be having a good time."

"Partying?" I asked.

"Oh yeah. From what I saw, there didn't seem to be much Yasmine wouldn't try."

I looked pointedly at him. "This from personal experience with her?"

He didn't flinch. "Told you, I never even talked to her. I passed the partying stage long ago. Guess you could call me a loner, just trying to live my life. You know what I mean? I'm looking for a place to settle and put down a root or two." He shuddered. "Never thought I'd hear myself say that. Not at twenty-eight."

"No?"

"Long story."

The server arrived with our dinners and after she'd set everything in front of us asked, "Everything look okay?"

"Perfect as always, Sylvie." Tripp flashed a charming smile that made Sylvie blush and spin away.

"Mine looks good, too," I called at her retreating back. When I looked back at him, color had risen on Tripp's cheeks.

"We had a night. She brought me one too many beers and we . . . never mind. Nothing going on now, though."

"I don't recall asking."

I turned my attention to the chicken pot pie in front of me. It was good. No, not good, amazing and not just because I was so hungry. At least the first few bites were amazing; I ate so fast I barely tasted any of it. Not even five minutes later, I was chasing the last bites of my pot pie around the ramekin and only had a few deep-fried cheese curds left. My embarrassment doubled when I noticed that Tripp wasn't even half done with his pot roast.

"I haven't eaten since this morning," I explained. "It's been a stressful day. I eat fast when I'm stressed."

Tripp shrugged. "Didn't really notice."

But Sylvie returned then to check on us. "How is every—" She stopped mid-question when she realized my plate was almost clean. "Oh. Are you ready for your cobbler?"

"Would you box it for me, please? I'll take it to go." I wouldn't risk embarrassing myself, and repulsing my dinner companion, by inhaling anything else tonight.

About two hours into the drive today, I realized that one of the benefits to taking responsibility for packing up the house was that I'd have time alone to get my head on straight. My plan was to learn to be more in-the-moment. I had developed a habit of going through my day without really paying attention to anything. My habit of eating before the food could cool was a big one to break. Maybe I'd try a cleanse. Hell, I'd try yoga or meditate or whatever other mumbo-jumbo the New Age gurus suggested if it would help get me out of my funk.

I forced a peppier disposition. "So tell me, what brought you to Whispering Pines."

"The town where 'All are welcome and those in need may stay.'"

"Sounds like you're quoting an advertisement."

"It's the village motto or something." He frowned and took a long chug of his beer. "They must have come up with it before it became a tourist destination."

"Why do you say that?" I tried to be more ladylike, more mindful or whatever the term was, and slowly placed one of the few remaining spoonsful of pot pie into my mouth instead of shoveling it in like a glutton after a forced three-day fast.

Tripp leaned back in his chair, a bitter edge to his voice as he explained, "I've been here for about a month. Been trying to get a job somewhere since day one, but the council won't approve me."

Council? Approve? I shook my head. "I don't understand."

"The good village folk of Whispering Pines, Wisconsin are very choosey about who they let stay here permanently."

"How can they stop you?" I felt myself getting worked up, like I did anytime I heard about an injustice. "You have the right to live here if you want."

"Sure I do," Tripp agreed. "If I want to live at the campground. No one will rent me a place to live if I don't have a job here."

"Don't care much for outsiders, hey?" That surprised me. I always felt comfortable here. Of course, I was only a kid then and my grandparents owned the land the village sat on. Guess my dad owned it now. What would he do with it?

"Depends. Tourists are welcome to visit and spend boat loads of money but . . ." Tripp inhaled deeply while rubbing his hands over his face. "Sorry. I'm just a little frustrated. I finally find a place where I want to stay . . . Maybe it's best if I just go." He took another long drink from his stein and sighed. "So. How long are you gonna be here?"

"Originally a week. Long enough to pack up the house and hire a crew to load everything onto a truck. I'm supposed to ship anything my family might want, sell what can be sold, and donate or dispose of whatever is left."

"But?"

"But someone broke in and trashed the place."

"Bastards," he hissed immediately.

I couldn't help but smile at the way he came to my defense.

"Now I've got to order a trash bin and do a mass cleanup before I can even get to the salvageable bits. And if the rest of the house is as bad as the two rooms I saw, I'll need more than one bin."

"I can help," Tripp offered a little too eagerly. "Since you're willing to hire a crew. I'm sort of desperate for money."

"Thanks," I said. "I'll keep that in mind."

I had to admit, I could think of worse things than seeing Tripp Bennett every day. He had this sort of hipster-lumberjack thing going on that was kind of appealing. Not that I was in the market for anything other than a friend. I noticed good-looking people, too, and he definitely fit that bill.

We sat in easy silence. As he finished his dinner, I stared around at the empty tables—some small and round, some larger and rectangular—or out the window next to us into the nighttime darkness. For as much as I didn't want to have to pack up Gran's house, I had been quietly anxious to return to this village of supposed misfits. Now that I was here, I sort of felt like Whispering Pines and its population of odd, quirky residents might be exactly what I needed. I'd never in my life felt as odd as I had lately.

"You okay?" Tripp asked.

How long had he been staring at me?

"Yeah." I gave a little shrug and echoed him. "Long story."

"I've got time." He scraped the last of his pot roast into a little pile and pushing it onto his spoon with his final bite of rustic bread.

"Thanks. Really, I'm just wiped out. I need to get some sleep."

When Sylvie brought our separate checks, I grabbed

both of them. "It's the least I can do for making you deal with a dead person."

Tripp, clearly a man comfortable with himself, sat back. "Not going to object. I'm seriously almost broke and meant what I said about helping." He held his beer stein out to me. "Thanks for dinner."

We left The Inn and started down the same path back to the parking lot, my unease over walking in the dark with a stranger all but gone. I prided myself on my instincts, and they were telling me that Tripp Bennett was okay. I made a detour through the pentacle garden. A visit to the pristine, white marble well at the center of the pentacle had been a requirement for Rosalyn and me every time we came here. Like everything, except Gran's house, the well seemed much smaller. My dad always had to boost me up. Now, I could look over the side without problem.

"Do you know what this is?" I asked.

"A well," Tripp guessed sarcastically.

I shook my head.

"A wishing well?"

"It's a negativity well. You whisper any negative thoughts or frustrations into your hands."

I demonstrated by cupping my hands next to my mouth. With my eyes closed, I thought about the events of the last six months. The tragedy of Frisky's death. My agonizing breakup with Jonah, my almost fiancé. The fact that every decision I made lately seemed to be wrong. I just wanted to move past it all and get my life back on track. I whispered all of that into my hands and then, as though holding a bubble full of wishes that might leak out, sealed my hands tight.

"Then you throw them into the well."

I reached as far down as I could and pushed my hands down toward the water. I stood there, half expecting to hear a splash. When I glanced over my shoulder, Tripp had an expression that said this was not at all a strange thing to do.

In Whispering Pines, it wasn't.

We followed the pea gravel pathway out of the pentacle and then took the red brick sidewalk to the parking lot. Between my full belly and the silence of the night, I felt relaxed and content, despite the day's earlier traumas.

Tripp paused by my car and opened the door for me.

"Thanks again for your help today," I said.

"Anytime. See you soon, Jayne O'Shea."

See me soon? Nice to know that neither being subjected to a dead body nor being forced to witness my born-in-a-barn eating habits had scared him off.

Chapter 5

FOR SEVEN YEARS, JONAH AND I had lived in an apartment on a busy street in the University area of Madison. After we broke up, I moved to my parents' house in a quiet suburban neighborhood. That had been a hard transition. Mostly because of the breakup, but also because of the lack of street noise. Four months later, I still had a hard time falling asleep when it was too quiet. The lack of noise was even worse in Whispering Pines. At least by my parents' house there was the occasional barking dog or car with a loud muffler cruising by. Here, the silence was overwhelming.

After half an hour of tossing and turning, I opened the French doors that led out to the sundeck. That helped. The sound of the water washing in and out of the boat area below offered something to focus on. A gentle breeze blew across my face. The fresh air, fragrant with lake water and pine, combined with the sloshing sound was surprisingly relaxing.

My body had just become heavy with sleep when I heard something outside. Voices. Someone was out there. Silently, I crept out of bed and over to Meeka. I had woken her when I got up to open the door, but she was once again sound asleep on her pillow. I roused her with a sharply whispered, "Meeka."

She jerked her head up and *ruffed* at me.

"Quiet, girl. No barking." Whoever was out there, I didn't want her scaring them away. Especially if it was the vandals, I wanted to get a look at them if possible.

Meeka yawned and stretched but didn't seem at all concerned about possible intruders.

"Come," I commanded, and we tiptoed onto the sundeck. A soft beam shone down from the crescent moon and shimmered on the water. I knelt next to my dog and softly asked, "Is anyone out there, girl?"

Curious, Meeka tilted her head, stuck her nose through the slats in the railing, and sniffed. Then she sat and wagged her tail across the deck's floor, clearing a fan shape in the accumulated dirt and pine needles. If someone had been out there, Meeka would have alerted me. Then I'd give her the signal, and she'd take off in a white blur, barking when she got to the intruder's location, just like she had with Yasmine's body.

Despite the fact that I was positive I'd heard someone, I couldn't see anyone either.

"All right. Let's go back to bed."

Just as I stood, a puff of wind blew in off the lake, and I thought I heard the sound again. A moment later, a stronger gust blew through, and this time I was positive.

Whoosh. Shush.

"It's the trees."

Intrigued, I leaned on the rail and listened. As the wind blew through, the fifty-foot pines swayed this way and that. The needles and twigs of the branches tangled and brushed together creating the *whoosing, shushing* sounds, the bigger branches creaking with the gusts. It almost sounded like the trees were talking to each other. Or me.

"The pines really do whisper here."

With Meeka back on her pillow, I crawled under the

covers and lay there, listening to the trees' conversation. It was comforting. Almost as if they were watching over me. And just as I was slipping from awake to unconscious, I swear I heard them say *O'Shea*.

~~~

I woke with a start, no idea where I was. After a long moment of panic and a glance out the open French doors, it all came back. The boat house. Right, I was in Whispering Pines to pack up Gran's house . . . except the house was trashed. I needed to let Mom know. I needed to call the insurance folks. And I needed to have the sheriff view the damage as well. I also had to report to the sheriff's station this morning to give a formal statement on poor Yasmine Long. No time for relaxing.

A glance at my phone told me it was already nine o'clock. It was almost eleven when I finally fell asleep last night. Ten hours? I couldn't remember the last time I'd slept that hard. Maybe the sound of city noise wasn't as relaxing as I thought. And maybe getting away from the chaos of my life—namely my mom, sister, and Jonah—was the best thing I'd done for myself in a long while.

I let Meeka out to do her doggie thing while I showered and dressed. My stomach grumbled. How could I possibly be hungry after that huge chicken pot pie and small mountain of cheese curds last night? I mentally added a grocery store visit to my already long to-do list for the morning, then grabbed the Styrofoam container of cherry cobbler from the little refrigerator in the kitchenette. I spooned the first bite of the dessert into my mouth and had reloaded the spoon before I'd even chewed twice. I stopped, with the spoon halfway to my mouth. I was supposed to eat mindfully so slowed down and paid attention. The cobbler exploded in my mouth—sweet, tart, buttery, flaky, and fabulous. Slow was good.

I took the container out onto the sundeck and found Meeka at the water's edge. She was chasing the waves as they went out, then spun and ran like crazy when they crashed back in.

"Come on in, girl. We've got an appointment this morning."

The little white terrier looked up at me, gave a final warning *yap* at the waves, and ran up the stairs. Meeka ate her kibble while I finished the cobbler, then sat by the door to wait for me.

I grabbed her leash and a couple of poo bags, and we headed for the Cherokee. One problem. I had no idea where the sheriff's station was. Problem number two: coffee. I could function well enough on cherry cobbler but not without coffee. We'd stop for a mega-cup in the village and ask directions. I'd seen a sign hanging from one of the scary witch buildings while walking with Tripp last night. 'Ye Olde Bean Grinder' sounded like a coffee shop to me. Fifteen minutes later, we confirmed that's exactly what it was.

"Are dogs welcome?" I asked before entering.

"Will your dog leave a mess?" the busy barista asked.

I looked at Meeka. "No mess. Right?" She gave a little half-bark. "Nope, no mess."

She waved us into the shop that was even more charming on the inside than it was on the outside. Cozy café tables dotted the sitting area, a stone fireplace sat tucked into the far corner. I silently wished for a good book and a dreary afternoon because this would be the perfect place to spend it.

While the barista prepared my favorite extra-large mocha with a double-pump of vanilla and extra whipped cream, I found myself staring at a covered dish of scones. My stomach rumbled again, and I mentally shushed it. Not only was I supposed to be working on eating more mindfully, I really should eat better, too. Cherry cobbler and scones weren't anywhere on a better menu.

"Could you point me toward the sheriff's station?" I asked as Violet, the barista—*early-twenties, five foot even, light-brown skin, long straight black hair, violet eyes*—set my drink on the counter along with a biscuit for Meeka.

"It isn't far," she said. "Hope you don't have a problem."

I took the first sip from my paper cup. This was quite possibly the best coffee I'd ever had. What was it about the food around here?

"Nope, no problem," I said.

"That's good. Because I heard there was some trouble over by the campground last night."

I added *nosey* to her description, but in a friendly, not annoying, way. Violet's statement was as loaded as a fishing hook with a fat worm. She was looking for information, but it wasn't my place to supply it. Word would spread soon enough.

"You staying at the campground by any chance?" she asked.

That I could answer. "No, I'm Jayne O'Shea—"

"Oh! You're Lucy's granddaughter."

"You knew my grandmother?"

Violet's smile melted my heart. "Everyone knew Lucy. She was The Original, after all."

I swallowed my mocha wrong and coughed. I'd heard Gran called many things, mostly by my parents, but that was a first.

"She was the what?"

"The Original," Violet said dreamily, as though my grandmother was a movie star. "Whispering Pines wouldn't exist if not for Lucy O'Shea letting people live on her land." Violet dug in her cash drawer and then slid my five dollars back to me. "Coffee's on the house. Any day. Any time. Always."

"That's not necessary."

"Seriously, your money is no good here."

There was no point in arguing, I knew a determined look when I saw one. My sister Rosalyn wore one like a fashion accessory. "Thank you, Violet. That's nice of you."

Violet smiled.

"So?" I prompted. "The sheriff's station?"

"Oh, sure." Violet pointed east. "Go past Shoppe Mystique next door. If you're looking for herbs, candles, crystals, or oils that's the place to go. Anyway, keep going and take a left past Treat Me Sweetly, the village bakery." Violet nodded at the scones. "I supply coffee for her, she supplies scones for me. Help yourself. The lemon-lavender are out of this world."

Not wanting to seem rude, I chose a scone. "Let me guess. She gets the lavender from Shoppe Mystique?"

"Where else?" Violet looked at me as though I hadn't been paying attention.

The scone practically melted in my mouth. The lemon invigorated while the lavender soothed.

"Oh my god." I held my hand in front of my mouth as I spoke. "So, magic of some kind is one of the ingredients?"

I was joking, but the hint of a smile on Violet's lips caught me off guard.

"Just past the bakery," Violet continued, "you'll find the Fairy Path. Follow that and you'll run right into the sheriff. Well, his building. And not literally, of course, unless you don't stop."

"I'm sorry?" I leaned in to be sure I'd heard properly. "The Fairy Path?"

Violet swatted the air. "That's our little joke because mushrooms tend to grow in circles along there. The actual fairies hang out on the other side of the creek near The Meditation Circle."

I blinked and decided it was time to move along. "Two shops down, take a left. Got it." I held up the coffee. "Thanks again."

A meditation circle? Fairies? Magical scones? Had the

village been this quirky when I was little? There weren't as many tourists then, but now that I thought about it, it always seemed like a fairytale land to me.

Just past the bakery, I spotted a hand-carved wooden sign, about a foot-and-a-half tall and a foot wide, at the start of a path that led through a thick grove of trees. 'Fairy Path' was carved into the sign with a fanciful font. About ten feet away, on the other side of the path, was a matching sign that read 'Sheriff – 0.5 mile,' an arrow indicated that through the grove was the proper direction. I started down the path, not at all surprised to find more signs advertising other locations: library, lower school, upper school, yoga studio, healing center.

"Suppose a healing center is like a clinic?" I asked Meeka who had stopped to investigate the mushrooms that really did grow in circles. Dozens of little houses, the size of shoeboxes, circled the bases of trees. Very cute. Another touch for the tourists, or did the villagers really believe in fairies? Did they employ a medical doctor in their healing center, or would I find a shaman if I walked in?

The path came to a fork. One sign pointed left toward the healing center and yoga studio, another pointed right to the schools and library. Dead ahead was a simple single-story square building, painfully utilitarian compared to the charming witch cottages surrounding the pentacle garden. A sign that read 'Whispering Pines Sheriff Station" hanging next to the door told me I was at the right place.

Chapter 6

MEEKA AND I ENTERED THE sheriff's station and found a large open space that was as no-frills at the outside of the building. Two jail cells took up the far left wall. Two rooms, one labeled 'Sheriff' and the other unmarked, with a small bathroom in between, occupied the wall to the right. Straight across from the front door at the far side of the room sat a single desk. If the name plate on the front edge of the desk was accurate, the desk belonged to Deputy Martin Reed. I had seen the man sitting there last night. He had come to my house to help investigate the crime scene, but I hadn't met him personally.

He looked up from his paperwork. "No dogs allowed."

"She's a service dog."

He narrowed his eyes at me and Meeka, then took a handful of trail mix from a plastic zip-top bag. "We figured you forgot you were supposed to come."

"I don't recall a time being set. I slept in." My tone held no apology, but I did my best to stay cordial. "All the driving I did yesterday must have tired me out more than I realized."

I guessed Deputy Reed to be younger than me—*early-twenties, thinning dirty-blonde hair, the bony frame of someone who either used illegal substances or was suffering from a chronic disease.* He made my instincts prickle, and I never questioned my instincts. What were they trying to tell me about the good deputy?

"Sheriff's in the interview room." Deputy Reed pointed to the door directly to his left. "Been waiting for you."

For whatever reason, he was trying to intimidate me. Good luck with that. I didn't intimidate easily. Also, I hadn't done anything wrong, unless sleeping in was an offence of some kind in Whispering Pines.

"Glad you could make it." Sheriff Brighton said and pointed at the empty chair across the simple wood table from him. "Have a seat."

On guard now, thanks to the deputy, I was prepared to be treated as a hostile witness, so to speak. I took the chair, immediately uncomfortable with my back to the door.

Sheriff Brighton made a show of placing his voice recorder in front of me. The only other items on the table were a file folder, open to reveal both handwritten and computer printed notes, and a pad of paper. He switched on the recorder.

"Let's talk about the victim found on your property yesterday."

"Yasmine Long."

The Sheriff looked up, eyebrows arched. He seemed surprised by my knowledge. "How did you know the victim?"

"I didn't, but her name is written on your folder's tab. And Tripp Bennett, the man who came to get you—"

"I know who Mr. Bennett is."

Sheriff Brighton sat straight and tall in his chair, an obvious attempt to be in control by making himself seem as physically imposing as possible. Whatever. I was well aware of police interview tactics.

"Tripp went to dinner with me last night," I said.

"You discussed the investigation?" This displeased

Sheriff Brighton, if the furrow at the center of his forehead and the accusatory tone meant anything.

"I didn't know there was a reason we shouldn't. We were both a little upset by the woman's death and the topic naturally came up. It's not like I revealed anything new to him. Tripp saw everything I saw. He volunteered her name and stated that Ms. Long had been staying at the same campground he is."

"Did you and *Tripp* know each other before yesterday?"

The sheriff put an emphasis on Tripp's name that I couldn't decipher. It didn't imply that Tripp had done anything wrong, but there was a definite vibe that indicated the sheriff didn't like him. Maybe it was because Tripp had stayed even though the village council hadn't approved him getting a job or a place to rent. Guess they really didn't like outsiders here.

"I thought you brought me in to discuss Ms. Long," I said.

Sheriff Brighton held my gaze longer than was necessary. "Yes. Miss Long. Give me the timeline of your day yesterday."

"You mean since I arrived at my grandparents' house?"

The sheriff lifted a shoulder. "Why not your whole day? It seems you'll be in Whispering Pines for a while. I like to know the residents of my village."

The hair on my arms stood up as Tripp's words about 'those who weren't approved couldn't stay' sounded like an alarm in my head. My family owned every square foot of the land beneath this village. They couldn't do a thing about me staying.

"Well," I sat straight in the chair, "I got up at about seven-thirty and peed. Then I took my dog outside so she could pee."

"Miss O'Shea," the sheriff interrupted, "is this a joke to you for some reason?"

"Sheriff Brighton, a girl died on my property. Or she

died elsewhere and someone dumped her body there. I take that very seriously. You, however, seem more concerned with learning about me and my relationship with Tripp Bennett, of which there isn't one, than you do with the facts surrounding the deceased woman. If you'd like to chat," —I held up my half-full paper cup— "Ye Olde Bean Grinder makes great coffee. I'd be happy to sit and get to know you, and any of my fellow villagers, there."

He squirmed slightly my use of the phrase 'my fellow villagers.' He really didn't like outsiders.

Beneath the table, Meeka leaned against my legs, sensing my irritation.

"Miss O'Shea—"

"*Ms.* O'Shea."

We locked eyes, Sheriff Brighton looking away first. He shifted in his chair and cleared his throat.

"All right. Why don't you tell me what happened from the time you entered Lucy's property?"

Lucy's property. Making sure I understood that it was my grandmother's and not mine?

"You knew my grandmother?" Of course he did. Like Violet at Ye Olde Bean Grinder had said, everyone in Whispering Pines knew Lucy O'Shea.

His stern expression softened slightly. "I knew her quite well. Lucy was a wonderful woman."

I softened a little myself at his reaction. I'd been stressed and exhausted for months. The sheriff was just doing his job. Right now, my job was to let him.

"I left Madison a little after eleven yesterday morning."

"Can anyone confirm that?"

"My mother can."

"When did you get here?"

"A little before five."

He nodded and jotted the fact on his notepad. "Then what happened?"

"Shortly after we arrived, Meeka started barking at

something at the perimeter of the yard. When I got closer, I saw the body. For the record, I'm confident she didn't touch the victim. She's trained to alert me and only attack if I'm in physical danger."

"Your dog is how big?" He checked beneath the table and held his hand about a foot off the floor.

I smiled at his implication. "Have you ever been bitten in the ankle or calf, Sheriff?"

He chuckled from deep in his belly. "Can't say as I have, Miss . . . Ms. O'Shea. Please, continue."

"As I stated last night, I called out to the victim but she was unresponsive. I checked for a pulse and found none." I took a drink of my mocha, giving myself a moment as an image of Frisky flashed before my eyes. "At that time, I knew I needed to contact your office and secure the scene."

"You sent Mr. Bennett for me."

"Yes, sir. My cell phone gets no reception here."

"No one's does," the sheriff said.

"I went inside the house to use the phone there."

I explained, in detail, the condition of the entryway, dining room, and sitting room. The broken furniture, destroyed items, and graffiti on the walls. Not pertinent to Yasmine's case, but I wanted to be sure my break-in was on the sheriff's radar.

"Is that all the farther you went?" Sheriff Brighton asked, noting these details on a separate sheet of paper. "Only into the entryway? Did you look in any other rooms?"

I shook my head. "I didn't want to contaminate the scene. You will only find my footprints in the grime on the floor. I didn't touch anything, not even the front door since the broken pane of glass alerted me to a break-in."

Sheriff Brighton glanced up from scribbling notes. His eyes narrowed and he studied me for a beat. "And then what happened?"

"I went to use the telephone in the sitting room; you will find my fingerprints there. The line was dead. Whoever broke in, yanked the cord from the wall. I went back outside and that's when I saw Mr. Bennett kayaking past the property. I called him over and asked him to get in touch with you."

"Why did you ask him to go? Why didn't you come get me yourself?"

"I wanted to secure the scene and guard the body from predators or the killer if he or she was to return. If she was murdered. We can't know that until the autopsy results come back, can we?"

The sheriff bristled visibly. "You chose to stay with the body so you could 'secure the scene.'"

"Yes, sir." I stared at my coffee cup on the table while the sheriff flipped through his notes in the folder.

"What is your timeframe for staying in Whispering Pines?" It was a standard question, but I couldn't help but think he wanted me out of here sooner than later.

I explained how it was originally going to be a week. "With the state of the house, that's kind of up in the air now."

Sheriff Brighton tapped his pen on the notepad, studying me as he did. "Ms. O'Shea, you seem to know a lot about police procedures. In fact, you sound like a cop."

He waited for me to respond, but since he hadn't asked a question, I stayed mute.

He chuckled softly. "I knew someone from your family would be coming to take care of the house. As I said before, I like to know the residents of my village. I did a little research. Your mom owns a spa. Dad is an archeologist. Your sister Rosalyn is a student at UW Madison." He looked up. "You worked for the Madison PD for nearly five years."

I didn't know how to react to that. "Got a lot of free time on your hands during the off season, do you, Sheriff?"

"Are you a cop, Ms. O'Shea?"

Damn. This wasn't supposed to come up. I didn't know anyone here, my plan was to be off the grid and incognito for a week. Enjoy a little solo time. I sighed.

"Until six months ago, yes, sir, I was a cop."

He nodded, confirming the facts. "What happened six months ago?"

"I stopped being a cop." What were the chances he'd let this subject go with that?

"Why? Were you terminated?"

I sat straight, clammy hands resting on my thighs. Meeka shifted and pressed even harder against me.

"My work history isn't relevant to this discussion. I'd prefer to not talk about it."

The sheriff was wrestling with something; I could see it on his face. Finally, he said, "You want me to investigate the break-in of your family home, correct?"

"Yes, sir."

"And you'd prefer that I track down the vandals, not just file a report. Correct?"

"That would be preferable."

"You're also aware that I now have the death of Miss Yasmine Long to investigate. And our tourist season is about to begin?"

"I'm sorry, Sheriff Brighton, but is there a point here?"

He stared at me for another long moment, wrestling again with whatever was swirling in his head, then he switched off the voice recorder and stood to close the interview room door. I tensed, my pulse rate increasing as I prepared for whatever was about to happen. Or so I thought.

"Deputy Reed out there," the sheriff began in a low voice, "is my nephew. I deputized him because he needs something to do. I dress him up in a uniform and have him walk around the village. He feels like he's doing something important, which he is. As you know, sometimes the simple presence of a uniform is all it takes to keep trouble under control."

That rubbed me the wrong way. Deputizing him

because he needed something to do?

"He knows the law and can handle doing minor enforcement. He keeps an eye on the drunks we throw in the cells to dry out. He can handle most of the administrative tasks." The sheriff paced the width of the room, working that bum leg. "But the boy isn't capable of investigating his way out of this building without a map. I'm basically a department of one and quite honestly, dealing with tourist issues this time of year takes all my efforts. Add a murder *and* a home break-in investigation to the mix . . ."

I tilted my chin up and stared him in the eye, sure he was about to tell me one of those things would have to wait. Logically, that would be investigating the break-in.

"What are you saying, Sheriff?"

He paused, wrestling one last time, then let out a resigned exhale. "I'm saying I need help around here, Ms. O'Shea. The hotels and cottages are reporting solid bookings for the next three months. I was going to put out an advertisement today, but as long as you weren't fired due to breaking a law or misconduct, I'd like to offer the job to you."

Chapter 7

I HAD A LIST OF things I'd been looking forward to doing while in Whispering Pines: Enjoying the peace and quiet of spending a week in a village barely big enough to be represented by a spot on the map. Spending a little time by or on the lake with my dog. I brought books—a sci-fi a friend recommended and a women's fiction in case life in space didn't do it for me—and my watercolors so I could finally try painting like I'd wanted to forever. There was also that 'focus on being mindful' thing. Of course, taking care of my grandparents' home was first on the list. That was it; that was my list. A job with the sheriff was nowhere on it.

"Before we go any further," Sheriff Brighton said, "tell me why you aren't a cop anymore."

I drained the now-cold coffee from my cup then walked to the water cooler in the corner. While I filled the cup, I debated if I wanted to talk about this, if I was even capable of talking about it. I didn't have to; it was my right to simply refuse.

Fine. He wasn't going to let this go. I dropped back into the chair. "What do you want to know?"

"Did you quit or were you terminated?" Sheriff Brighton asked without missing a beat.

"I quit."

He sat there, silent, waiting for me to continue.

"About a year ago—" I paused to calculate. Wow, yes, it had been that long already. "Almost a year ago exactly, I was named detective."

"How old are you?"

"Twenty-six. Twenty-five at the time."

His eyebrows raised in surprise. "That's impressive."

I nodded. "Something I'm very proud of."

"Go on. What happened to make you step away from that?"

"In a nutshell, my partner was having some personal issues. I tried to help him, encouraged him to get counseling, but for reasons I'd rather not explain, he wouldn't go. I should have reported him so he could get help, but instead I tried to help him myself." I shook my head. "Things got worse and worse until one day he lost control."

I paused to clear the memories trying to worm their way in.

Finally, Sheriff Brighton cleared his throat. "What happened, Detective?"

The use of my title brought me back. I scrubbed my hands over my face. I could do this. Maybe telling someone other than my therapist would even help.

"One of our CIs was a woman named Fr—" My voice broke. "Frisky. She called herself Frisky Fox. She was an older woman, late-forties but looked well into her sixties." I laughed, remembering the vibrant woman with the big laugh and ready hug. "Life had worked Frisky over good. Anyway, after getting busted on some minor charges, she became an informant. What that meant, in Frisky's case, was doing all she could to keep the kids in her neighborhood out of trouble. One day we saw her car and, since we hadn't heard from her in a while, pulled her over just to chat."

Sheriff Brighton sat quietly, folded hands resting on the table.

"This particular day was a bad one for Frisky. It was the one-year anniversary of her brother's death. The next day was the second anniversary of her nephew's death." I was about to explain further but it wasn't my story to tell. "Frisky self-medicated that day, high or drunk . . . or both, and was belligerent as hell. When we pulled her over, she got out of her vehicle."

"Weapon?"

"Unarmed. She just wanted to be left alone, and us getting in her face upset an already strained situation. I'd never seen her like that. She'd always been calm to the point of pacifism, but that day she was ranting and raging. Randy kept yelling at her to get back in her vehicle. The more he yelled, the more upset she became."

The scene started to play out in my head. The panic on both Frisky's and Randy's faces. My inability to calm either down. The million regrets that raced through my mind in the second it took Randy to aim his weapon at her.

"Randy shot her."

"You feel responsible," Sheriff Brighton said.

I nodded. My role in the event and resulting feelings of guilt had been the topic of most of my sessions with Dr. Maddox.

"She wouldn't have hurt us. I'm positive of that," I said. "Not sure which I agonize over more, Frisky's death or the fact that I didn't report my partner sooner."

The sheriff closed his eyes, as though afraid to ask his next question. "You reported him?"

"I had to." I slouched back in the chair and traced a scratch on the table with my finger. "For a couple of weeks, I didn't say a word and it ate me up. The other officers and detectives knew as well as I did that Randy had been self-destructing. Finally, after weeks of staying awake all night gorging on sweets, I told my captain everything."

Sheriff Brighton winced.

"It was the right thing to do," I insisted, "for Randy and

the public. But the other officers, the other detectives in particular, turned on me."

The sheriff nodded his understanding. Loyalty among the brethren. I'd crossed that line.

"The worst thing for me," I said, "isn't being supposedly disloyal to my partner, it's knowing that I could have prevented a woman's death."

"A no-win situation." The sheriff shifted uncomfortably in his chair, massaging his right hip.

"Sir, are you okay?" I nodded at his leg.

He waved it off. "Lifelong problem. I'll be fine. How long ago did you quit?"

"I stuck it out for about a month after Frisky died, seeing a shrink three days a week. Six months ago, I couldn't face one more day of going in and getting harassed, so I emailed my resignation." I smiled. "Last night was the first decent night's sleep I've gotten since."

Considering I found a body on my property, I had prepared for nightmares. Maybe the whispering trees kept them away.

"Do you suppose staying busy would help?" Sheriff Brighton asked.

"Look, I didn't come here with the intention of staying. It was only going to be a week. Considering the condition of the house, it's going to be longer now but still not permanent."

"What about a part-time temporary job?"

This made me cautiously curious. "What did you have in mind?"

"Dealing with those tourist issues I mentioned earlier." He waved a hand in Deputy Reed's direction. "He can handle the office work. I need someone with experience who I can trust to handle law and order among the tourists. Wander around the village, walk along the beach, cruise around the rental cottages and the campground. Talk to people and let them know we're around and available should they need us."

I shifted in my chair. "That would sort of be a demotion for me, wouldn't it?"

"Don't know that you can do detective work part-time."

Couldn't argue with that. I had to admit, being with the public was my favorite part of the job. Accepting his offer would also get me back into the profession I loved.

"So, what, drunk and disorderly calls? Babysit the rabble-rousers?"

"Both of those," the sheriff said. "Then there's tracking down the occasional kid who wanders off. Vandalism is a problem at times, but not like what you say happened at your house. Spoiled rich kids come up with their parents and get bored because of the cell phone reception issue. And when kids get bored, they tend to get into trouble. Your house probably got hit because it's isolated."

I picked at the hem of my T-shirt. Was this really how I wanted to spend my time here? My plan was to read and paint when not packing. Maybe take out the boat or a kayak. What if I wasn't ready to get back to work? I'd made a lot of progress learning to trust myself again, especially over the last few weeks. It would really suck to backslide.

"Thanks for the offer, Sheriff, but I don't think so."

"At least take the day to consider it," he pleaded. "Let me know tomorrow."

"Fine. Anything else you need from me regarding Yasmine Long?"

Sheriff Brighton looked over his notes. "Not right now. I'll stop by to investigate your house later today. Did you call your insurance people yet?"

"No cell service, no landline." I frowned. "Any chance I could use the phone here? I need to call my mother, too, and let her know what happened to the house."

"Sure. Use that one." Sheriff Brighton gave a nod at the phone in the corner by the water cooler as he gathered his papers. "I'm serious about the job. We really could use you."

Chapter 8

AFTER RETRIEVING MEEKA'S COLLAPSIBLE DISH
from my bag and filling it with water from the cooler, I
called my mother.

"Do you know how many times I tried calling?" she
demanded in lieu of a polite greeting. "Did you get my
messages? Why didn't you call me?"

For a moment, I felt guilty about not answering that call
yesterday. But it likely would have dropped within a minute
or two anyway.

"There's no cellular service here, Mom, and there's a
problem with the house line. I'm calling from the sheriff's
station."

"Sheriff? Good lord, what happened?"

I explained the vandalism, which led her on a ten-
minute rant about not only how big a nuisance the house
was, but how we should have taken Gran out of it and put
her in a nursing home long ago. Not that my grandmother in
any way needed a nursing home. Then Mom went on about
how my selfish father needed to ". . . get back to this country
and take care of this fiasco himself. I told him, multiple
times, she's his mother. Why should I—?"

She cut herself off mid-rant and a humming sound came

through the receiver. I could picture her—eyes closed, chin up, jaw clenched as she shook her head back and forth in a sharp, crisp motion. Her version of meditation always made me think she was having a seizure.

While she pulled herself together, I started a good points/bad points list of reasons for accepting or rejecting Sheriff Brighton's job offer. Even though I didn't really want it.

"Jayne!" Mom demanded.

"What?"

"Have you listened to a word I've said?"

When had she started speaking again? I scrambled for a response. "Of course. You're not at all happy about this."

She sighed heavily. "You're sure you can deal with this? It won't be too stressful?"

I held back my own tired sigh. She sent me here. She insisted. "I'm fine, Mom."

"If taking on this much responsibility will be too much for you, I'm sure your sister or I can find the time to deal with it."

Dr. Maddox had helped me realize that my problem was a lack of confidence. This was why I couldn't stand up and do things like reporting Randy; I didn't trust that I was making the right decision. Not a good trait for a cop. Unfortunately, this inability to stand up carried through the rest of my life, too. I desperately wanted to tell my mother that I didn't need help running my life. The problem there was that she didn't trust me anymore than I trusted myself.

"I want to do this," I said. "Packing up the house is a good assignment for me. Do you think there's anything in particular Dad will want?"

"He hasn't mentioned anything. It's been years since he's seen any of it. Box up the contents of his bedroom. He can decide what's worth hanging on to and what can be sent to the landfill."

Lovely. No sense bringing up any warm-n-fuzzy

memories. She'd just start humming again.

"You're sure you can take care of this?"

It was part plea—"Please, darling, take care of this for your poor, ultra-busy mother."—part insult—"Seriously, Jayne, are you capable of doing even this one thing for me?"

She got like that when control started slipping through her fingers. Vandalism, or any kind of setback, hadn't been planned for on the packing-up-the-house schedule. If Dad was around, she'd take all of this out on him. Which was why he hid in the desert for most of the year.

"I'm on it, Mom. I'm looking forward to being busy again. I haven't seen all of the house, so I don't know the extent of the damage. Regardless of the break-in, the house needs a lot of attention if we want to get top dollar for it."

My businesslike tone took her by surprise.

"Well, yes. Of course. We'd be renovating anyway, I guess. Is that something you're willing to take on? We could hire a general contractor." She paused, her nails *tap, tap, tapping.* "Even if we do that, someone will need to be there to keep an eye on things and make sure they're actually doing what they say they're doing. You can't trust those people, you know. They'll steal you blind."

Suddenly, being five hours from Madison for a month or more, perhaps the whole summer if I stretched things properly, seemed like an unexpected gift.

"I'm fine taking this on," I said. "I'll get references from the locals and take bids. And I'll consult you every step of the way."

"Maybe not every step," she said. "I trust you. Of course I trust you."

No, she didn't. Still, she was going to let me handle the sale of the house. Maybe she was busier at the spa than I realized. Or she cared less about the house than I wanted to believe. Either way, this was big because a substantial amount of money was involved. She gave me all the insurance information and promised to transfer funds into a bank account I could draw from until the settlement came through.

"One other thing you should probably know about," I began and told her about Yasmine.

"Will that affect the sale, do you think?"

"Really, Mom? A woman died and you're worried about resale value?"

"Of course not," she objected a little too strenuously. "You make me sound like a coldhearted beast. The poor girl."

In the background, someone was asking a question about an inventory order. When she returned to me Mom said, "You only brought enough clothing and whatnot for a week."

"Right."

"I'll send a box. Would you like me to send some of your clothes, too, or will you go shopping there?"

By 'box' she meant a supply of the best of the best hair and skin supplies from her uber-popular Melt Your Cares Day Spa. I had to admit, my hair was super-silky and my pores were exactly the right size. The thought of me going even one day without the proper beauty regimen was probably making her eye twitch. The thought of my mother going through my clothes, and deciding what would be proper for me to wear in Whispering Pines, set both of my eyes off like a couple of good ol' boys playing *Dueling Banjos*.

"Just the box will do, I'll go shopping. Supporting local businesses is always a good idea." Mom was all about connections. "I buy from them, and they'll help make sure I get quality help for the house."

"Good plan. Okay, then." The change in her tone signaled she was ready to sign off. "I'll get that box ready and on its way this afternoon. Let me know if you need anything else."

Next, I called the insurance company who promised to

have an adjuster to the house tomorrow. Then I called the phone company to get service restored and a line run to the boathouse. Finally, I scheduled internet hook-up in the boathouse. After waiting on hold for fifteen minutes, I had a guarantee that someone would be there in the next twenty-four to seventy-two hours. Was a range that big really a guarantee? Seemed like more of a promise to get around to it.

"Get your business taken care of?" Deputy Reed asked when Meeka and I left the interview room.

By the challenging look on his face, it was obvious he had a problem with me. The sheriff, his uncle, must have told him I might be coming on board. Or maybe he just had one of those resting bitch faces.

"Yes, thank you. Is the sheriff still here?"

"No, he's off investigating a murder." He looked at me like I was dense or that Yasmine's death was somehow my fault because the body was found on my property.

My cop's eye turned on, and I stood back to study him. When he wasn't glaring, he was fidgeting.

"Something wrong, Deputy Reed? You seem upset."

"Someone died." Now he wouldn't look at me at all. "We don't get a lot of that around here. Maybe an accidental drowning every few years but never a murder. Is that reason enough for you?"

"Sure it is." I offered a moment of silence for Yasmine. "Don't recall it being labeled a murder, though. That's not a word the sheriff used with me."

Reed didn't respond.

"Do you have any idea what might have happened? Tripp Bennett told me Yasmine had been in the area for a few weeks. Did you know her?"

"Why would I know her?" He snapped and crammed more trail mix from the now nearly-empty bag into his mouth.

"Sheriff Brighton told me that one of your

responsibilities is patrolling the village. Is that true?"

"Yeah." He sat a little straighter and pushed his shoulders back.

"I just wondered if you ever saw Yasmine while you were out and about."

He took time brushing trail mix crumbs from his hands. "Possible, I suppose."

Everyone noticed her, Tripp had said of Yasmine. Deputy Reed seemed like a healthy, surely-hormonal young man. If his job was to patrol the village, there was no way he would have missed the sudsy girl in the yellow bikini.

"What difference would it make if I did?" He turned his glare back on, his voice growing louder and increasingly defensive. "Why do you care anyway?"

"Yasmine died on my property," I stated calmly. "Other than the fact that she's a human being, isn't that reason enough?"

He flinched a little every time I said Yasmine's name. Instinct told me that Deputy Reed was hiding something. Or he was flat-out lying.

"See you around," I promised. "Turns out I'll be here for longer than I'd planned."

He grunted and I felt his eyes boring a hole between my shoulder blades as I left the station.

Chapter 9

TREAT ME SWEETLY WAS ONE part old world bakery, one part vintage ice cream shop, and one part Willy Wonka candy store. The interior was bright and cheery while being warm and cozy at the same time. It was also far busier than I'd expected. Yes, it was a Sunday, but the official start of summer was still a week away. All six of the shop's café tables were occupied as were the two picnic tables and three benches outside. The employees were scurrying around like chipmunks, scooping ice cream on one side of the store, boxing up pastries or bagging candies on the other. What must it be like during peak season?

"What can I get for you?" The woman behind the counter asked. *Mid-forties, round face, reddish hair, slightly overweight.*

"It's busy," I said dumbly.

"Isn't it great?" She smiled with genuine happiness, as a shopkeeper should when business was good. "The villagers are getting their fill before the tourists arrive. There will be a constant line then, and we won't slow down until after the autumnal equinox."

"The autumn what?"

"Autumnal equinox. It falls around September twenty-second, depending on the sun, and marks the start of autumn. Things will die down and then we'll get a little activity during winter solstice." She laughed. "I could go on all afternoon about this, but as you can see, I've got customers. What can I get you, sweetie?"

Ice cream. I had to go grocery shopping, but if I went when I was hungry, I'd get nothing but junk food. I stared into the freezer case, like everyone before me had, and analyzed every container carefully. This decision could make or break my afternoon, after all.

"I'll have a double with strawberry ripple and lemon basil." There. Fruit. And there was some sort of nutritional value in basil. I read that somewhere.

"Are you visiting or passing through?" the woman asked as she scooped.

"Visiting, in a way. I'd planned to only be here a week, but it's going to be longer."

She laughed. "You make it sound like a business trip. Who comes to Whispering Pines for business?"

"It's kind of like business, I guess. I'm here to pack up my grandmother's house."

The woman stood straight up, nearly bumping her head on the freezer door as she did. "Lucy O'Shea's house?"

She wore the same giddy, slightly-awed expression as Violet over at Ye Olde Bean Grinder.

"I'm Jayne, Lucy's granddaughter."

The woman sighed and placed a hand to her heart. "Your grandma talked about you and your sister all the time. What's her name?"

"Rosalyn."

She pointed the ice cream scoop at me in confirmation. "Rosalyn. She adored you girls."

A wave of warmth washed over me at the proclamation.

"It's lovely to meet you, Jayne." The woman finished adding lemon-basil on top of the strawberry ripple. "I'm Honey. That's my sister." She indicated the woman across the store at the bakery counter. *Mid- to late-forties, round face, blonde hair with a touch of red, five-six.* "Sugar, this is Lucy's granddaughter Jayne."

There was that same expression again. The one that said she'd just met someone important. I knew Gran had been a sort of celebrity around here, being the village founder and all, but I hadn't expected that to rub off onto me.

"Your names are Honey and Sugar?" I confirmed, amused.

"Running a sweet shop seemed like the obvious choice." Honey handed me a cup filled with four, generous scoops of ice cream, not two like I'd expected.

"I only wanted a double," I objected, but not too strenuously.

"Around here," Honey said, "we fill the cup. So a single cup fits two scoops, a double fits four. She reached for my cup. "If you'd like me to take some away—"

"No-no." I held it away. "This is fine. I'll remember for next time. How much do I owe you?"

"Nothing. On the house."

Sugar appeared next to me and tucked a small cookie along the edge of my cup. A tiny purple flower was visible beneath a glittering coating of sugar.

"No charge for Lucy's family," Sugar explained, leaving no room for argument. "Biscuit for your pup?"

"She'll love you forever," I said and accepted the treat for Meeka. "Thank you, both."

As I turned away from the counter, one of the pink metal café tables was being vacated. Meeka lay beneath my chair, contently nibbling her biscuit, and I forced myself to eat slowly while looking around the shop. Warm brown wooden shelves loaded with old-fashioned candy jars lined the wall next to me, each jar stuffed full with brightly-colored candy—taffy and toffee, candy necklaces and buttons, root beer barrels and lemon drops, jaw breakers . . . What a fun place to work.

I'd made it to the last spoonful of lemon basil and was about to start the strawberry ripple when the shop door opened. The most striking woman I'd ever seen walked in. I stared at her with the spoon suspended halfway to my mouth. *Late-twenties, five-five, wavy raven-black hair that hung to her elbows, ivory skin.* A wicker basket hung from her arm, overflowing with small plant bundles.

"Blessed be, ladies," the woman chirped.

The woman wore short black shorts and a black corset vest beneath a long sheer black overdress, and black booties. A flowing jacket, in a beautiful olive-green chiffon embroidered all over with flowers and plants, fell past her knees and completed her outfit. Stunning. She was absolutely stunning.

"Good morning, Morgan," Sugar said. "I hope you've got some pansies in there for me."

Morgan reached into her basket, the numerous bracelets encircling her wrists jangling with her every move, and plucked out a small bundle of flowers.

"I remembered. I've got a bounty of other flowers and herbs for you today as well. The Goddess has already blessed my garden, and there are still five weeks until summer solstice." She placed the pansies and the rest of the basket's contents on a stainless steel table behind the serving counters. "Does the arrival of pansies mean you'll have fresh sugar cookies soon?"

"I plan to start them as soon as we get a break," Sugar said. "Your delivery is just in time. Jayne here got the last pansy cookie."

Morgan spun to face me, her chiffon jacket billowing around her, just as I inserted the last bite of cookie into my mouth.

"Guilty as charged," I mumbled around the pastry.

"Morgan," Honey lowered her voice as though she had a secret to spill, "this is Jayne O'Shea."

Morgan closed the distance between us in two confident

strides. She pulled out the chair across from me and in a smooth, fluid motion, lowered into it. I prepared for the same starstruck treatment I'd gotten from everyone else that morning. Except the sheriff and his deputy, of course.

"Jayne O'Shea." She placed her hands palms together near her heart, her reaction more one of relief than being in awe of my presence. "So glad you arrived safely."

Glad I arrived safely? She said it like she'd known I was coming. She couldn't though. Neither my mother nor Rosalyn had told anyone. We just got the email from Dad with the go-ahead two days ago.

"I hear you had a little trouble out at your place last night," Morgan said.

"Trouble?" Sugar asked.

"What trouble?" Honey added.

Morgan narrowed her heavily-lined and shadowed eyes at the women and then rose from her chair as gracefully as she'd lowered onto it. She held up a hand, flicked her fingers in a *follow me* motion, and floated out of the shop. On the other side of the threshold, she paused and looked over her shoulder at Honey and Sugar.

"Blessed be."

Feeling almost compelled to trail after her, I shoveled the remaining strawberry ripple into my mouth and stood after the brain freeze faded.

"Thank you, ladies. The ice cream and cookie were wonderful."

"We'll see you again?" Honey asked.

"Oh, yes. I'll be back," I promised and tossed the empty container into the receptacle by the door. I paused to attach Meeka's leash and hurried to catch up with Morgan.

"What an adorable creature."

Morgan bent and offered the back of her hand to Meeka who sniffed it, wagged her tail, and looked to me for approval. It was a good sign whenever my dog trusted someone.

"Friend," I gave the command letting her know it was okay to interact with this stranger. "This is Meeka."

Meeka immediately shoved her head under Morgan's hand, hoping for an ear scratch from nails coated with lacquer as black as Morgan's hair.

"We hardly had a proper introduction." Morgan straightened and held a thin hand out to me. She wore rings on each of her long fingers—all were silver, many looked like twined vines, a few held small crystals. "Morgan Barlow. I'm delighted that you're here."

I accepted her hand. "Jayne O'Shea. You act as though you've been expecting me."

Morgan tucked her hand beneath my upper arm like we were long-lost, reuniting friends.

"You have a lot of questions about many things." Morgan led me south around the pentacle garden toward a path that ran alongside the lake. "Let's walk. I'll try to ease your mind of some of them."

Assuming that she meant she had information about Yasmine Long's death—that had been the topic that propelled us from the sweet shop, after all—I went with her.

"So, you knew Yasmine Long?" I asked.

"Yasmine? Oh, yes. I was familiar with her." She paused. "Being an Original can be a bit overwhelming. There's a level of responsibility that comes with it."

Confused, it took me a moment to realize she had switched topics. "I have no idea what 'being an Original' means."

She gave me a look of pity. "They haven't told you anything, have they? Let me help you understand."

They who? Haven't told me anything about what? I felt like a coma patient who had just come to and found that years had passed while I was out.

"Understanding sounds like a good idea," I agreed, switching to fact-gathering cop mode.

"An Original," Morgan began, "is what we call the first

settlers of Whispering Pines. Family members of the first settlers also qualify. Your beloved grandmother was *The Original*, our founder. Your grandfather obviously supported her decision, but we didn't see much of him."

Gramps traveled a lot with his job in land development or general contracting . . . something like that. Gran hated city life and convinced him to buy the land Whispering Pines occupied. But moving all the way up here, alone in that big house on two thousand acres? She must have been lonely. Maybe she'd hoped for more children, but my dad was their only child. No wonder she agreed to let people live here.

"What do you know about the village's founding?" Morgan asked.

"Not a lot." The sun's glare off the lake blinded me, so I slid my sunglasses off the top of my head into place. "I know that my grandparents purchased the land in the early-sixties. I know that they designated the ten-acre thumb of land jutting into the lake as private for themselves. In the mid-sixties, The Inn was the first building built on the remaining acreage and others soon followed." I glanced at Morgan and found an expectant look. "That's it, that's all I know. And that the village primarily follows the Wiccan religion, but I don't know why because my grandparents weren't Wiccan."

Morgan smiled, as though she had a secret. Had my grandparents been Wiccan? Why would they hide that?

"Your knowledge is indeed limited," Morgan agreed. "The first thing to clear up is that my home, my grandparents' home actually, was the first structure built." Morgan gestured to our right. "It's almost directly north of this spot, just across the creek. Our grandmothers met in the early-sixties at a gardening show. They hit it off immediately and the more they talked, the more truths they revealed to each other. My grandmother was one of the few followers of Wicca in this country at that time."

"You're saying Wicca is a relatively new religion?"

"There have always been nature-oriented or Pagan religions. And by Pagan, I mean a religion other than Judaism, Islam, or Christianity. Wicca became popular in England in the 1950s and spread to America about a decade later."

"So why form a community in nowhere northern Wisconsin? It's so secluded."

"Wiccans tend to be very private." Morgan frowned. "People don't understand us. Most think that we worship the devil, perform human sacrifices, and dance naked in the moonlight. That's not at all true. Well, some dance naked but that's entirely personal preference. If a comparison helps, Wicca is similar to Native American spirituality in that both revere nature and its gifts. That's a very simplistic explanation, but this was the discussion our grandmothers had. Your grandmother couldn't tolerate that mine might be discriminated against because of her beliefs."

I smiled, remembering some of the spirited 'discussions' Gran and Dad used to have. "Yeah, my grandmother was a big believer in speaking your truth."

Morgan placed a hand over her heart. "Which is one of the many reasons why we miss her so very much."

I gave a nod of thanks as a little jolt of jealousy stabbed me. It wasn't fair that strangers knew my grandmother so well while Rosalyn and I barely saw her. Because of some stupid family feud, our time together became limited to short visits when Gran and Gramps came down to Madison. We'd have dinner somewhere or spend a rare overnight at a hotel where we could swim and Gran would tuck us in with bedtime stories.

"After my grandparents moved here," Morgan explained, "word started to spread. Followers of Wicca heard about a place where they could live without fear of persecution and made pilgrimages here. Lucy didn't turn them away, but she couldn't let everyone stay in the house.

That's when The Inn was built, so people had somewhere to live while their homes were constructed."

"But more than just Wiccans live here."

Morgan nodded. "In the mid- to late-1800s the Spiritualist movement, psychics and mediums holding séances to communicate with the dead, was all the rage. There are still many who believe in Spiritualism and feel just as ostracized as Wiccans. They found their way here as well."

The fortune tellers over in The Triangle.

"You're saying Whispering Pines is a community of different religions," I said as I stepped out of the way of a biker coming toward us on the path.

"At first. Then the carnies found their way here. Few are as harassed as the freak show folks." She smiled. "They have a lovely little circus setup in a clearing in the northeast forest. Very popular evening entertainment with the tourists."

A night circus? That sounded like fun. I'd have to check it out.

"Really," Morgan continued, "anyone who doesn't fit in elsewhere is welcome in Whispering Pines."

"Then why can't Tripp Bennett get a job here?"

She gave a small smile. "Because Tripp could fit in anywhere. Just because someone wants to stay, and plenty do, doesn't mean they belong. We want to keep it a safe place for those who need it."

"Sounds like reverse discrimination." My ire, as Gran would call it, was rising.

"I understand why you would think that. Remember your grandmother's intensions, though. If we fill up with everyone who wants to stay, where will those with a true need go?"

I needed time to digest that thought.

"You'll come to understand." Morgan's words sounded more like an expectation of assimilation than an explanation.

"This is why I said, being an Original comes with responsibility."

"Are there others?"

"Originals? Of course. The thirteen of us who sit on the village council all descend from the first families. Some are Wiccan. Some Spiritualist. Some Carnies . . ."

"Thirteen members on a council? Sounds like a coven."

I was joking and, quite honestly, losing patience with this whole discussion. The head-to-toe black clothing. The jewelry with the moons and pentacles. The goddess-blessed herbs and flowers delivered ceremonially to Sugar and Honey. Morgan certainly played the role of witch, or whatever, well. She'd have to work a lot harder to convince me, though. I had seen plenty of strange things during my time as a police officer. I'd walked into homes where whole rooms were devoted to an altar set up with daggers, candles, incense, containers of salt, and small cast iron cauldrons, whatever those were for. I understood that followers of Wicca truly believed they were casting spells of some kind, but I did not for one second believe in witchcraft. And after talking with Morgan, I couldn't help but wonder if my grandparents had gotten swindled out of nearly two thousand pristine lakeside acres.

Morgan's eyes glittered as she acknowledged, "We do have a coven."

Of course they did.

"It's for the Wiccans who live here," she continued. "We gather together for rituals and celebrations. Not all Wiccans choose to be in the coven. Many are solitary practitioners. You'll be here for a while, you'll come to understand."

"What's the council?" The one that refused to let Tripp rent a place to live.

"The council rules over the village. Most of the council members are business owners and have a direct interest in the goings on here. You've already met five of the thirteen—myself, Violet, Honey, Sugar, and Sheriff Brighton."

A village council to create rules and regulations made sense, but my head was spinning over the rest of what she said. I understood that Wicca was a recognized religion, and I was trying to remain respectful of that, but was she serious? Covens? Rituals? Discriminating against perfectly decent, normal people? Was this how her grandmother got Gran to let her live here? Smoke and mirrors and confusion? And how did she know I'd met Violet and the sheriff?

"You're staring at me," Morgan pointed out.

I was. Throughout our discussion, a sense of déjà vu hovered around me, growing stronger and stronger. "You seem familiar to me."

"We've known each other for a long time."

At first, I figured this was more of her spiritual, moons and pentacles talk. That we were neighbors in a past life or something like that. Then a memory flashed in my mind. Rosalyn and I in the pentacle garden playing with a little girl with long black hair.

We would always find her there, tending the plants or weaving herbs into long necklaces. She talked about the phases of the moon and the best times to harvest crops. We thought she was so weird.

"Oh my god. You're *that* Morgan."

"I am."

"You had a rooster. A solid black rooster."

She grinned. "I still do. Pitch is in my garden right now. He is excellent at keeping the soil loose and richly fertilized."

Great. Now I was imagining rooster poop in the flower on that sugar cookie.

"Wait. You can't mean he's the same rooster. That was nearly twenty years ago."

"The same rooster," Morgan said. "Looks like we're at your car."

I blinked, surprised to find we were in fact standing behind the Cherokee.

"How did you know this is my car?"

Morgan looked skyward then laughed and gave me a wink. "I have my ways. We'll see one another again soon, Jayne O'Shea. Blessed be."

I was halfway to the grocery store before I realized Morgan never did tell me how she knew Yasmine.

Chapter 10

SUNDRY, WHISPERING PINES' GENERAL STORE, sold pretty much anything that wasn't available in the main village: groceries, office supplies, hardware and tools, medications not of a holistic nature. . . Equally charming with its cottage-style exterior and sit-and-stay-awhile interior, it fit perfectly into this old-world environment.

On the way home with my groceries, I passed a twin of the massive "Welcome to Whispering Pines" sign. It even had an identical 'Blessed Be' plaque hanging at the bottom. Out of nowhere, I was bombarded by memories of Mom mumbling, "Tree huggers," or something similar every time we came to visit.

"That's not what Wicca is," Dad would object.

"What's a tree hugger?" Rosalyn asked.

"It's someone who hugs trees, silly," I answered with total sincerity.

What did I know? I was only eight at the time, Rosalyn four.

"A tree hugger," Dad had explained, "is an environmentalist, someone who cares a lot about nature. Wiccans do worship nature and often synchronize their rituals with the phases of the moon." He waved his hand as though wiping words from a whiteboard. "That's a very basic definition. A detailed explanation would take a great deal of time. My point is, tree huggers are environmentalists and Wicca is a religion."

"They think they can perform magic," Mom said. "It's complete lunacy."

"Who's to say they can't?" Dad glanced at her and grinned. "Point of information: the word lunacy comes from the word lunatic, which holds the root word *luna*, which means moon. Long ago it was thought that people went temporarily insane based on the phases of the moon."

"Oh god," Mom groaned.

"Like werewolves?" I had asked, bouncing in my seat. "Are there werewolves in Whispering Pines?"

"I've never seen one," Dad said. "And to my knowledge no one ever has."

That didn't stop me from hoping. If we ever visited during a full moon, I'd sneak outside in the middle of the night and listen for howls. One time I heard some, but Gran said that was a gray wolf that prowled the area, not a werewolf.

Dad had loved Whispering Pines. He acted like an excited kid every time we planned a visit. Mom, on the other hand, was as averse to the village of *tree huggers* as it was possible to be. She was averse to anything that wasn't middle-of-the-road or generally accepted by society. Maybe that was the reason for the feud. Maybe my grandparents had practiced Wicca. That, as far as Mom would be concerned, would place them far from the middle. If that was it, why had it taken until I was ten years old to boil over?

I shook my head, scattering the thoughts, and pulled to a stop in front of the garage. I let Meeka out of her crate and stood there and stared at the lake. It was so peaceful. A dozen or so boats zipped across the vast blue surface. A week from now, the lake would be crammed with boats and jet skis. The atmosphere in the village would be different, too. It would be noisier and crowded with people, some doing stupid things—happy, laid-back vacation stupid things, but still stupid.

After not even twenty-four hours, I felt more relaxed, far less stressed. Was being in Whispering Pines specifically the reason? Or was it because I was on my own and I'd feel this way regardless of location? Tomorrow, I would set up my easel and try to paint. Or maybe I'd sit in the sun and soak up some vitamin D while reading a book. Until the insurance people came, then I'd have to get busy on the house.

I was also supposed to let Sheriff Brighton know my decision about the job tomorrow. I'd said I wasn't interested, but it was an honest offer that deserved honest consideration. After talking with Morgan and others around the village today, I had a new understanding of how much Gran meant to the place and its people. I almost felt responsible to them now, like a family member should be here to fill Gran's role. Accepting the sheriff's offer would allow me to stick around. That was crazy, though. Sure, they gave me free coffee and ice cream, but only because I was Lucy O'Shea's granddaughter. No one really cared if I stayed here or not.

The thing was, until the day Frisky died, I had loved every aspect of being a cop. Quitting had been a reaction to my fellow officers harassing me, not because I didn't enjoy the work. Being a deputy in this tiny town would be a quiet way to return to law enforcement.

Except, I was here to pack up the house.

I couldn't make this decision right now. It was a beautiful day and it felt good to be in the sunshine. I had until tomorrow to give the sheriff an answer. No need to stress about it right now.

After running the groceries up to the apartment, I whistled for Meeka. Her furry head poked out from around a corner of the boathouse.

"Let's go for a walk."

She looked at her leash in my hand and took off in a white blur.

"Fine," I called after her, "but you're on the leash at the end of the driveway."

I swear she understood more English than just dog commands. When I got to the end, she was sitting there waiting for me. I praised her and after I'd clipped on her leash, she tugged me toward the campground. Didn't matter to me where we walked, so I let her take the lead.

We wandered along the one-way road, circling to the south side of the grounds first where we found a few RVs docked on the pads. At the north side, a handful of tents had been setup. When we were almost back to the entrance, we came to an old red pickup next to a popup trailer. Tripp had mentioned he had a truck. He hadn't described it, but I knew this thirty-year-old F350 had to be his. Far from swanky, it had a homey feel that seemed to fit the man I'd gotten to know a little last night.

He'd been so easy to talk to. Maybe he could help me with this job decision. I looked down at Meeka. "What do you think? Should we see if Tripp is home?"

She wagged her tail double time.

I stepped under the awning hanging off the side of the popup and around a picnic table beneath it. "Tripp? Are you in there?"

An instant later, Tripp's face appeared on the other side of the screen. The second I saw him, I wondered if just showing up this way was okay. Maybe he had company.

"Jayne." He gave a big grin that made a dimple appear in his left cheek. "What's up? Come on in."

I almost objected and said we should sit outside, but considering half of his home was mesh, it was practically the same thing.

The inside of the popup was much nicer than the outside. It was old, yes, but clean and bright. All of the wood cabinets were covered in a coat of crisp white paint. The floor was faux-bamboo linoleum. The cushions on the bench seats were covered with chocolate-brown upholstery. Red, yellow, and brown plaid curtains hung randomly around the mesh perimeter. Everything appeared to be new or newer.

"Impressed?" he asked with a grin. "Amazing what stuff off of the closeout shelf and a gallon of paint can do, hey?"

"This is really nice. You did all this yourself?"

"Can't sew. Had to have someone else do the curtains and cushions. A lady with a sewing machine needed her garage painted, so we swapped. But yeah, I did the rest. Rewired and re-plumbed the whole thing." He shrugged. "Nothing fancy, but it works for me. Now that you see what I'm capable of, maybe you'll let me help with your house?"

He really was desperate for a job.

I didn't commit to anything but didn't say no either. "The insurance people are coming tomorrow. I'll know more after that."

"So, what're you doing here?" He ran a hand through his blonde curls and gave that dimpled grin again.

He was sweet, but this was stupid. What made me think stopping here was a good idea? If I needed help with a decision, I should call my best friend, Taryn. She was currently in Mexico with her boyfriend, though.

"We were just out walking," I said. "I'm trying to make a decision and needed to clear my head."

"Maybe I can help."

He held a hand out to the bench seats with their newly-covered cushions. I sat, Meeka dropped to the floor next to me, and Tripp took the other bench. I offered him an awkward smile and all I could think was that I should leave.

He barely knew me. How was he going to help?

"What're you struggling with?" Tripp twirled a finger near his head. "I can see your wheels spinning."

All right. I was here, might as well give it a go.

"I went to see Sheriff Brighton this morning. You know, to give him my statement about Yasmine? He ended up offering me a job."

The moment the words were out of my mouth, I thought of how Tripp had been trying to get a job here for nearly a month. The look on his face said he thought the same thing. Damn.

"I'm sorry." I slid to the end of the bench. "I should go."

"Jayne, it's okay. Tell me about it."

I inhaled and blurted, "I'm a cop."

Tripp didn't flinch. At least I could be reasonably confident he didn't have any outstanding warrants for his arrest. Those who did tended to bolt when I told them that. They'd either rush away or pretend their phone was ringing and then announce that they needed to leave.

"I *was* a cop." I dismissed that part with the wave of a hand. "Long story. Anyway, the sheriff needs help keeping the tourists in line and asked if I was interested in temporary work."

"What's stopping you?"

For the second time that day, I told the story of Frisky's death and the fallout I suffered because of it.

"That sucks," Tripp said when I was done.

None of the "It wasn't your fault" or "You have nothing to feel guilty about" responses I got from family or friends. I appreciated that. I had accepted my role in what happened long ago and didn't want to brush aside the importance of it.

"Again, I ask," Tripp said, "what's stopping you from accepting the offer?"

I rubbed my hands up and down my thighs. "It feels like every decision I've made lately has ended in disaster. Guess I'm afraid of another disaster."

"Don't you think that doing normal stuff will help you get past this? Or heal. Or whatever the right term is."

After a moment of consideration, I agreed, "Accepting the job would be a step back toward normal life. It would only be until I'm done with the house and ready to go back to Madison. And if it turns out I can't handle it, I can step down."

He was staring at me.

"What?" I asked.

"I think you have a plan."

"I think I like this plan. Why are you still staring at me?"

"You're a cop." He gave a half-grin. "That's kinda hot."

"That's exactly why I chose the profession," I said, not missing a beat. "So guys would think I'm sexy."

He blushed and started to apologize, but I waved it off.

"Why *did* you choose it?" he asked.

"It just kind of fell into place for me. During my freshman year in college, I got to be involved with an FBI kidnapping investigation."

"Wow. Someone you knew?"

I nodded, but didn't want to go into the details. "It's a long story, but boils down to the fact that I was so impressed with how the FBI followed the clues and found the girl, I declared criminal justice as my major."

"Is that what you want to do? Find kidnap victims?"

"No, that's too close for me. I've tracked down kids that wander off or run away, but the ones that are taken? Not sure I could do that day in and day out. Becoming a detective hit my radar right away. To dig in and track down the truth behind crimes, I knew that's what I wanted to do."

He smiled, but only with his mouth. "I envy people who know where their place in the world is."

Once again, I felt like I'd said the wrong thing. Time to lighten the mood.

"I picked up groceries today. Got some bratwurst and

coleslaw and stuff." I didn't want this to sound like a date request. That's not what I wanted. Tripp was friendly and easy to be with. That's exactly what I needed in my life right now. An easy-to-be-with friend. "Interested?"

"I'd love a brat." Tripp held the door open for me and then locked it behind us. "Don't know why I bother with that. The walls are made of netting. Not too hard for someone to get in if they wanted to. Besides, the only thing I own worth stealing are my tools, and those are locked up tight in my truck."

"It's your home. Whether it's a popup or a mansion, you don't want anyone violating your space. Wait 'til you see what they did to my grandparents' house. Talk about being violated."

As we headed down the driveway toward the boathouse, Tripp gave me a playful shoulder bump. "This makes two nights in a row. Careful. I'm going to get used to your company."

Chapter 11

THE NEXT MORNING, I WOKE with a sense of purpose that I hadn't felt in six months. Instead of driving the two miles to the village, I pulled one of the kayaks and a paddle off the wall in the boathouse garage. It was only three or four hundred yards across the bay. A snap even for out-of-shape me.

"Want to ride with me?" I asked Meeka.

She jumped into the kayak and waited with tail wagging.

As I pulled on a life vest, I thought of the many days I had pulled on a bullet resistant vest. This wasn't at all the same, but a little sense of excited longing tugged at me. Maybe I really was ready to go back to work.

While I paddled, Meeka sat in the well between my legs, her front paws on the edge so she could look over the side. Every few minutes she barked at something.

"What do you see? Fish or your own reflection?"

Without warning, she dove in.

"Silly dog. You're not getting back in here now."

Of course, I kept an eagle eye on her the whole way. I'd yank her back in the boat in a blink if she struggled even a little.

As I got closer to the marina, a small beach area came into view. That looked like the best place to attempt getting out of the kayak. As I came to shore, a boy—*seventeen or eighteen, five-nine, kinky afro, medium-brown skin, blindingly white teeth*—came out of the shack that served as the marina office. He took a couple of steps into the water, pulled the boat the rest of the way to shore, and helped me out.

"Thanks," I said. "There's no graceful way to get out of one of these things."

"Not going to argue that. I'm Oren. I work here at the marina."

"Nice to meet you. I'm Jayne."

"I saw you launch from the O'Shea property. You family?"

"I'm Lucy's granddaughter."

Oren nodded mournfully. "Sorry to hear about your granny. She was one cool lady."

"Thanks. It's nice to know that so many people cared about her." I gestured toward the village. "I've got a few things to do. Can I leave my kayak here?"

"Of course. I'll put it in the rack on the other side of the building."

"Perfect. Meeka, come."

Still playing in the water, she dog-paddled to shore and shook herself off.

We stopped at Ye Olde Bean Grinder for a mocha and treats before continuing to the sheriff's station. Something in the woods along the Fairy Path caught Meeka's attention. I didn't see anything there, but she was so insistent I let her explore for a minute. She seemed especially curious about something near one of the mushrooms circles and at the base of a couple of trees.

"Goofy dog. Do you see fairies?"

I laughed and tugged on her leash, gently as opposed to her attempt to dislocate my arm. Most likely she was detecting decomp from a dead animal. She knew not to alert me, by sitting and barking, if it was anything other than human remains. She'd been well trained. Or rather, the Madison PD had paid a lot of money to train her. The problem was, Meeka operated on her own schedule. Her rogue behavior meant she couldn't be trusted as either a narcotics or cadaver dog, even though when cooperating she could detect both as well as any K-9.

After another minute of her resisting the leash tugs, I issued the command, "Working."

She stopped snuffling at whatever had so captivated her and looked up at me, tail waving excitedly. By the time we got to the station, she had figured out we weren't really working and turned her back to me.

"Sorry, but there wasn't anything there."

To make amends, I held out a bit of my maple bacon brown sugar scone. A sniff, a chomp, and a wagging tail later told me I was forgiven.

"Good girl. You can play in the woods all you want when we get home."

We were fifteen or twenty paces from the station when I heard voices through an open window. Angry voices.

"I've never seen such sloppy work," a woman said, her words crisp and clipped, her tone demanding.

"Don't worry. I'm taking care of things," the sheriff said, as soothing as the woman was angry.

"Are you? From where I stand, things are completely out of control here. First Morgan and now the girl. That's how you 'take care of things'? Are either of you capable of doing your jobs?"

A male voice murmured something I couldn't make out. I also couldn't tell if it was the sheriff or Deputy Reed. Whatever was said, it had calmed the woman enough that I assumed it was safe for me to go in now. Just as I reached for the handle, the door flew open, making me wonder if I had latent witchy abilities that were just waking up. Or maybe I could use The Force and never knew it. I chuckled at my own wit and looked up to see the woman who was so blatantly displeased with Whispering Pines' law enforcement officials.

Five-six, strawberry-blonde hair twisted into a tight bun, body size hard to determine due to her formless shin-length dress. She was still facing inside with her hand on the door.

"Take care of this, Sheriff. I don't want to hear any more grapevine gossip."

Her deceptively soft voice had a razor-sharp edge. She spun to leave and nearly collided with me.

"Pardon me." Her words were a command rather than a courtesy.

"Not at all." I stepped aside and swept my hand forward, as if laying out an invisible path for her to follow.

She closed the gap between us to half a foot, stared down her narrow ski slope nose, and pierced me with her sharp blue eyes. A tight smile altered her stern, scrubbed clean pale face, but that didn't help with the friendly factor at all.

"Tourist?" she asked with a hiss.

Why did she care? "Visitor. I'm here to take care of my grandparents' property."

Her eyes narrowed and through pursed, disapproving lips she said, "O'Shea."

She sniffed, glared down at Meeka who had huddled close to my legs, and then spun so quickly her slipstream almost pulled us along. I watched her and after a few seconds my body released a massive shiver. Who was this woman?

"Another satisfied customer?" I quipped as I walked inside.

Deputy Reed looked up from his desk, sighed, and looked away again. "What do you want?"

"Service with a smile would be nice." He ignored my snark. "I'm here to see the sheriff."

Sheriff Brighton came out of his office. "Did you think

of something to add to your statement? Or do you have some good news for me?" He looked skyward briefly. "Please, let it be good news."

"I'd like to accept your offer of a temporary position," I said, standing at attention. "There are a lot of things I need to take care of while I'm here, so part-time is all I can manage. Any hours are fine. Let me know which days and times are most crucial for you and that's what I'll do. Does that work?"

The sheriff's shoulders visibly relaxed. "I'll take whatever you can offer."

"You're sure you only want me to patrol?" Seemed like a wasted resource to me. "I can help with the Long investigation."

The sheriff shook his head. "I've got that pretty well under control, and I can't let you investigate your own house. Patrol is where I need help."

We shook to seal the deal, and he led me into his office where we took care of paperwork. I would officially be on the payroll starting tomorrow. He didn't keep uniform shirts stocked so would order a couple for me. They would arrive in a day or two. As a detective, working in civvies was standard for me. Wearing a uniform again would be strange.

"That woman," I said as I signed the last form, "the one leaving as I arrived, she seemed upset. Anything I should be aware of?"

"No, nothing for you to worry about." Sheriff Brighton placed my paperwork in a file folder and wrote my name on the tab in precise block letters. "She's Yasmine Long's aunt. Stopped in to see where we were in the investigation."

Had she been looking for information? Cause of death maybe? The preliminary autopsy reports should be in soon. Would he tell her what those findings were or wait for the final report, which would likely take a week or two. Maybe that was it, she wanted information now and the sheriff was making her wait. Except her words echoed in my ears: *First*

Morgan and now the girl. That's how you take care of things? I knew who Morgan was, did 'the girl' refer to her niece Yasmine? Seemed like a cold way to talk about a deceased family member. Maybe something else had her upset.

As Meeka and I left, I couldn't help but notice that Deputy Reed's jaw was tensed and his nostrils flared, but for the first time his attention wasn't on us. In fact, he'd barely acknowledged us at all. What was going on around here?

Chapter 12

SINCE I WOULD BE STAYING longer than originally planned, I needed more clothes. The insurance people would be at the house in about an hour, so I didn't have a lot of time. A woman, who introduced herself as Ruby, was tending the flowers outside a little craft shop across the Fairy Path from the sheriff's station. She recommended Quin's, a few dozen yards away.

"He's got an eclectic line of clothes there," Ruby said, giving my jeans and T-shirt outfit a onceover. "But what else would you expect in Whispering Pines?"

I thanked her and continued along the path toward the pentacle gardens. I noticed the sign before but hadn't realize Quin's was a clothing shop. A peek in the front window revealed a riot of color and patterns from racks of dresses, shirts, and pants. Sweaters filled freestanding shelves. Not a T-shirt or sweatshirt in sight.

A sign on the door instructed customers to, "Please leave your pets on the porch."

"Stay, Meeka. I won't be long," I promised as I hooked the handle of her leash into a clip bolted to the front of the building.

"Welcome. Women's items are on the right, men's on

the left," a man greeted from behind the counter at the back. *Six foot even, slightly heavy build, silver-gray ponytail hanging just below his collar.* He wore a shirt with a solid red front and right sleeve, a solid black back and left sleeve, and contrasting red or black triangles running down the center of each arm. Using a handheld steamer, he removed wrinkles from a pair of flowing pants printed with stars and moons.

As I flipped through a rack of dresses, I was sure I wouldn't find anything in this shop that would fit with my normal wardrobe. Although . . .

"This is pretty." I held up a peasant-style dress. White with blue peacock feathers printed around the collar and along the bottom of both the skirt and elbow-length sleeves. Where would I even wear a dress? When not patrolling the village, I'd be packing the house. A dress wouldn't be appropriate for either activity. "It's not really my style, though."

"No, that will look fabulous on you. The blue in the feathers matches your eyes perfectly," the man said from behind me. He nodded toward one of two fitting rooms. "Give it a try."

I held the dress up and looked in a mirror. He was right, the icy blue shade did match my eyes. There was no harm in trying it on. A Jayne O'Shea revamp was part of the plan while here, after all. I stepped into the changing room, slid off my clothes, and slipped the dress over my head. The peasant top fit snuggly across my bust, but the skirt disguised my belly, which had gotten softer and rounder over the last six months.

"What do you think?" the man called from the other side of the fitting room curtain.

"I think . . ." I bit my lip. Did I? Should I? Maybe I'd wear it to that circus Morgan mention. It looked okay on me. Feminine but not frilly. And the cool, airy fabric would be nice on humid summer days. "I think I like it."

I held the curtain aside for his opinion, and he gave an appreciative nod.

"Wonderful." The man's already low voice held a bit of a sexy growl that made me flush. "I knew you would like it. I've gathered a few other pieces for you to try as well."

He handed me a couple more dresses, a half-dozen fluttery tunic shirts, and the pair of pajama-style pants he'd finished steaming. The guy had a gift for picking the right clothes. He'd seen me for all of sixty seconds and chose not only the right styles and colors, but the correct sizes, too. I couldn't stop myself, nor did I want to, and told him I'd take the peacock dress and three of the tunic shirts.

"Matching jewelry?" He held up earrings with one hand and a necklace with the other. The already delicate items seemed even more so in his thick hands.

"I'll stop with the clothes for today." Airy, flowing clothing was one thing, jewelry would push me into a girly world I'd never been in.

While he rang up my order and placed the items in a simple cloth sack, I gazed at a display of harlequin dolls on a shelf next to the counter. They all had porcelain faces painted stark white, but otherwise each was completely different from the next. One was dressed in traditional harlequin garb with a half-red, half-black pointed jester's hat. Another doll wore all black, except for one pant leg covered in black-and-white triangles. A third had the traditional harlequin triangle pattern on his pants and tunic, but instead of the face being painted with makeup, he held a black mask in front of his eyes.

"This must be where the name Quin's comes from," I said. "Harlequin?"

"Most don't catch on that fast," he complimented.

"They're great." But a step closer altered my opinion. The traditional red and black doll had only nostrils and no nose. The all-in-black was missing a hand. I suspected that the harlequin holding the mask had no eyes. Misfit dolls sold in a village full of misfits? "Unusual, aren't they? How long have you been collecting?"

"I don't collect." He took my credit card and plugged it into his reader. "I make them."

"You made these? Like in a kiln?"

With his flamboyant clothing choices, for both himself and his shop, and his affinity for making deformed dolls, this man was a living example of misfit.

I mentally scolded myself. Maybe he was close to someone who suffered with a physical disability and was honoring them through his creations. Artists had a different way of looking at the world. Did that mean they all qualified for misfit status?

"I do have a kiln," he confirmed. "It's in my studio at home. I give classes twice weekly, Wednesdays and Saturdays during the tourist season, only Saturdays once the season ends. You should come. If you buy a ten-class punch card, the first class is free." His low voice was soothing. "It's quite cathartic. At times, I go into a trance, almost like I am the conduit and the dolls are making themselves."

Maybe he could give me pointers when I broke out my watercolors. Or I could try sculpting, that might be fun.

"Do you only instruct on how to make dolls?"

"My students are free to create whatever they choose. I, however, make only harlequins. I've been fascinated with them since I saw one in a play when I was a boy. My grandmother had a talent for making the most beautiful porcelain baby dolls. Whenever possible, I sat with her and tried to mimic her style. Turned out I'm not good at copying and my style . . ." He gestured at his display, letting me fill in the blank.

Is to make misfit jesters? Had his creations always had something not quite right about them?

"Are they for sale?" I asked to fill the gap in conversation as we waited for my credit card to process, not that I had any desire to buy one. China dolls freaked me out, and clowns were flat out creepy. Harlequins were the lovechildren of the two and took the creep factor to a whole other level.

"These are for sale. Others I give away."

His demeanor seemed to darken with that last statement. It was slight, but it was there. His eyes took on a vacant gaze. A slight, sinister smile turned his lips. I didn't need a cop's instincts to tell me something was off about this guy. Uncomfortable and ready to leave, I reached for my bag.

"You're sure that's all I can help you with?" He pulled the bag back, holding it just out of reach.

"I'm sure." I leaned over the counter and snatched it from him.

"You know where I am. Stop back if you decide you want more." He extended his hand out to me. "I'm Donovan, by the way. It's been a pleasure meeting you, Ms. O'Shea."

I froze, my hand locked into and dwarfed by his. On the inside of his right wrist, Donovan had a small tattoo. The same Triple Moon Goddess symbol as on the village's welcome sign, scattered throughout the village, and the pendant on Morgan Barlow's necklace. On anyone else, it would be an innocent tattoo. On Donovan, my instinct said it meant something more.

"You know who I am?" I asked, my mouth drying.

"Word travels quickly here." Donovan tightened his grip on my hand. "It took me a few minutes, but now I see a lot of Lucy in you."

Donovan's acknowledgment that I was Lucy O'Shea's granddaughter was nothing like the warm welcome the others in town gave me. His suddenly tight, icy smile and squinting, blank eyes were the opposite of warm. For whatever reason, he did not like my grandmother, or me by association. I tried to pull free from his grip but couldn't. After another uncomfortable second or two, he released me and the smile and friendly disposition from when I first entered the shop returned. It was like watching fog evaporate from a window to let the sun shine through.

"Welcome to Whispering Pines, Ms. O'Shea."

I swallowed and held up the bag. "Thanks for your help."

As I backed toward the door, a sudden urge to strap on my service pistol hit me. It was the first time, literally, that I had even thought of my 9mm in months. I left my Sig Sauer subcompact in my bedroom closet in Madison. Before Frisky's shooting, I carried all the time, my service Glock while on duty and my Sig when not.

I dropped to the porch floor and clutched Meeka to my chest, my heart hammering. My own voice in my head scolded me: *Bad decision. Yet another bad decision. You're all alone up here. You should've brought your weapon.*

Meeka squirmed at first and then realized I needed her comfort. She nuzzled her nose into the crook of my neck and went limp, letting me hold her until I'd calmed again.

"It's no big deal," I said, my fingers entwined with her fur. "Not everyone here is going to like us." I pulled her away and looked into her furry face. "Right?"

She wagged her tail and licked my cheek until I laughed. God, I loved this dog.

With Meeka's leash in my shaking hand, we walked along the Fairy Path toward the lake to retrieve the kayak and go home. We had just come to the fork in the path by the sheriff's station when I heard a familiar voice.

"How hard can this be to figure out?"

I stopped walking and peeked around a large maple tree to find Morgan Barlow and Sheriff Brighton in a heated discussion.

"The break-in happened more than a week ago," Morgan said, "and you still have no suspects?"

"Even on a slow week, a hundred people go through your shop." The sheriff gestured up into the trees. "It's not like we have cameras posted to record the comings and goings."

She glared at him. "You're not even going to try, are you?"

"They're beans, Morgan. A handful of beans."

"I gathered those beans during the harvest festival," Morgan said. "I have a supply at home, but I was going to plant those beneath the new moon in a few nights. I'll have to bring some to the shop. My stock will be greatly diminished this season."

"Can't you just order more?" He shrunk from the withering look she leveled on him. "I'll keep searching, but don't get your hopes up. I really don't think we'll be able to figure this one out."

"You understand that it's not just about the beans. It's that someone broke into my shop. There were very few tourists that day which means it might well be one of our own."

"I understand that," Sheriff Brighton said with more compassion. "You feel violated. I would, too."

"Thank you for understanding." The acidic edge in Morgan's voice softened but hadn't disappeared completely.

The sheriff went inside the station, and Morgan started up the Fairy Path toward the village center. There was no way for me to avoid her.

"Jayne," she greeted with a smile. "Blessed be."

"I couldn't help overhearing." Better to confess than get caught hiding information. "Your shop had a burglary?"

"I can hardly believe it. Everyone in the village knows that if they have a true need and no means to pay, I'll share my stock freely. There's no need to steal from me." Morgan sighed and shook her head. "It used to be that we never even had to lock our doors. Now, I'm tempted to put bars on the windows and install one of those cameras the sheriff is so quick to say we don't need."

"I understand how you feel. My grandparents' house

was vandalized."

"I heard. I'm so sorry." Morgan placed both hands over her heart, rings clicking together.

"I have no idea if anything was taken, mostly it was just destruction. The thief took beans from you? Is that what I heard?"

"Castor beans."

"As in castor oil?" I asked, amused by a memory. "Gran used to give us that as a laxative when we ate too much of her good cooking."

"Oh, yes. Castor oil has many medicinal benefits. I sell bottles that have been charged by the light of the full moon in my shop. I use the beans in spell bags and witch bottles." She frowned. "There weren't many, a handful. I'll need to come up with an alternative for bags and bottles this season."

"I should get going." She lost me with talk of witchy gardening techniques. "The insurance people will be to the house soon to check out the damage. Sorry to hear about your troubles."

"And I yours," Morgan echoed and then blessed me again.

Stolen beans? Was this what I'd signed on for with this job? A summer of investigating crimes that were the equivalent of 'he stole my ball' on a schoolyard?

No, I couldn't think that way. Morgan was right, a break-in was a break-in.

And in a village where relatively little crime happened, maybe there was more to this. Her break-in, my vandalism, and Yasmine's death so close together? I didn't believe in coincidences. Somehow, this was all related.

Chapter 13

THE INSURANCE ADJUSTER, AN ELDERLY gentleman with snow-white hair named Mr. Proctor, let me enter the house with him, but I stood in the doorway of each room while he noted the damages. As he moved through the rooms efficiently, I imagined what the vandal had been thinking each step of the way.

I yank on the cabinet door until the top hinge pulls free. I leave it hanging and move on to the next cabinet. Here, the entire door comes off. I reach in and pull one armful after another of dishes out and let them smash to the floor.

"At least a good amount in here can be salvaged," Mr. Proctor said.

I frowned at a piece of a coffee mug I recognized. It read "World's Best Gran—" The piece that completed the word 'Grandpa' buried somewhere in the rubble. I picked up the shard of the gift Rosalyn and I had given him for Christmas years ago, careful not to cut my hand on it. We moved to the great room.

I take a butcher knife from the kitchen drawer, stab it into one of the three leather couches and slice it open, and move on to a second . . . I hoist a table lamp above my head and hurl it across the room.

"The lamp is a loss," Mr. Proctor notes, "but the couch

cushions can be recovered."

In Gramps' normally cozy den:

I toss papers from the desk like confetti. I pull books from the built-in shelves, tear the covers off some.

Envisioning how a scene ended up in the condition it did rarely gave me trouble. Determining motive, however, was trickier. I couldn't even begin to understand the motivation behind this. Maybe because this incident was personal. At least, it sure felt that way.

"They did quite a job on the place," Mr. Proctor said, frowning. "Luckily, your grandparents kept meticulous records."

Pictures of the contents of each room filled a four-inch thick three-ring binder labeled "Insurance" we found in Gramps' den. There was even a spreadsheet with the estimated value of each item.

I chuckled. "That's my Gramps. Meticulous to the point of anal. If you're going to do something, he used to say, do it to the very best of your ability. Otherwise, why bother?"

The best of his ability just saved me a huge headache. It would have taken forever to come up with values for everything in this huge house. Still, the original one week that had turned into one month was quickly becoming one full summer.

Fortunately, the upper floor hadn't gotten quite the same treatment. The vandals must've run out of steam. There, clothing had been tossed around the rooms, dresser drawers as well. The mattresses were flipped off the beds. Just cleanup really, very little actual damage.

"Your grandparents were good, longstanding clients of ours," Mr. Proctor said. "I'll make this claim my top priority and put a rush on getting a settlement check out to you."

"I appreciate that." I saw him to the front door. "Is it all right for me to get started on things now?"

"Absolutely. Sorry so much of it will end up in the trash."

After he walked away, I absently reached to my back pocket for my phone to call Mom with an update, forgetting I didn't have connection. In Madison, I would have gone insane without a cell phone for three hours let alone three days. Here, it almost felt out of place. I carried it with me anyway, out of habit mostly, but maybe I'd want to take a picture of something. Like the graffiti all over the walls. I'd get shots of all the tags later, for now I needed to talk to my mother.

Meeka was not at all interested in going back to the village. So, after settling her into the boathouse, I went to Ye Olde Bean Grinder to see if Violet would let me use the phone there.

"Course you can." Violet handed me the handset and then placed a mocha with double vanilla and extra whipped cream in front of me before I could even ask. Day three and not only was I a regular, the barista knew my beverage of choice. That was unexpectedly comforting.

I chose a corner stool and dialed Mom's number.

"Every room?" she asked when I was done explaining the damage.

"There wasn't damage to every room," I corrected. "Every room does need cleaning and updating. Unfortunately, they didn't touch the lovely peachy-gold tiles in the master bathroom or the salmon-pink ones in the others."

"Maybe we could hire someone to break in and take care of those, too," she joked.

I was simultaneously pleased and flabbergasted to hear that she had a sense of humor about this. But, "Careful. I am an officer of the law, you know."

I debated not even telling her about the deputy position. It was only temporary, after all, and I might change my mind about it completely in a day or two. The backlash would be worse if she found out from someone other than me, though.

"Are you sure that's a good idea? You're all alone up there. What if you have problems?"

Her tone was not that of a concerned mother. It was that of a mother who didn't want to deal with a setback.

"I told the sheriff about the shooting. He says I can step down at any time if it turns out to be the wrong choice. And I've made a few friends up here already, so I'm not completely alone."

"Three-day friends aren't the same as family," Mom said.

And family who harassed me about every choice I made wasn't the same as friends who supported my decisions.

"I'm not sure it's right, but that's your decision," Mom said. "I'll wire funds into your bank account today and you can get started on the house. We need to get this done quickly so we can wash our hands of Whispering Pines."

Except, I wasn't so sure I wanted to do that. Other than the misfit aspect, which was starting to grow on me, I liked it here. Of course, Gran and Gramps had left everything to Dad, nothing here was mine. I was simply the worker bee, making everything pretty again for a new family. My stomach turned every time I thought of someone else living in my grandparents' house.

"I'll have phone and internet in two days, give or take," I said.

"Good. Remember that the salon is busy now. Lots of summer dye jobs and lighter haircuts." She sighed. "And dozens and dozens of wedding parties."

She had little patience for diva brides.

"I'll only call if something important comes up," I said.

"That's not what I meant. You can call any time. Or email is good, too. Be careful up there, Jayne."

I placed the phone back in its cradle on the wall and thanked Violet for the loan. While I'd been talking with my mother, the coffee shop filled up. With an eclectic group of patrons that could only be found in Whispering Pines. One older gentleman was dressed as though he was about to have high tea with the Queen in a black tux with tails, black top hat, and walking cane. A couple of tables away from him, a woman sat sipping her beverage and reading a paperback novel with a tinfoil hat on her head. At the table next to her, a man pushed his chair back, stood to leave, and managed to get one of his feet tangled up with a leg of his chair. As if expecting it, the tinfoil lady put out an arm to catch him just as he started to pitch forward.

"He does that every time," Violet said with a fond grin.

"He trips?" I asked.

"Yep. That's Mr. Powell. You name it, he'll get stuck in it, trip over it, or fall into it. Happens every day. Every single day. We all know to look out for him."

I eyed the tinfoil lady and top hat man. "Anything unusual going on in here that you see."

Violet looked up from filling the coffee bean container and glanced around at the tables and stools at the counter. "Unusual? No. Why?"

"No reason." Apparently, tuxedos and tinfoil hats were acceptable attire. "I need to order a Dumpster. Any idea who I should call?"

"Ask Mr. Powell. He runs a landscaping company. He also takes care of plowing the roads around here in the winter."

"Seriously? A man that accident prone works with heavy machinery?"

"He doesn't operate the machinery anymore. We made him stop after the backhoe incident."

I arched an eyebrow. "Do I want to know?"

"There's a section of the creek just east of the village limits that tends to flood the road in the spring," Violet explained. "He was trying to widen the ditch and managed to flip the backhoe. Not an easy feat. He wasn't in any danger, but the seatbelt buckle jammed so he hung there for almost an hour before his guys came to cut him free."

"Good decision to keep him away from the equipment." I waved goodbye to Violet and caught up with Mr. Powell outside.

"Not a problem." He gave me a salute, poking himself in the eye with his thumb in the process. "I'll have an extra-large receptacle there by morning."

Now that I'd seen the state of the whole house and had a bin on the way, my next task was to make sure Tripp still wanted to help me.

Chapter 14

"THIS IS GOING TO BE a massive project," I explained to Tripp when he joined me at the picnic table outside his popup. "Along with tossing a ton of stuff, there's also going to be a lot of renovating involved. The bathrooms look like they were last updated in the eighties and all the carpeting upstairs needs to get ripped out. Anyway, it would take me more than a week just to do the cleanup by myself. Are you still interested in helping?"

"I can start right now, if you want," he said, relief and excitement clear on his face. "Why don't we go over and come up with a plan?"

My attention had shifted from him to the people in the tents across the campground. Ten of them, all late-teens or early-twenties.

"Is that the group Yasmine Long hung out with?"

Tripp nodded and pointed. "See that tent set way back in the woods?"

A good twenty-five yards beyond the cluster of tents of varying sizes and colors—two orange, one army-green, and one blue—was a small tan A-frame all by itself.

"Yasmine's?" I guessed and Tripp nodded. "We'll go check out the house in a minute. I've got a few questions for the group."

"I thought you were on village patrol," Tripp teased. "Can't stop yourself from investigating?"

"It's my nature." My 'nosey' nature as Rosalyn used to say. 'Inquisitive,' Dad always corrected. "If there are questions that need to be asked, I ask them. Drove my teachers and coworkers crazy."

As I got close to the tents, the group members waved or called out greetings.

"How ya' doing?"

"New to the camp?"

"Welcome."

"I'm actually staying in the house down the road." I pointed in the general direction of the house, watching their reactions. Were any of them the vandals? None of them reacted so probably not. "I also work for the sheriff here in Whispering Pines. I've got a couple of questions about the young woman who died a few days ago." I nodded at the lone tent. "I understand she stayed here? Did any of you know her?"

The group members exchanged looks with each other as mournful comments of "Yasmine" and "nice girl" and "didn't know her that well" rang out. One girl—*five-three, black hair woven into approximately fifty small braids that hung to her waist, pale beige skin, dramatic makeup*—turned her back to me and the group. She busied herself with her backpack while tossing nervous glances over her shoulder.

If this was a dangerous neighborhood, I'd be prepared for a gun to come out of that backpack. Out of habit, I put my hand to the spot on my right hip where my 9mm normally hung. An unwelcome flash of one of the many, many times Jonah begged me to quit popped into my mind.

"Don't you get it?" he would plead. "How do you think it makes me feel, knowing that the woman I love is out on the streets, going into dangerous situations without backup?"

He wasn't any happier when I became a detective and had a partner with me at all times. He simply wanted me to quit, but I was never sure if that was for my safety or his political aspirations. He said I should get a safe office job somewhere. I deciphered that as, "Get ready to be a politician's wife," since he was steadily climbing the ranks in local government. My jokes about it being to his benefit to have someone on the inside at the MPD never sat well with him.

I blinked and tensed even more as the girl with the braids turned partway toward me. She had a rolled-up fleece blanket in her hands and until she had it fully unrolled, my hand stayed uselessly at my hip. She wrapped the blanket around her shoulders like a shawl and clutched it with one hand while freeing her braids from beneath it with the other.

"I knew Yasmine," the girl said. "A little."

I stepped closer and could smell the weed on her from five feet away. "What's your name?"

"Keko Shen."

I nodded in the direction of Yasmine's tent. "Would you step over there with me and tell me what you know?"

"You got a badge?"

"Not yet. I just started with them this morning." I smiled and shrugged. "Small town. Limited inventory."

Keko's eyes narrowed and she tugged the blanket tighter around her.

"You're not in any trouble," I assured. "I just have a few questions."

"You sure sound like a cop." Keko looked at the group and shrugged a shoulder.

We followed the compacted-dirt pathway the twenty-five yards through the bushes to the little tan tent.

"How well did you know Yasmine?"

"Not that well," Keko said. "I met her the first day I got here."

"When was that?"

"About two weeks ago."

"Why are you here? Vacation? On your way to somewhere else?"

Keko shook her head and her face brightened with a smile. "I came to learn about herbs and plants and stuff. There's this woman here, Morgan Barlow. Word is, she's the most skilled green witch in Wisconsin. Maybe the whole Midwest."

"Green witch?"

"Yeah. You know, healer stuff. Morgan knows how to mix herbs and roots and flowers and stuff. She can fix just about anything with the right blend. She's real powerful." Keko's smile turned a little wicked. "She knows how to unfix things too, if you know what I mean."

I got another whiff of weed and was about to dismiss this part nature girl, part goth girl as a stoner girl, but my instincts tingled, telling me to pay attention. "Unfix?"

"You know." Keko looked around conspiratorially and whispered, "Black magic."

Black magic? Oh, geez.

"Okay," I said, trying to keep a straight face, "so you arrive in Whispering Pines and meet Yasmine right away?"

"Pretty much." Keko stared over my shoulder into the woods as she talked. "She was already living here at the campground."

"What do you mean 'already' living here?" Paranoia got the better of me. I spun quick to verify there wasn't anything behind me. Nothing but trees.

"She came to visit her aunt," Keko said, "but that didn't go so well. Yasmine ended up living in the campground after like a day."

Yasmine's aunt? The angry woman from the sheriff's station. "Do you know what happened?"

"They had a fight." She dismissed this, like fights bad enough to get you kicked out of your home was a common occurrence for her.

This was the same thing Tripp had told me, that Yasmine had a fight with her aunt. That's good. I liked it when stories jived. I reached for the notepad I carried in the pocket of the jacket I always wore while on duty, remembering a second later that I wasn't wearing a jacket, nor was I on duty. I did have my phone, though. I pulled it out and opened a voice recorder app.

"Are you okay with me recording this? It's not like a formal statement or anything. It's just for me, so I remember what you said."

"Yeah, that's cool."

"Do you know her aunt's name?"

"Something weird." Keko kicked the toe of her black combat-style boot repeatedly into the ground as she tried to remember. "Flavia! That's it. Ain't that weird?"

"It is unusual." I liked unusual names. Made tracking the person down much easier. "Did you ever see the aunt? Can you describe her?"

Keko shook her head. "Never saw her, but Yasmine used to pick on her a lot." Keko gestured around her head like she was pulling her hair back. "Guess she wears her hair in a bun so tight her eyes get squinty. Yasmine used to hold her hair back then purse her lips and look down her nose and pretend to be her."

Sounded exactly like the woman at the sheriff's station. "Does this Flavia wear long baggy dresses?"

She shrugged and shook her head. "Dunno."

"Do you know what they fought about?"

"No clue," Keko said too quickly. "Something stupid. Something about Yasmine not being pure. Whatever that means. Yaz was really wasted that night she was talkin' about it. Wasn't making a lot of sense. And she wouldn't talk about it no more after that."

Pure? Was that the same thing as being an Original? Or did purity have to do with Yasmine's peepshow-like style of washing cars?

"I heard she was trying to make money," I said.

"Yeah. She didn't have enough to get back to Milwaukee after her aunt kicked her out. She was planning to stay here, as in permanently, but her aunt wasn't too happy with Yaz's career choice." Keko laughed. "Don't know if you know what Yaz looked like, but damn, the girl was stacked and had the tightest ass I've ever seen." Keko's cheeks flushed red. "Not that I check out girls' butts or anything like that. Anyway, she put on this teensy little bikini and set herself up at either the parking lot by the creek or over by the hotels next to the lake. She'd get buckets of water from either the creek or the lake, get herself all wet."

Keko mimicked carrying a bucket clutched to her chest instead of by the handle.

"That's how she carried it?" I asked.

"Yeah. Said it added to the show."

"The show?"

"No one's gonna pay fifty bucks to have some chick wash their car. But a girl in a bikini with her nips poking out? It was a total show. She made good money."

"She must've been cold," I said and shivered. "That was two weeks ago and it still isn't bikini weather."

Keko laughed again, but this time it sounded hollow. Like the high school girl who didn't make the cheerleading squad but was trying to convince you how happy she was that her best friend did. And for someone who claimed she didn't know *Yaz* well, she sure had a lot of answers.

"Did you ever help her?"

"Washing? Yeah. She let me help once. We figured two girls would earn twice as much. Didn't work out that way. She said she could make more on her own." Keko's face darkened for a moment. "Guess I understand. Like I said, she made good bank."

"Did she have enough to go back to Milwaukee?"

"Made enough, sure. But she decided she was gonna

stick around for the summer. It was almost Memorial Day, and she had her performance down to a freakin' science. She knew she wouldn't make that kinda money back home flippin' burgers or whatever." Keko's shining, almost proud smile faded to a frown. "Then she got sick."

"Sick how?"

She pulled the blanket off her shoulders and hugged it in front of her like a protective shield. "First, she started puking a lot. She said her stomach hurt real bad. Then her head started hurting and she got diarrhea. It was bad."

"Do you think she caught a bug or something?"

She shook her head. "Food poisoning."

"What makes you think that?"

"Because she went to The Inn with this guy one night." Keko huffed and shook her head again. A heavy scowl tugged at her brow.

What did that reaction mean? Disappointment maybe? Disgust? Whatever it was, she clearly didn't approve of Yasmine's date.

"It was right after that she got sick."

"Have you heard of anyone else getting sick that night? If it was food poisoning, it's likely more people contracted it, especially since The Inn has such a small menu."

"No, didn't hear of no one else. Besides, with food poisoning you're better in like a day. I know, I had it before. Yaz kept gettin' worse. I told her to go to the doctor. I was plannin' to drag her there that next morning."

"You mean the morning after she died?"

Keko nodded somberly. "I shoulda took her right away. Food poisoning don't last that long. You know?"

"Depends on the person and whatever caused the poisoning. E coli, for example. Some people get sick from it and get better. Others get sick and die."

"Guess that's true."

"So, this guy she went to The Inn with. Do you know his name?"

"Yeah, I do." She gave a half pout, half frown that was full of attitude. "That guy you work with. Martin Reed."

Chapter 15

WHAT WAS I SUPPOSED TO do with this information? Yasmine Long goes out to eat with Martin Reed, gets sick, and a few nights later she dies? I couldn't go to the sheriff with this information. Could I? He must know that his nephew went to dinner with the victim. Whispering Pines had a population of less than one thousand. They all seemed to know everything about each other, down to when to put out an arm to catch a fellow villager from falling.

Maybe Keko was wrong about this. Maybe she only thought Yasmine had gone out with the deputy. She was high on weed, and who knew what else, right now. Maybe she was confusing the details. After all, I asked Martin flat out if he knew Yasmine. He insisted he didn't.

Then again, I hadn't been sure I believed him.

"Thanks for your help, Keko," I said and switched off the recording app. "Will you be around for a while? In case I have any follow up questions."

"I'll be here. At least through next weekend."

Keko joined her friends again while I stood by Yasmine's tent, staring at the zippered doorway.

"Hey guys?" I called out to the group. "Has anyone come by to look through Yasmine's things?"

"Haven't seen anyone" and "Me either" and "Don't know" were the responses that rose from the group like the cloud of tobacco smoke that surrounded them.

"Have any of you been inside since Yasmine died?"

"Why would we do that?"

"Couldn't pay me to go in there."

"Do you know what she was doing in there? Put on a hazmat suit first, lady."

I turned back to the tent, absently patting my nonexistent jacket pocket for the third time in twenty minutes. This time I was looking for a pair of rubber gloves. Instead, I used the hem of my T-shirt to grab the tent's zipper pull, but Tripp interrupted me before I could open it.

"What are you doing?" he asked.

"I can't believe the sheriff hasn't been here yet. It's been nearly three days since I reported Yasmine's death. As far as I know, the only pressing thing he's got going on right now is investigating a break-in at Shoppe Mystique."

"A break-in?" Tripp asked.

"Someone stole some beans. Must be magical beans considering the commotion Morgan is making over them." I shook my head. "Sorry, that's not very professional. I actually got calls for reports similar to that all the time in Madison." I laughed out loud. "One day, an eight-year-old kid called 9-1-1 because his stuffed pig was missing. He was sure the neighbor's dog had climbed in through his bedroom window, on the second floor, and run off with it."

"Did you go on the call?" Tripp laughed along with me.

"I was in the neighborhood and you never know when they're in real trouble and saying anything, no matter how weird, in order to get some help. So yeah, I went. His mother was horrified when I showed up at the door. Since I was there, I searched his room and found the missing pig stuffed between his mattress and the wall. My first successful missing person recovery. Or missing porcine, in this case. Then we had a discussion with him about only calling 9-1-1 in an emergency."

"But it was an emergency to him, right?" Tripp asked with a look of empathy.

"If you could've seen the way that boy clutched that pig. Honestly, I've returned children who wandered away at festivals and the parents didn't react with that much emotion. So, yeah, I guess stolen beans qualify as legitimate."

"Don't you think you should let Sheriff Brighton search the tent? Aren't there procedures or something?"

"I might be breaking rank, but I am following procedures," I said. "I'm just going to take a peek."

I unzipped the tent door and immediately gagged as the unmistakable smell of sickness hit me like a slap to the face. A sleeping bag, pillow, and thin sleeping pad covered one half of the small A-frame. Clothing, two backpacks, a tote bag, and empty food containers cluttered the other side. Using my phone's camera, I took pictures, documenting the contents of Yasmine's tent from my crouched position in the doorway, careful to not cross the threshold and contaminate the scene. Besides, I had no idea what Yasmine died from and didn't want to catch whatever bug might still be crawling around in there.

From beneath one of the pines, I found a tree branch long enough to reach across the tent. I used it to pull the tote bag close to me. After a quick peek inside the tote, I walked over to Keko's group.

"I've another question." I directed it at Keko, but spoke loudly enough that they could all hear. "Do you have any idea how Yasmine ended up down by the lake? Did she tell you where she was going?"

"All I heard her say was that she felt like she was going to puke again," Keko answered. "Two whole days, she never left that tent except to go to the bathroom. Sometimes she didn't make it in time."

That explained the smell.

"She had the runs real bad," a guy with a full mountain man beard added. "She couldn't make it all the way to the toilets over there." He pointed to a small wooden building set up near the middle of the campground. "She did her thing behind some trees over by her tent. I'd stay away from that area if you know what I mean."

"I know what you mean." I made a face. "Sorry, I didn't catch your name."

"Duane. Duane Crawford."

I jotted the details on a note taking app in my phone.

"You don't know why Yasmine would have wandered down by the lake?" I asked.

"She wasn't making a lot of sense," Keko said. "Kinda delirious or whatever."

"If she'd been vomiting and had diarrhea that badly," I said, "she was most likely dehydrated. Delirium can result from severe dehydration. Regardless, when a person is that sick, it's hard to think clearly."

Keko frowned. "She probably went to do her thing by the tree and went the wrong way. Or maybe she just wanted some fresh air and got lost."

"Any chance that someone lured her to the lake?"

"Lured her?" Keko asked. "Why would you think that?"

"I heard that she entertained guests in her tent." I could be way off with this, it was just a hunch, but if it was true these people might know.

Duane snickered. "Dudes."

Keko spun on him. "You make her sound like a hooker."

"Well," Duane began.

"Shut up," Keko snapped with more anger than seemed appropriate. "She wasn't no hooker."

"If she had men in her tent," I said, "there could've been a significant other looking to enact a little revenge on her."

"If?" Duane asked. "New night, new dude."

Keko glared at him but didn't disagree. She added, "Not

those last two nights. She was too sick."

I thanked them and went back toward the tent but didn't stop there. At the moment, I was trying to see everything through Yasmine's eyes.

I've never been this sick. Everything hurts and I can't think clearly. There's nothing left in my stomach, I've been puking for two days. I drop to my knees as my stomach clenches again and dry heave. The cool, moist night air feels good on my hot face. My tent has become toxic with my stench and sickness. Maybe being outside, breathing in some fresh air, will help clear my confused head.

Walking through the woods, I stop every now and then to lean against a tree and wait for the forest to stop spinning. When it does, I take in a deep breath and walk a little further. Wait. Am I heading back to the tent? The trees are obscuring the moonlight, so it's too dark and I can't tell which direction I came from. Walking again, I stumble, or maybe I tripped on something. I put my hand out to steady myself against a tree. Except my hand misses and I collide face first into the tree. Now I have an abrasion on my left cheek . . .

"Jayne!"

I blinked and looked around, Yasmine's dark night cleared away and the current daylit woods came back into focus. I was me again. Behind me, Tripp stared like I'd lost my mind. I hadn't, only slipped into someone else's for a minute.

"Where are you going?"

Squinting, I could just make out the lake through the dense forest. "I'm walking the path Yasmine likely took to end up at the lake. That's a tactic I use sometimes. It helps me get a better idea of what the victim might've been thinking or experiencing."

I glanced at the lake, grateful that the last thing she saw was something peaceful and beautiful.

Tripp followed me back to her campsite where I peeked in the tote bag again, this time taking a picture of the contents. I moved items around with the stick. Money littered the bottom of the tote, and a quick estimation put it at five hundred dollars or more.

"Either she got turned around while wandering or she knew she was about to die." I tapped the tote with the stick. "This is her purse. Her wallet, which surely has her ID and credit cards, is in here along with a lot of cash. She planned to come back. No woman would leave with the intention of not returning and not take her purse. Especially with this much money in it."

Tripp knelt next to me. "She left her tent, for whatever reason, got lost or turned around and died before she could make it back."

"Or she was taken and murdered."

"Why do you think that?"

I gestured at her group of friends. "Duane says she couldn't walk across the campground to use the toilets, but suddenly she was able to make it two or three times as far to the lake? I'm thinking that maybe someone took her there." I studied the group some more. No one seemed skittish over my presence. No one seemed anxious to run or for me to leave. "I believe them. If Yasmine was murdered, I don't think it was any of them. It's upsetting that none of them tried to help her sooner. Of course, they all seem so wrapped up in themselves, I'm surprised they noticed her at all."

"You saw her," Tripp said. "The dudes definitely noticed her."

I scowled at him. "Always about sex with men, isn't it?"

He returned the scowl. "This isn't about sex. This is about a woman *wanting* to be noticed."

I was about to object, but he stopped me.

"Oh, come on. Suppose some super-ripped guy walked past you right now. Or maybe he's walking around the village. All he's got on is a Speedo and flip flops. Along with being ripped, he's filling out that Speedo with a nice sized package. You're saying you wouldn't notice him?"

I cleared my throat. "I guess I see your point. Although

not a Speedo. No one should wear those. Regular old swim trunks are better."

"Good to know," he said. "My point is that Yasmine had some real problems. The bikini thing didn't start until after her aunt kicked her out." He paused, staring into the tent. "So why did the aunt abandon her?"

"Good question. And I agree, something was definitely not right in Yasmine's world."

I moved things around inside the tent with the branch, snapping a picture every few seconds. Condoms, a box of new as well as a few used, were tucked between the sleeping pad and the side of the tent. The unmistakable stench of vomit wafted from the sleeping bag, and this time I nearly puked myself.

I poked at empty pastry boxes with Treat Me Sweetly's logo imprinted on them, paper coffee cups from Ye Olde Bean Grinder, a few Styrofoam containers from The Inn, and a couple of plastic treat bags with pink Valentine hearts all over them.

"Are those containers used?" Tripp asked. "I mean, is there food still in them?

"They've all been here a while. Anything left is crusty. Why, you hungry?"

He made a face at me. "No, but any bears around here might be. We're supposed to lock our food in our cars or in the bear boxes." He indicated a large metal container closer to the other tents. "Bears can't open them so anything inside is safe."

"Why is this a concern?" I asked.

"I'm surprised one hasn't shredded this tent yet," he said. "Probably the people around the campground have kept them away, but bears have a tremendous sense of smell. They're attracted to anything that could be food, even things like lotions and toothpaste."

"You're saying we should get this stuff out of here."

"Isn't this a crime scene or whatever? Shouldn't you tell

the sheriff or the deputy?"

"With the speed at which they operate? This is a public safety issue now. I can't risk the other campers getting attacked due to division of responsibilities. Do you have any plastic bags?"

"You're such a rule bender."

Tripp went to his popup and returned with a few bags. Using the stick, I pulled the items to the edge of the tent and, because I was as anal as my grandfather with his insurance binders, photographed every item with my phone. Since the items had all been piled together in the tent, there was no need to bag them separately.

Once I'd collected all the visible food containers, I checked inside the two backpacks. The first, a small red hydration pack, the kind with a drinking tube connected to a water bladder inside, had nothing food related or smelly. The second, a larger orange nylon pack, had toiletries. Tripp said those should go. City girl learned a nature lesson today. I placed those items in a separate bag.

"I think we've got all of the smelly stuff," I said. "I'll leave the rest for the sheriff. I just need to check underneath the sleeping pad."

I pushed it up and found a small harlequin doll, like the kind I saw at Quin's. There was nothing at all charming about this one. Like the deformed dolls at the shop, this one was dark and scary, but even more so. The clothing was the traditional pants and tunic of the harlequin, but solid black except for the shoes which were red. The doll had a black hat, like a swim cap, covering its head. The face was painted more like a skull than a mischievous jester. It had empty black sockets instead of eyes. The cheekbones jutted out severely as did the chin.

"That's creepy as hell," Tripp commented. "It looks dehydrated, like a shrunken head or one of those apple head dolls my grandma used to make and sell at craft fairs."

"That's what I was just thinking, that it looks

dehydrated." I took a picture of the doll where I found it and then pulled it closer to the tent door. I snapped more pictures, front and back and close-ups of that face. What were the chances that Yasmine would own a harlequin doll that just happened to resemble the way she looked when she died? Right down to her red Converse sneakers. Another visit to Quin's felt in order.

I pulled the tent's zipper back down, and grabbed the bags. Tripp held his hand out to take them for me.

"Thanks," I said of his chivalry, "but chain of custody dictates that I not let these bags out of my possession until I hand them off to the sheriff. I'm going to run them over to him right now. Should I swing by to pick you up afterwards? We can check out the house then."

"No need to pick me up. Do your thing. I'll meet you at the house in an hour."

Chapter 16

A SMALL FOUR-STALL PARKING LOT behind the sheriff's station was, according to the sign, for "Employees Only". Since I was one now, I took advantage of the perk and pulled in next to the station's van instead of walking the three-quarters of a mile from the lot by the creek. With garbage bags in hand, I entered through the back door and found Deputy Reed at his desk as usual. He glared at me. As usual.

My immediate reaction was to confront him on his statement about not knowing Yasmine Long. Just as I opened my mouth to do so, I decided to keep this tidbit to myself for a while. If he was lying, there was a reason for it, and lies had a way of rising to the surface without prompting. Curiosity might be one of my flaws, but patience was one of my strengths.

"What're you doing here?" Martin greeted with a snarl.

"Work here now." I wouldn't let him get to me. "Is the boss in? Never mind, saw his car in the back."

Sheriff Brighton was in his office on the phone. He held up a finger for me to wait and pointed at the chair across from his desk. I sat, waiting while he finished his call, and noted that his office was sparsely decorated. The only accessories were a large framed map of Whispering Pines, a framed print of a sunrise over a lake, and another of a lush garden. There was nothing else of a personal nature, no family pictures on the credenza behind him, no doodles from a grandchild, no 'World's Best Dad' mug with dried drips of coffee running down the side.

"What's that?" The sheriff hung up the phone and nodded at the bags on the floor next to me.

"Food containers and toiletries from Yasmine Long's tent."

He fixed a stare on me. "And why do you have them?"

"I stopped by the campground to let Tripp Bennett know the insurance company says we're free to begin working on the house. He'll be helping me with cleanup and repairs. While I was there, I started up a conversation with a young woman named Keko Shen. One topic led to another and she mentioned that no one had been out there to investigate Yasmine's tent."

"And you took it upon yourself to do so? I remember stating, pretty clearly, that your job was to patrol the village and be among the tourists. Not investigate crimes."

"Ms. Shen and the rest of her group are tourists, sir. Keko has been staying at the campground for a number of weeks. Turned out she knew Yasmine . . . sort of. She told me how Yasmine had been raising eyebrows around the village."

The sheriff's jaw clenched. "That she did. We like to keep things wholesome around here, innocent fun. First and foremost, Whispering Pines is a family community. Tourists enjoy visiting, but this is home for the rest of us. Parents don't want to see the kind of display Miss Long was putting on around young eyes."

"Keko also told me that Yasmine was here to visit her aunt. A woman named Flavia?"

Sheriff Brighton put a hand to his forehead, as though just the mention of this woman's name stressed him.

"Same person we talked about yesterday. You crossed paths with her at the front door. Remember?"

"I remember. It seems she and Yasmine had a falling out."

The sheriff pursed his lips and shook his head. "I wouldn't know. A 'falling out' doesn't fall under legal problems."

"Unless things turn deadly because of it."

He rubbed his bad hip but said nothing.

"Anyway," I continued, "sad how Yasmine got sick so suddenly."

Did Aunt Flavia have anything to do with that? It could be coincidence, although I didn't believe that. Not when the coincidence involved death. Yasmine's 'illness' seemed to come on and progress quickly after she left her aunt's place. Maybe the food poisoning had nothing to do with the food at The Inn. Maybe the aunt had slipped her something.

"Miss Long had been sick?" the sheriff asked.

"According to the group at the campground, she'd been very sick. I assume the ME will be testing for poisoning during the autopsy?"

"Poisoning?" Sheriff Brighton sat back, surprised. "You think she was poisoned?"

"Keko Shen thinks Yasmine had food poisoning. That's not likely, though. There would be more than just one case. Do you know of any other reports of foodborne illnesses in the last week?"

"No, none. If you don't really believe that's what it was, why do you think Dr. Bundy should test for it?"

I shrugged. "Because she got so sick so quickly, it could be some other kind of poisoning. No harm in testing, right?"

Sheriff Brighton stared at me, as though deciding if my concern had any merit. "All right. I'll ask him to include a tox panel."

"Thank you, Sheriff." I stood, the garbage bags still clutched in my hand. "Where would you like me to put these?"

The sheriff motioned to the bolted down, floor-to-ceiling cage that lined the far wall of the room. "Set them by the cage. I'll take care of logging everything. The bags have been with you the whole time?"

"Haven't left my sight for even a minute."

"Very good." Before I could cross the room, he called me back. "Ms. O'Shea, we had a nice little chat here. I appreciate you taking an interest in the Long case, but don't misinterpret my willingness to listen to your thoughts as encouragement. Leave the investigation work to me. In four days, possibly sooner, Whispering Pines is going to be full of tourists. I need to know that you'll be doing the job I hired you to do."

I looked shamefully down at the floor. "I apologize for stepping out of line. I'll spend more time in the village meeting the tourists and locals. It's just, I understand bears might be attracted to the food containers and toiletries. I was concerned and assumed you wouldn't want anything to happen to the other campers. Or for possible crucial evidence to be destroyed."

Once again, the sheriff studied me with his well-trained eye.

"You were clearly on track to be a fine detective, Deputy O'Shea. I understand it's hard to turn off training."

His use of my new title caught me off guard. A reminder of what was expected of me.

"Yes, sir." I nodded and left his office.

"Messin' around in business that ain't yours, hey?" Deputy Reed asked and popped a handful of trail mix into his mouth.

"Just trying to be as much help as I can be." I forced myself not to confront him on Yasmine Long.

"Sheriff don't like people sticking their noses where they don't belong."

"I take it eavesdropping on conversations with other

employees isn't included in that directive?"

Reed's face flushed red. Angry, not embarrassed. "I suggest you watch yourself, O'Shea."

I strode toward the back door, but couldn't hold back any longer. I didn't take well to threats. "I almost forgot. I wanted to verify something I asked you about earlier. You said you didn't know who Yasmine Long was, correct?"

Martin's jaw worked and his eyes narrowed. "I don't recall that. I do recall you asking if I ever saw her before. I recall answering that I supposed it was possible."

Shrewd. Maybe Deputy Reed wasn't as clueless as I thought.

Chapter 17

AFTER LEAVING THE SHERIFF'S OFFICE, I still had more than thirty minutes before I needed to meet Tripp at the house. I'd been to many of the little shops in the village but not Morgan Barlow's Shoppe Mystique. This felt like the perfect time to pay a visit. Perhaps I'd learn more about green witches and black magic while I was there.

Shoppe Mystique resembled the other cottages in the village with its dark-stained wood and single-story stature. Unlike the others, it was surrounded by a garden that was already lush and full, even though the temperatures had only recently warmed enough to not require a jacket during the day. The front porch, with its pots overflowing with plants and flowers, practically beckoned people to come and poke around inside, or simply relax outside on one of the rocking chairs.

Inside, the first thing I noticed were dozens of bundles of drying herbs and flowers hanging from the rafters. I expected to be suffocated by scent, but instead I felt wrapped in fragrance so warm and welcoming, I wanted to stay and explore every corner.

"Blessed be," Morgan greeted from behind an old waist-high wooden table to the right of the door. She smiled as though my appearance in her shop was the best thing that had happened to her all day.

"Why am I not overwhelmed with the smell of plants?"

Morgan held her hands up in a *beats me* gesture. "Sometimes a thing on its own stands out far more than when within a group."

Couldn't argue with that. Flavors mingled to form the perfect meal. Individuals got lost in crowds.

"Please, look around." Morgan swept a hand across the shop.

I had already crossed from the door to the left side of the shop. Two massive bookcases stood in the corner, one along each wall. Apothecary-style glass bottles, the old-fashioned kinds with cork plugs, filled every shelf. Each bottle had a tea-stained label indicating the contents. Wandering clockwise around the space, I came to a three-foot square wooden table loaded with bottles and jars filled with creams and cosmetics and a basket of handmade soaps. A sign hanging on the front of the table read "Lotions and Potions." As I made my way around the perimeter, I came to more tables and free-standing shelves with candles of all shapes and sizes, crystals and stones, oils and incense. More filled baskets were tucked beneath tables. Strings of lights twinkled like fireflies in the rafters above the bundles of drying plants. Everywhere I looked, I found something else charming.

In the far right corner from the front door, I came to a table stocked with earthenware mugs, a rack of loose-leaf tea, a carafe with hot water, and a covered plate of scones.

"Help yourself," Morgan encouraged and pointed to the little room next to the tea table. "Take a seat and I'll join you."

I sniffed the different teas, settled on one labeled "Clarity," and took my steaming mug into the little room. One wall held a case full of books about the Wiccan religion, witchcraft, and topics such as how to use crystals and plants for healing. On the wall opposite the bookcase was a large stone fireplace. Cozy wingback chairs and a worn velvet loveseat invited the reader to grab a book and stay for as long as they wanted.

"What do you think?" Morgan asked cheerily.

"Of Shoppe Mystique?" I settled at one end of the loveseat and sipped the tea. Just that fast, my stress dropped another level. First being near the lake relaxed me and now a mug of tea? At this rate, I'd be mellow as a yogi within a week. "It's the most welcoming place I've ever been. I feel like I've been hugged."

"That's exactly what I strive for." Morgan joined me on the loveseat, lowering gracefully onto it like she had the chair at Treat Me Sweetly, her folded hands resting on her lap. "What questions do you have for me?"

How did she know I had questions?

"Do you know a young woman named Keko Shen?"

Morgan sighed, indicating that she did know Keko and was exhausted by her. "She comes in every day."

"She told me she wants to learn witchcraft from you."

I'd issued the statement as a challenge, a *how crazy is that* joke, but Morgan didn't flinch.

"Keko is a follower of Wicca," Morgan said. "She's been studying for a few months and says she's ready to commit herself to it. However, she's hoping there's a fast track for everything. In particular, to becoming a green witch."

"That's what you are? That's what she wants to learn from you?"

Morgan nodded.

"What exactly does being a green witch mean?" I bit back the cynicism trying to burst free, reminding myself that this was Morgan's religion. "Do you perform witchcraft?"

"Not the kind you're envisioning." Morgan's smile was knowing. She was used to skeptics like me, which was why she lived here in the middle of nowhere. "It's not like what you've seen in movies and on television. I use the gifts that nature and the universe provide and combine them to bring out their medicinal properties for healing or self-care." She waved a long-fingered hand at her shop. "All of my lotions and creams, my candles, my oils . . . I infuse them all with herbs, plants, or flowers of some kind. This is nothing radical. Long before pharmaceuticals were created, plants were our medicine."

I sat straighter on the loveseat. Like everything else in this shop, including its proprietress with her hypnotic disposition, the loveseat soothed me. If I got any more comfortable, I'd never make it to the house to meet Tripp in time.

"A green *witch* provides medicine and cosmetics," I confirmed and scolded myself for the slight emphasis I'd placed on witch.

"That's right."

"So, you don't perform magic?"

"Of course I do," Morgan said as though it should be obvious. "Again, not the kind the entertainment industry would lead you to believe. I can't move things across a room with the power of my mind. I can't transform a person into a toad. I can use elements from nature to bring about what a person needs. It's no surprise to me that you chose the tea you did. Clarity is my own blend of passionflower, chamomile, and valerian root. You're feeling calm and more centered, less anxious. Aren't you?"

"I am," I admitted.

"Some might call that magic."

I studied Morgan for a moment. "Keko says you 'can fix just about anything with the right blend.'"

Morgan didn't miss a beat. "Just about."

"She also says you can unfix things. That you perform black magic." I leveled a stare on her over the tea mug. "That true?"

Morgan released a displeased sigh. "Magic doesn't have a color. Witches, at least those with whom I'm familiar, use what nature provides to practice their craft. As a green witch, I combine plant life for medical purposes. A traditional witch works with the cycles of the moon and the spirit world. A water witch, as the distinction implies, gets her or his power from water. These are all elementary definitions, of course. A full understanding of each type of witch would take a very long time."

I shifted positions to sit sideways and face her. "What's your definition of black magic?"

"As I said, magic doesn't have a color. We do sometimes refer to magic as light or dark. You could directly substitute the words 'positive' or 'negative.' The end result of any casting comes from the witch's intent. I, for example, perform my magic with a positive intent. I intend only to help others."

She was avoiding the question. "Are you capable of performing negative magic?"

A slow smile turned Morgan's mouth. "Now you're asking the right question. However, there are two things you need to understand. First, the prime rule, so to speak, of Wicca is to do no harm. That's why most of us work with positive intent. Second, the magic a witch performs comes back to her or him. If I were to perform negative magic, I would attract negativity and become negative myself."

"Sounds like karma," I mused.

"Exactly. What you put out into the world comes back to you."

A small clock on the mantel over the fireplace chimed twice.

"I need to get going." I set my nearly empty mug on the small square wood table in front of the loveseat. "One last question. What do you think Keko meant by unfixing?"

"First, understand that unfixing doesn't necessarily mean something negative. It simply implies a reversal from a current state. Second, you're asking me about Keko, but you really want to know about Yasmine Long."

I hesitated before nodding.

"Yes, by 'black' magic Keko could mean murder. Although, Goddess willing, I hope not."

The entire time we had spoken, Keko gave me mixed messages. She claimed to not know Yasmine well, but had a lot of answers to my questions about her. She responded with angry emotion to Duane's comment about Yasmine having men in her tent. She was not happy about Yasmine going to dinner with Deputy Reed. That was a lot of emotion for someone she claimed to barely know. Combined with what Morgan had just confirmed, Keko Shen was firmly on my suspect list.

I scooted to the edge of the loveseat and pushed myself up to stand. As Morgan followed me to the front of the shop, we walked past a table with a sign that read Amulets, Talismans, and Charms.

"What are these?"

Morgan ran a finger across a stand of necklaces. "Amulets are worn for protection and to ward off negative energy." She plucked a stone with a symbol carved into it from a basket. "Talismans bring power and positive energy." She returned the stone and reached into another basket for a small glass vial with a four-leaf clover inside. "Charms are more of a superstition item. They offer mental assurance more than magical protection."

Closer to the door, I noticed a two-shelf case hanging on the wall next to the long wood table that served as the checkout counter. A spinner rack covered with handmade wreaths, both round and pentacle shaped, stood in front of the case, making it hard to get to. The shelves were filled with jars of plants, like those on the larger shelves I had inspected when I first came in.

"Why aren't those herbs with the others?" I assumed they were rare or expensive.

"Those," Morgan said, "are the dangerous plants. I like to keep an eye on them."

I was about to ask more about these dangerous plants when a trio of women walked in, squealing over the lovely shop.

"Let me know if you'd like me to help you pick out an amulet or talisman," Morgan offered.

I looked quizzically at her, biting back a laugh. "You think I need mystical help?"

"People require assistance for many different ailments. Some ailments are medical as in an illness. Some are physical as in an assailant." Morgan held my gaze with a look of compassion laced with concern. "Some ailments come from within, demons that won't leave us alone." She touched my shoulder lightly. "Blessed be, Jayne."

Chapter 18

IT WAS VERY KIND OF Morgan to offer an amulet to protect me from my own brain, but I didn't believe in any of that. The atmosphere and the aromas swirling around Shoppe Mystique, along with Morgan's confident, calm disposition, had lowered my defenses. The further I got from Shoppe Mystique, the more my logic returned.

Morgan wasn't joining forces with the universe to make positive, or negative, things happen. She didn't make magical necklaces that could save you from your personal boogeyman. What she did was blend plants. Like she had said, herbal medications had been used for centuries. Basically, she drugged me with tea and a soothing voice.

Morgan's collection of dangerous plants was quite large. Did Keko know about them? Did her desire to learn black magic include a spell to repel? As in repel Yasmine from this life by using a deadly blend of plants? I had many more questions for Morgan; I'd have to go back. Right now, though, I had to meet Tripp.

By the time I got to the house, I was almost fifteen minutes late. Tripp was there, comfortably lounging in one of the Adirondack chairs on the front porch. His hands were propped behind his head, eyes closed, looking like he hadn't a care in the world. I couldn't find a single thing that classified him as a misfit, yet he still seemed to fit perfectly with the Whispering Pines easy-going mentality. No wonder he wanted to 'put down a root' here.

I hurried up the boathouse steps to let Meeka out and returned to Tripp on the porch.

"All that time with the sheriff?" he asked as I got closer, eyes still closed.

"Not all of it." I sat in a chair next to him and mimicked him by leaning my head back, closing my eyes, and taking a moment to breathe in the pine-scented air. "I had a few questions for the local green witch."

"Morgan Barlow?"

I spun to look at him. "You know about the witch stuff?"

Tripp laughed, a comforting baritone sound from deep in his chest. "Spend more than a couple days here and you're sure to hear about the witches."

Witches. As in more than one of them in Whispering Pines. Seemed Morgan was being honest about the coven. Could I believe her about the rest? At the moment, my instincts were stuck in neutral regarding her. I had research to do on Wicca, among other things. My internet couldn't get turned on soon enough.

"This stop to visit Morgan," Tripp began, "is it pure coincidence that it ties to your conversation with Keko Shen this morning?"

"I'll be living here for a while, it's only neighborly of me to patronize the village shops. Is it my fault the conversation turned to witchcraft?" I paused, waiting for him to respond. He didn't. "I think she drugged me with tea."

Tripp shook his head, not buying a word of it.

"Anyway," I continued, "the sheriff isn't doing enough. In my opinion."

"You'll need to get used to that. People here work on Pine time." He settled into the chair again. "My term, not theirs. And, this isn't your problem. Right?"

As we sat on the porch, listening to the wind through the trees, I thought more about Keko. Which made me think of Yasmine. Which made me realize I hadn't asked Sheriff Brighton why he hadn't been out to investigate her tent and collect her possessions. I hadn't found anything odd, except for that harlequin doll, so the collection of her items wasn't the issue here. The issue was why, after so many days, hadn't he been out there to collect them?

Maybe he hadn't realized there was a tent to check out. Except, the aunt had stopped by the station yesterday. Regarding her niece's death, he said. Surely, he would have found out about Yasmine living at the campground from her then. Was that why Flavia was unhappy? Because the sheriff wasn't investigating?

Morgan had also accused him of not investigating during their argument along the Fairy Path. *You're not even going to try, are you?* In her case, he wasn't looking for the bean thief.

"Stop it," Tripp said.

"Stop what?"

"Whatever you're debating about."

"I'm not—"

"Your leg is bouncing. You're debating."

I stared at him for a moment. "You'd make a good detective."

He was right, though. I was hired as a deputy, not a detective. I got up and unlocked the front door.

"Shall we?"

Tripp slapped his hands down on the arms of the chair and pushed himself up. "Let's do this."

This was the third time I had seen the destruction inside, and it wasn't any easier. Even though Gran had never been one to get attached to material possessions, this would have upset her greatly. Until Gramps had died, nearly ten years ago, they had traveled the world. Many of the bits and pieces and shards littering the floor had been souvenirs from those trips. Even the once-beautiful blue damask sofa in the sitting room, where Gran had read bedtime stories to me and Rosalyn, had been acquired on a trip.

"I saw it in the window of this little shop in Ireland and had to have it," Gran said anytime someone commented on it.

Gramps would roll his eyes. "Cost more to ship it here than the thing is worth." But Gramps never denied her a thing. Not even her desire to turn their stunning two-thousand lakeside acres into a Wiccan village.

Tripp followed me in, his eyes scanning the damage. He went into the dining room first, not saying a thing until he had visually inspected everything. "A little wood putty and some new hinges and the doors on the china cabinet will be fine. It's pretty beat up so it'll need refinishing." He laid a hand on the dining table. "This, too. Luckily, it only got scratched."

"That's good news," I said. "At least they aren't a total loss."

"Everything's dusty and full of debris right now. Things will look better once we've got that much cleaned up." He followed me across the hall to the sitting room and motioned at the beloved sofa. "The fabric is a loss, but it can be recovered."

We wandered through the rest of the house, assessing damage. While Tripp formulated a cleanup plan, I took pictures of everything with my phone's camera—the broken things, the scratched floors, the graffiti on the walls.

"This is a great house," he said when we got to the fifth of seven bedrooms. "You're really going to sell it?"

"Not my choice. My parents want to get rid of it." I studied his expression a little more closely. "What are you thinking?"

"That this would make a great bed-and-breakfast. Sure, all the bedrooms and bathrooms need updating, but you said you planned to do that anyway."

I could see what he meant. There were tons of little nooks around the house where comfy chairs could be set for reading or quiet conversation. The dining room was big enough to seat at least a dozen people. The great room, which ran almost the full length of the house, had three couches—two of which needed repairing—and a half-dozen chairs scattered about. Plenty of room for guests to spread out.

Tripp looked at me and nodded. "You see it, too, don't you?"

I shrugged, not willing to wish for anything regarding this house. It wasn't mine to wish on.

"With this location," he continued, "you could get top-dollar listing this place as a rental. Or, like I said, turn it into a bed-and-breakfast. I mean, look at this view."

He spread his arms wide in front of the spectacular wall of windows that looked out at the lake. It was breathtaking. Even in the winter, when the lake froze over and covered with snow, it was beautiful.

My mind started spinning along with his. My parents would have no desire to run a B&B, but did I? That would mean I'd have to buy the place from them. I didn't have that kind of money. Or a job that made enough to secure a loan that big. Mom was a business woman, though. A good one. Maybe I could convince her this was a good investment and work out a deal. As I stood there, I could picture guests milling around, kids playing in the yard . . .

What was I doing? Why was I even thinking about this?

"So," I said, "now that you've seen the project, are you still interested?"

"Is that a formal offer?"

I'd spent five years in law enforcement reading people, deciding if they were being truthful or trying to pull something over on me. I didn't sense anything but sincerity from Tripp.

We negotiated an hourly wage and shook on it. Tripp, grateful to be earning a paycheck again, gave me a low, flourishing bow.

"I promise, milady, to treat your home as if it were my own."

"Speaking of your home, feel free to move your camper over here. Unless you want to keep staying at the campground."

"I'll move it," he said immediately. "The campground is going to fill with tourists in three days. Music playing all night, listening to other people snore and . . . doing other things, isn't my idea of pleasant living conditions."

"I'm staying in the boathouse," I said. "Feel free to use one of the bathrooms in here. And the kitchen. Other than needing cleaning and minor repair, it's usable."

"I'll move my home down here tonight."

I gestured for him to follow me. "Let's go to the boathouse and have a beer to celebrate your new job."

I hadn't realized how late it was getting. We'd been wandering the house discussing cleanup and renovation ideas for nearly two hours.

"Burger?" I asked.

"I could eat a burger," Tripp said.

After I gave Meeka a scoop of kibble, I fired up the gas grill, took out some burger meat, and grabbed two New Glarus Spotted Cow ales from the little kitchenette fridge. By the time the burgers were ready, the sun was low on the horizon and a cool wind was blowing in off the lake. I turned on the portable deck heater and flicked on the gas flames of the tabletop fire pit.

"You sure know how to throw a party," Tripp said and tapped the neck of his beer to mine.

I stared out at the reflection of the trees and the pink and orange shades of sunset on the softly rippling water. It was perfectly peaceful. As if on cue, a loon sang out, giving me goosebumps. Emotion snuck up on me, stealing my voice.

When I could speak again, I said, "I think I understand why my grandparents loved it here."

"You're starting to see why I want to stay?"

"I am." I took a slow pull of my ale.

"You've been feeding me a lot," Tripp said, "and I appreciate that. Soon as I get my first paycheck, I'll buy groceries and stock the refrigerator in the house. Anything in particular you like?"

I was already so comfortable in the little boathouse apartment, I hadn't even thought of using the house's kitchen. With just myself to cook for, there was no reason to. I enjoyed Tripp's company and would be happy to have dinner with him every night. Stocking the bigger refrigerator was a good idea.

"Usually, I open a can or warm up something from a box." I was supposed to be reinventing Jayne O'Shea, though. No reason that couldn't extend to the kitchen. "I like grilling. I can handle simple things with just a few ingredients."

"I have to say," he held up his burger, "you're good at grilling."

My face flushed with warmth. Time to turn the conversation to a new topic. "I told you my story. Where'd you come from, Tripper Bennett?"

I'd been curious about his story since he first told me he'd been here for a month. It felt like too personal a question at the time. Now, I figured it was okay to ask.

He took another bite of his burger, followed by a half-dozen potato chips and a few baby carrots, then a long drink of his beer. He was stalling. Maybe it wasn't okay to ask. I remained quiet, letting him decide what to say and when. If he wanted to tell me anything at all. He certainly didn't have to.

"I'll need another beer for this," he finally said. "Want one?"

"Yes, please." I watched as he went inside to my tiny refrigerator and pulled out two more Spotted Cows. As he handed one to me, Meeka climbed onto the oversized lounge chair next to me and rested her chin between her paws.

After a sip and a resigned sigh, he said, "I moved in with my aunt and uncle in California when I was thirteen. Within the year, I started running. Every other week, give or take."

Him being on the track and field team was my first thought. Then I got it. "You mean you ran away?"

"I ran away," he confirmed. "One night my uncle came into my bedroom and told me that if I stayed put until my eighteenth birthday, they'd give me a thousand dollars in cash, the keys to that old red truck, and their blessings."

A hundred questions were already swirling in my head. Why did he live with his aunt and uncle? What happened to his parents? The military? Death? Prison? Why did he keep trying to run? I forced my patient side into play and waited to see what more he'd reveal.

"My birthday, coincidentally, was the day after high school graduation," Tripp continued. "That meant not only would I be eighteen and a legal adult, I'd have a high school diploma, too. No matter how badly I wanted to leave, even I saw the intelligence in that plan." He shrugged, scratching his chest beneath his black-and-white checked flannel shirt. "So, I stayed."

I filled my mouth with burger to stop from asking the questions on the tip of my tongue.

"Why did I live with them?" he asked. "That's what you're wondering. Right?"

I smiled around my mouthful. "Mm-hmm."

He sighed and chugged half of his beer. This was tough for him. "My mom took off for 'a chance' when I was thirteen."

"A chance?"

"A guy with a job offer. A chance, she claimed, she

couldn't pass up because it was going to make all the difference for us." Tripp stared into the fire pit, his light hazel eyes sparkling from the flames. "My dad took off soon as he found out Mom was pregnant. She never heard from him again. Her employment skills involved waitressing and an occasional modeling gig." He smiled at the fire. "My mom was real pretty."

I propped my feet on the fire pit table and knocked one against his. He shifted his eyes to me, and I gave an encouraging grin, silently letting him know that his story was safe with me.

"Last time we heard from her was New Year's Eve when I was sixteen. She was in Seattle, or thereabouts, and swore that was the year. 'I've got a tryout for this bigtime modeling gig tomorrow, baby,'" Tripp said in a falsetto and blinked. "She was so happy that night. 'I'll send for you when I get that job. You can ride in an airplane, and I'll pick you up at the airport.' Like I was a little kid." He paused, obviously reliving the call. "She gave us all these details about the job and the agency. I believed her. Hell, my aunt . . . her sister even believed her, and my aunt never believed anyone about anything." He shook his head. "We never heard from her again."

I felt bad for him, for the kid he was then as well as the abandoned and still-hurting son he was now.

"When you ran," I asked while scratching Meeka's ears, "you were going to find her yourself."

He popped the last bite of his burger in his mouth, nodding as he chewed.

"You headed to Seattle with your thousand dollars and your truck?"

"I had four thousand dollars by that time," he reported proudly. "I worked all the time, saving because I knew I'd need it. I was determined to find either her or a trail that would lead to her."

"How did you know where to start?"

"I went to the modeling agency where she said she had that tryout. It was a legitimate place. She didn't get that bigtime job, but some little clothing boutique in Spokane liked her look. They said she went to Spokane."

"And you did, too."

"Yep." Another swig of beer. "Spokane to Walla Walla and then Portland. Portland to Casper to Denver to Omaha."

"Were those all modeling jobs?" I shifted in my seat, rousting Meeka who jumped down with a scowl.

His eyes hardened a little. "Men. One after another."

"And you were able to track them all down?"

"If not them, someone who knew my mom. It wasn't always quick or easy, but I'm persistent and determined. She's my mom. What else was I supposed to do?"

"You've been searching for ten years?"

"Nah. I searched for five, letting my aunt and uncle know where I was every step of the way. I know how hard it is to wonder where someone you love might be. I couldn't do that to them. I drifted from place to place, picking up odd jobs wherever I could find them. I stayed for a whole year in Fargo, North Dakota. Liked it there." He let out a chuckle. "My aunt called me her Wayfaring Stranger after some old Johnny Cash song. Since I seemed to fit in anywhere and nowhere, I couldn't help but head toward this place called Whispering Pines when I heard about it. 'You'd fit perfectly there,' this one old guy told me. So, here I am. Trying to fit in."

"You never heard anything more from your mom?" I asked.

"Not a word." He got quiet and cleared his throat. "I just wish I knew. I don't need her to take care of me anymore, but if she needed me I'd sure like to be there for her." He stared at the flames again and softly repeated, "Just wish I knew."

We chatted about a variety of topics after that, nothing nearly as deep as the conversation about his mom, and time got away from us. It was around one in the morning when I drove him back to his camper. Tripp complained the whole way that he could walk up the driveway.

"I'll move my camper over in the morning and get right to work on the house," he promised as he got out of the Cherokee.

"No worries," I said with a wink. "We can work on Pine time, too."

As I tucked into bed a few minutes later, I looked across the room to Meeka on her pillow.

"I think I could get used to life here."

Meeka responded with a sleepy little *ruff*.

I couldn't remember the last time I'd felt so at ease. It was partly the beer and partly being around Tripp. A lot of it was being by the water. I'd never realized how much it soothed me. The gentle sound of it sloshing up on shore. The smooth-as-glass surface when nothing disturbed it. The intrigue of what lay beneath.

I closed my eyes and listened to the sound of the pines whispering to each other as I fell asleep.

Chapter 19

I WOKE, AFTER NOWHERE NEAR enough sleep, to a beeping sound. After quickly pulling on some clothes, I went out onto the sundeck to see what was going on. A flatbed truck, with an enormous, rusty red garbage bin on the back, was in the driveway. When Mr. Powell said early, he meant early; it wasn't even eight o'clock. I padded barefoot down the boathouse stairs and across the yard to the truck.

"Where do you want it?" the driver called from the cab.

The circular driveway made a loop in front of the house and garage before meeting itself back at the main drive. I pointed to the area closest to the house's front door. "There, I guess."

Clearly a pro, the driver spun the truck around and had the huge bin in place in no time. "That good?"

"As a yard ornament, not so much. As a refuse collector, it's perfect."

"Sign this, please." He chuckled and handed me a clipboard with a multi-part invoice attached. He tore off the bottom copy and handed it to me. "Give a call when you're ready for me to come get it."

I had gotten halfway to the boathouse when Sheriff

Brighton's Tahoe pulled up. I figured Pine time meant slow and late, not whenever they were ready even if that meant the crack of dawn.

"Y'all sure are early birds around here," I called out as I crossed the yard again. "Haven't even had my first cup of coffee and you're my second visitor."

Sheriff Brighton got out of his truck and pulled a cardboard box out of the back.

"These were delivered late yesterday. I ordered two uniform shirts for you. Thought I'd drop them off on my way to the office." He reached into his pocket, pulled out a badge with a gold star, and placed it on top of the box. "Welcome to our little station. Glad to have you."

My emotions unexpectedly got the best of me. I blinked and cleared my throat. "Thank you, sir. Happy to be here."

"The number of tourists is starting to rise." Sheriff Brighton said this with the same tone he'd likely use if concerned about the body count at a massacre. "Start patrolling the village today. The sooner you make your appearance known, the sooner we'll keep the stupid stuff under control." He stuck his right leg in his truck, winced as he pulled it out again, and rubbed his hip.

"Sheriff? Are you okay?"

"Had this bum leg my whole life," he explained. "My left leg is a little shorter, a little weaker. The right one has had to compensate for fifty-seven years. It's been complaining for the last five."

"I'm sorry to hear that. Maybe Morgan has an herb blend for you."

"Oh, Morgan's got about a dozen remedies for me. I've tried a few and they help a little, but nothing takes it away completely." Slower this time, he lifted his right leg into his truck. "Stop by the station later to pick up your belt and service weapon."

I flinched internally. Was I ready to carry again? Would I ever be able to draw a weapon without thinking of Frisky and my partner Randy? Thankfully, Dr. Maddox's office number was in my phone in case of a setback. She had told me coming here would be a good test, but neither of us had ever considered the possibility that the test would involve employment and a service weapon.

"I'll send Martin to have a set of building keys made for you first thing this morning as well."

"Thank you, sir. I'll be there in a couple of hours."

Sheriff Brighton gave a crisp nod, eased himself the rest of the way into his truck, and drove away.

As I showered, I warned myself to follow the sheriff's directives. I was a patrol officer. My assignment was to keep the citizens and visitors of the village of Whispering Pines safe and out of trouble. My job was not to worry about Yasmine Long.

Except, as I dried off—with a wonderfully fluffy towel, thank you, Gran—I couldn't stop thoughts of Morgan and Keko . . . and Deputy Reed from tumbling through my mind. It seemed a safe bet to me that Yasmine had been poisoned, whether via food or some other means. Did Keko know how to combine plants into a poisonous concoction? Had she poisoned Yasmine? Morgan surely knew how. Had *she* poisoned Yasmine? Then there was Deputy Reed. How did he tie into this? He could have slipped something into Yasmine's food at dinner that night.

Deputy Reed had opportunity, but I didn't know if he had means or motive. Morgan had means, but I didn't know if she had motive or opportunity.

As a suspect, Keko checked all three boxes. She seemed jealous of Yasmine. Her emotions flared when I mentioned the men Yasmine had in her tent. That seemed like motive to me. She had means by being in Shoppe Mystique so often, although Morgan didn't mention if she'd purchased anything during her visits. Finally, staying in the campground with Yasmine provided Keko with plenty of opportunity to slip something to her.

My brain buzzed with trying to keep this all straight.

Investigating Yasmine's death wasn't part of my job, and I knew that, but I also knew I wouldn't be able to leave it alone. There was nothing preventing me from developing my own personal conclusions. To do that, and to help quiet the buzzing in my head, I needed a suspect board. A mobile white board like we had at the station in Madison would be best. I didn't have access to one of those, but the wall over the table here in the apartment would work.

In the mirror, I saw Meeka watching me from her cushion. Disapproving. Almost like she could see the thoughts spinning in my head.

"I need to write this stuff down," I said partly to Meeka, but mostly to myself as I pulled on my T-shirt and jeans again. "That way I can stop thinking about it while we patrol the village today."

There should be paper in Gran's office. I grabbed the ring of house keys from the little kitchen table. The moment I opened the door, Meeka raced down the boathouse stairs ahead of me and tore around the yard, burning off energy. I smiled, thinking of how much fun the little terrier would have on patrol today, meeting people and exploring the village. Like me, that's what she liked best about the job, being with the public. She hadn't liked searching for drugs and finding cadavers seemed to depress her, so she was retired after only three years of service.

I'd been thrilled to adopt her; a decision Jonah wasn't even a little happy about. He complained constantly about having dog hair all over the house, even though Westies don't shed that much. This only cemented my love for Meeka. Despite my heartache at our breakup, I was sure I ended up with the right companion.

"Do your thing," I told her now as she snapped at bugs. "I'm going into the house for supplies."

I entered through the French doors at the back of the house this time and was immediately assaulted by the graffiti painted all over the walls. At first glance, they looked like some sort of gang symbols. But I'd seen plenty of gang tags over the years and these didn't look like any I'd seen. A few looked familiar, like items on that amulet table in Shoppe Mystique. Were they Wiccan symbols? Was there a Wiccan gang running around Whispering Pines? More likely it was the bored rich kids Sheriff Brighton mentioned.

Regardless of who had done it, I just wanted to paint over the markings, sand and re-stain the hardwood floors, and repair the furniture. I pictured people sitting on cozy newly-covered sofas, gathered by the fireplace to read or simply be together to talk and laugh.

Tripp's bed and breakfast idea was infiltrating my thoughts again. I pushed it away. Other matters required my attention right now. Besides, Dad wanted the house sold, gone forever from the family. Gran's heart would break to hear him say that.

A little room . . . correction, a *tiny* room off the kitchen served as Gran's office. It must have originally been a pantry. Seriously, there were closets in the upstairs bedrooms that were bigger. Somehow this room had escaped the vandals. It's sliding pocket door was closed so maybe they thought it was a closet and passed it by. Gran's newer, touchscreen laptop still sat on the built-in desk. A blinking light on the printer indicated it was still powered up and waiting for the next job request.

My vision blurred with tears as I wondered when the last time was that Gran had sat here. To say we were shocked when word of her death came didn't begin to describe it. Even Mom, who hadn't seen or spoken to Gran in years, had shown emotion. The conclusion from Sheriff Brighton was that Gran had died while getting ready for a bath one night.

Gran loved her baths. She'd get a glass of Chardonnay, light candles, and sprinkle lavender-infused sea salt in the water . . . which she probably got from Morgan. On the night in question, she either slipped on some water on the floor, tripped over the floor mat, got tangled in her bathrobe belt, or who knew what. However it happened, she hit her head, lost consciousness, and fell into the prepared bath where she drowned. A freak accident.

As I stood there, sniffling, I thought of how she and I had stayed in touch. We didn't talk on the phone often, but Gran had developed a fondness for emailing, the reason for the high-tech laptop. With my crazy work schedule, I was never home or available when she wanted to chat, so we emailed. Gran always talked about the weather up here and would end each email with a few words about the lake's mood that day — *the lake is peaceful and smooth . . . moody with little whitecaps . . . angry with pounding waves* . . . I'd laugh at how she personified the lake, but now that I'd been here for a few days, I was starting to understand.

I never told anyone about the emails, not even Jonah. It was possible Gran had been emailing Rosalyn, too, but I liked to think that Gran liked me best. I touched the edge of the laptop, envisioning her furiously typing away, her beautifully manicured pale blue fingernails clacking on the keys. I choked back a sob. Never again would I find a message from Lucy O'Shea waiting in my inbox.

A gust of wind outside made the house creak, startling me from my memories. I needed to get what I came for so yanked open the overhead cupboard doors. Behind the first, I found papers and manila envelopes piled in messy stacks. The next cupboard, just as cluttered as the first, was stuffed with office supplies. That's what I'd come for. I grabbed a mostly-full ream of paper from the top shelf, pulling down an envelope stained with coffee mug rings along with it. I had to laugh at the coffee rings. They were all over the desk, too. My sweet, sloppy grandmother.

I tossed the envelope back into the cupboard and poked around for tape, highlighters, scissors, and anything else that seemed useful. During my excavation, I unearthed a small cast iron cauldron with a faint tri moon symbol etched on the front and two votive candles, one white and one purple. The cauldron was filled with sand and held long incense sticks. A strong sense of déjà vu struck me. Something about the cauldron was familiar. I spent a minute trying to force the hidden memory to the surface, but it stayed stubbornly in the shadows of my mind.

From a third cupboard, I found an empty printer paper box. I unplugged the printer and piled it along with the rest of my bounty, including that intriguing little cauldron, into the box.

I had just opened the French doors, ready to leave, when the wind gusted again. At that moment, I swear I heard a whisper. It came from behind me, from inside the house. I spun, expecting to find someone standing there. Of course, no one was. It had to be the wind. Or maybe . . .

"Gran?"

No response. Of course, there was no response. I knew she was gone, I had accepted that. Still, a part of me had been hoping to find her standing there.

Angry, embarrassed, and if I was being honest, disappointed, I scolded myself. "It was the wind. You did not hear your grandmother's voice. Quit being stupid."

Outside on the covered patio, I leaned against the house and pulled myself together. It was the little cauldron. The déjà vu feeling gave me the heebie-jeebies. It was probably that I had seen one like it in Shoppe Mystique. Nothing magical. No woo-woo. Just a tourist's souvenir.

The real problem was, I was still mourning Gran's death. If I didn't get a handle on my emotions, I'd never be able to pack up this house.

"Ten minutes," I called out to Meeka, who stood on the end of the pier, barking at something in the water. Fish, I assumed from the playful tone of the yaps, and not a dead body.

Why was my first thought always a dead body? Lord, I

was so morbid.

Inside my apartment, I set the boxful of office supplies on the sofa. As much as I was itching to put my thoughts together on a suspect board, I was equally eager to get to work in the village.

Eager, until I opened the box Sheriff Brighton had dropped off. One glimpse at the black T-shirts and black uniform tops and I broke out in a sweat. I mopped the rivulet running down the center of my back with a bathroom towel, then reached out shaking hands and took one of the black T-shirts from the box. Slipping it on was fine. I could be anyone in jeans and a T-shirt. But the uniform shirt, with the patches on the shoulders and over the breast pockets brought back a flood of memories.

Like a slide show, images flipped through my mind. The way Randy and Frisky were both so out of control that day. The look on Frisky's face when she realized she'd been shot. Standing in my captain's office to report Randy. The anger on my fellow officers' faces when they learned what I'd done.

After laying the uniform shirt down on the bed, I backed away, like it was a bomb ready to explode. I paced the apartment, from bedroom to living room, and then stepped into the bathroom and stood in front of the mirror.

"You can do this." I stared into the mirror, talking to my reflection as though it was me. "Frisky's death was not your fault. Yes, you should have reported Randy sooner. That was a horrible lack of judgement, but you're a good cop. You won't let that kind of thing happen again." I stared at myself until my dark bobbed hair and ice-blue eyes blurred. I repeated the words, 'you're a good cop,' again and again until I stopped shaking and started believing it. "All you'll be doing today is walking around talking to people. The same thing you've been doing for the last four days."

Reflection Jayne nodded, ready to try again.

I picked up the shirt from the bed and stood in front of

the mirror, watching reflection Jayne put first one arm and then the other into the sleeves. I watched her button each button, silently reassuring her that this was okay, this was good. By the time the last button was buttoned and the shirt tucked into her jeans, reflection Jayne looked like a cop. Or a sheriff's deputy, as the case would be. The color of the uniform, black instead of MPD blue, helped. I had come away from the shooting and the resulting fallout a different person. It seemed right that I looked different now, too.

Meeka came running into the apartment, slid to a stop on the wood floor, and looked up at me. Her tail started wagging at top speed, and she gave a short, happy yip as though sensing I needed someone's approval. Then she sat, awaiting assignment.

"To the car, sidekick," I ordered in my Batman-to-Robin voice. But since I was in uniform, Meeka had gone into K-9 mode. She went to the door, sat, and looked up at her leash. She was right; we needed to play our roles now. Meeka was clearly able. Was I?

Chapter 20

I PULLED INTO THE CAMPGROUND and over to Tripp's popup. A few more tents had moved in since yesterday, but most sites were still empty. I let Meeka out but instructed her to stay by the Cherokee. She crawled underneath it.

"Tripp?" I called softly as I rapped on the camper door. There was no answer, so I tried again. "Tripp? It's Jayne."

"I thought we were running on Pine time," came a muffled response. "It's only eight-thirty. Is this the kind of boss you're gonna be?"

"I don't care when you get to work," I responded with a laugh. "And it's after nine. I just wanted to let you know I won't be around until later this afternoon."

"Hang on."

Shuffling noises came from within the popup followed by a thump and a curse. A few seconds later, the door opened.

"Stubbed my toe thanks to —" He stopped talking mid-sentence. "Look at you."

I held my hands out to the side and looked down at the uniform, feeling oddly proud and self-conscious at the same time.

Tripp stepped out of the camper, examined the badge pinned over my heart, and tugged on my stubby ponytail. "Gotta say it. The uniform is kinda hot."

I flushed as he continued his inspection. "What are you looking for?"

"Duh. Handcuffs."

"Haven't gotten them yet." My heat level grew, despite the fact that I'd heard the same or similar comments from numerous people—men and women alike. I hadn't expected it from Tripp. "Anyway, I wanted to let you know that the garbage bin arrived. You can start whenever, but police pup and I will be patrolling the village this morning. You have the key?"

He jerked a thumb over his shoulder at the camper. "In there."

"I'll set a schedule with the sheriff. Then I'll have a better idea of when I can help around the house."

"Okay." Tripp grinned and leaned in to give me a quick kiss on the cheek. "Have a good day at work, honey."

I laughed, realizing how domestic the whole conversation sounded, and turned to leave. When I did, I noticed that along with the new tents in the area, the one at the far end was missing.

"Where's Yasmine's tent?" I asked.

Tripp squinted down to the far end of the campground. "Dunno."

I headed that direction and stopped outside the cluster of tents where Keko and her posse had made camp.

"Anyone awake?" I called and clapped my hands like an annoying summer camp counselor. "Hello?"

"Yeah," a man's voice grumbled from inside one of the tents. "Gimme a sec."

The army-green tent shook a bit as the zipper went up and Duane Crawford stuck his head out. The second he saw me standing there, his head dropped forward.

"What's going on?" He didn't seem at all surprised to

see a uniformed officer standing outside his tent. "Who's in trouble?"

"No one's in trouble, Duane."

He narrowed his eyes, trying to place me. "You were here yesterday. Asking all sorts of questions about Yasmine."

"I was. I've got one more." I gestured toward the spot where her tent used to be. "Any idea what happened to her tent?"

"That deputy came and took it."

I spun to find Keko strolling our way, her mass of braids dripping and a towel draped over her shoulders. Since she wasn't wearing a swimsuit, I guessed she just left the showers and not the lake. Was she an early riser or just getting ready for bed?

"Deputy Reed?" I asked.

"Don't know his name," Keko said. "Looked kinda sickly. How come you're wearing a uniform today?"

"Just got it. I told you I was working with the sheriff."

"Right." Keko hesitated before responding, in a way that said she didn't remember that at all.

"So, this deputy. He just took everything?" I confirmed.

"Yeah. At first, I figured he was a thief," Keko said, "the way he shoved all her stuff in the back of his van."

"He put everything in bags first, right?"

Keko burst out with a laugh. "Nope. He didn't even empty the tent. He pulled the tent poles out of the ground, rolled it all up, and threw the whole thing in his van. Don't think he was here even five minutes."

That didn't even come close to proper collection procedure. Either Keko couldn't see what Deputy Reed was doing, or she was too stoned to be a reliable witness. An investigation took a long time—documenting information about each piece, properly bagging each piece, photographing everything. Of course, I had taken thirty or forty pictures. Maybe they were planning to use mine?

Regardless of procedure, the thing that made the least sense was, why Deputy Reed? Sheriff Brighton had come right past here to deliver my uniforms. Why wouldn't he stop and do the collection himself? He'd told me that Reed wasn't an investigator. Why let him collect everything? What was going on around here? I don't think they bothered to check the woods around the house where Yasmine's body was found. Didn't sound like the sheriff had ordered a tox panel. They didn't come out to investigate her tent for four days. When they did, it was a grab-and-go. My captain in Madison would have the balls of any of his detectives who pulled something like this.

"Did you talk to the deputy at all?" I asked.

"The only thing I said," Keko began, "was who was he and why was he takin' Yasmine's stuff."

"And no one had been poking around that tent since I was here?"

Keko stared blankly. "Couldn't say. Didn't realize I was supposed to be babysitting it."

I sighed. "You weren't. Thanks for your help."

"What's going on?" Tripp asked when I returned to his camper.

"No clue." I paced, getting more frustrated with things by the moment. "It's like they aren't at all concerned about what happened to this girl. Something doesn't feel right."

"Could it just be Whispering Pines versus Madison?"

Maybe. I assumed that an officer of the law would follow proper procedures, no matter where the officer worked or where the crime happened. Maybe I was just naïve.

"Hadn't considered that," I said.

"It's not your job, you know."

"That doesn't mean I can just turn my back on this," I said too loudly, too defensively. I closed my eyes and counted to five. "If you were in my shoes, could you?"

"No, probably not."

"I've got to go to the station and pick up my belt and weapon. I'll ask about Yasmine's things. Maybe Keko got it wrong or there's a simple explanation."

Tripp grabbed my arm, stopping me before I got to my vehicle. "If something is off here, I think you should be careful."

The hair on the back of my neck stood up. "What do you mean?"

He locked eyes with mine. "I spent time in a lot of small towns since leaving California. They run according to their own rules and tend to be protective of their own. And, when they're tucked into the middle of nowhere, like Whispering Pines is, they tend to get left to their own ways."

"Pine time," I confirmed, but with darker meaning.

Maybe Deputy Reed wasn't capable of proper evidence collection, but it didn't take a lot of skill to dispose of it. More and more, I felt like Reed was involved in Yasmine's death, and now it looked like he might be trying to cover it up, too.

~~~

I parked behind the sheriff's station and found Deputy Reed the only one inside.

"Aren't you supposed to be patrolling the village?" he said, his voice laced with venom. "While I'm on desk duty."

Patrol had been his responsibility, and I couldn't tell if he was more sad or angry that it had been given to me.

"Came to pick up my belt and weapon," I said. "And keys. Sheriff Brighton told me you'd get some made for me."

He tossed the set at me. Correction, he threw the keys at my face. Luckily, I caught them before they made contact. Who knew all those years covering first base in high school softball would have a practical purpose.

I leaned across his desk. "Look, Sheriff Brighton told me you needed help around here over the summer. I happen to be available. Patrol wasn't my choice, it was assigned. If you've got a problem with that, take it up with our boss. I'm not looking to get in your way. You, actually, aren't even on my radar."

Not in a professional sense, at least. He was number two on my suspect list, behind Keko Shen and before Morgan Barlow.

Deputy Reed's face slackened and turned into the pout of a kid who'd just been grounded from his favorite toy. "Whatever." Reed pushed back from his desk and strode over to the sheriff's office where he unlocked the door. "He left your weapon in his credenza, said I could give it to you."

"Credenza? The sheriff stores weapons in a piece of furniture?"

"It's lined with half-inch steel."

That worked.

An empty nylon Sam Browne belt, presumably mine, sat on top of the desk. I secured it around my waist while Reed unlocked and opened the credenza door.

"Desk work isn't all you're going to be doing, right?" I asked in a peace-offering sort of way. "You'll get out in the field sometimes, won't you?"

He shrugged. "Depends on what the *sheriff* says."

A little angry at Uncle Sheriff as well as me? Or maybe he was just angry at the world in general. Reed struck me as that kind of guy.

"Well, you got to go out and collect evidence this morning," I said, the picture of innocence. "Didn't you?"

Reed froze, the gun case in his hands, and slowly looked over his shoulder at me. "What do you mean?"

I think you should be careful. Tripp's words sounded in my ears.

I flipped a casual hand westward. "This morning over at that campground near my house. I hired one of the guys staying there to help me with some work. I stopped by to let him know he could start today and noticed that Yasmine Long's things were gone. One of the other campers mentioned that you'd been by to collect everything."

Reed spun on me. "Who told you that?"

His anger ratcheted up another level, and I was suddenly concerned that if I mentioned Keko's name she could be in danger of retaliation.

"It was no big deal." I laughed, trying to diffuse the situation. "I was there a couple of days ago and got to know some of the campers. I noticed Yasmine's tent then. I cleared out the garbage to keep the bears away. Remember?"

Reed's stiff shoulders relaxed a little. "Yeah."

"I noticed her stuff was gone today."

I took hold of the small gun case in his hands and tugged gently so Reed would let it go. Inside was a Glock 19 and two empty magazines. I squeezed my hands into fists as they started to shake. Could I do this? Could I carry again? In my mind, I chanted *not your fault . . . you're a good cop . . .* Fortunately, Reed had turned back to the credenza to retrieve of box of ammo. By the time he faced me again, I'd managed to get back in control. Externally, at least.

I gave a nod at the box. "Thanks. Is there a range around here? Somewhere I can practice?"

"There's a setup in the woods about a quarter mile past the Meditation Circle. We don't have any official targets, so I just draw my own on paper and stick it to the hay bales set up there."

I filled both magazines with bullets, loaded one magazine into the Glock, and secured the other on my belt. I prayed I wouldn't need the weapon. Other than to do damage to some hay bales, I had no intention of firing it.

The tool belt got heavier as I added a set of handcuffs and keys, a flashlight, baton, and a canister of pepper spray Reed removed from the credenza. "Taser?"

"Taser?" Deputy Reed laughed. "Lady, maybe you'll need to handcuff a drunk, but that's about as much as you're likely to do." He nodded at the Glock. "Don't know why Sheriff Brighton got that for you. You aren't gonna need it. Neither of us have ever even needed to take ours out of the holster. All you really need to carry is the cuffs."

I was about to give him a lecture about being prepared, about how I never knew what I'd encounter on any given day so planned for anything. Then I thought, *Pine time*, and let it go. Besides, I was secretly giddy that I'd likely never need to draw the weapon.

"Why even bother with uniforms, then?" I joked.

Reed looked confused. "How will the tourists know who we are?"

Couldn't argue with that.

As Reed locked the ammo back into the credenza, I glanced at the heavy-duty shelving in the cage lining the far wall of the office. The station's evidence locker. The only thing on the shelves behind the gate was a clipboard with a log sheet attached.

"Seriously, though, what happened with Yasmine's things? The locker's empty."

"Couldn't tell you. Sheriff Brighton took it all with him."

"Took it all?"

"You deaf?" he mocked, raising his voice. "That's what I said. He took it all."

There went my theory that Deputy Reed was trying to dispose of evidence.

"I'm not the enemy, Deputy," I said. "I'm here to do a job, same as you."

Reed put his hands on his hips, looked down at his shoes, and sighed. "He said something about bringing it to Dr. Bundy, the ME, for a thorough search."

Not an apology for being a jackass, but I chose to take it as one.

"That makes sense," I conceded. But the way he wouldn't look at me didn't make sense at all.

Reed returned to his desk and wiggled the mouse to wake up his computer.

"I'll need login ability, too." Hopefully, the request wouldn't set off another tantrum. "To write up reports on the drunks and all that."

Really, I had no reason to dislike Reed. Except for his juvenile behavior and that fib about not knowing Yasmine. The fib still stuck in my craw. Why would he lie about that?

Fortunately, whatever had been poking at Reed had subsided. He opened the proper screen and created a sign on for me. Excellent. Now I could find out if the deputy or the good sheriff were hiding anything else.

Chapter 21

IT WAS A BEAUTIFUL LATE-SPRING day in Whispering Pines. An excited buzz circulated among the locals that even a newcomer like me could sense. Tourists would start pouring in for the long Memorial Day weekend over the next day-and-a-half and the summer season would officially be underway.

The shops were all fully staffed as they made last-minute preparations—stocking shelves inside, weeding and watering flowerbeds outside. In the last two days, the plants in the commons' pentacle gardens seemed to double in size, almost as if by magic, and were now bursting with color. The same way Morgan Barlow's gardens had been all along.

"Looks like we've got a new sheriff in town."

I turned to find a teenage girl reading a book beneath the shade of a tree a few yards from the lake—*wavy light blonde-brown hair, very light brown skin, thin but not skinny.* Bare feet poked out of ripped jeans, and the pale turquoise blue shade of her tank top matched her eyes exactly.

"I'm not a sheriff." This girl mesmerized me. "I am a deputy. Part time, just for the summer. I'm—"

"Jayne O'Shea," the girl completed. "I've heard about you. I'm Lily Grace."

She gave no indication if that was two first names or if Grace was her last name. Her jewelry, a ring that resembled a miniature crystal ball and a pendant at her neck that looked like a gray cat's eye staring out of her chest, caught my attention.

"Let me guess," I said, "you're a fortune teller."

Lily Grace lifted a thin shoulder. "That's what they tell me." She held her hands up to me. "Want me to do a reading?"

"You don't sound so sure of your abilities."

She leaned toward me and in a conspiratorial tone said, "It's all for fun, you must know that. Wagons and scarves and" —she shook her ring at me— "crystal balls. Please."

I put a hand to my heart as if shocked by this news then leaned close to Lily Grace and whispered, "You mean to tell me you're taking money from tourists and not giving them what they pay for?"

She paled and looked around to make sure no one was listening. "It's not like we're stealing from them. We give a reading, that's what they pay us for. Some are even accurate."

I leveled my cop glare on the girl and then burst out laughing. "Relax. It's not like I'm going to arrest you. Some people take this stuff really seriously, hey?"

Lily Grace nodded, her hair and oversized silver hoop earrings bobbing along with her head. "My grandmother, the great Cybil—"

"Is that what she goes by? The Great Cybil?"

Lily Grace shook her head. "Just Cybil. I tack on the rest, but never to her face."

"Understandable."

"Anyway, some people come every year just to get an annual reading from her. A few come twice a year. A couple come every month."

"She must be good."

The girl shrugged again and leaned back as though

bored now. "I guess."

"And you give readings, too?"

She sighed hard. "That's what I've been trained to do."

"Trained? I thought being able to tell a fortune was a gift people were born with."

"Yeah, well, I'm a freak among the freaks around here." She held her hands out again and gave me a questioning look. "So?"

"What the heck." I sat next to her on the ground and ordered Meeka to sit, too. Her butt dropped immediately and she stared at the lake.

I placed my hands on Lily Grace's and watched as the girl closed her eyes. A look of serenity softened her face. After a few minutes, she began to sway slightly, as though she'd gone into a trance. If this was an act, Lily Grace deserved an award for her performance.

A second later, her eyes snapped open, and she jerked her hands away from mine.

"What?" I asked and then laughed. "Did you see something disturbing in my future?"

Lily Grace looked confused. "I saw something."

"Isn't that what's supposed to happen?"

She stood, paced three steps away and then back, shaking her hands as though she had something stuck to them. Then she sat back down, pulled her legs into crisscross, and straightened them out again.

"You don't understand." She blew out a slow breath, still freaked out over whatever her vision had showed her. "I *saw something.* I never see anything. When I tell you I'm a freak among freaks, that's what I mean. I'm a fortune teller who can't tell a fortune."

"Wouldn't that make you normal then?"

"My grandmother has been telling me since I was three that I was destined to be a fortune teller, that it was in my blood. I've just been going along with it. I'll be a senior in the fall. I've got one more summer and I'm out of here. I want to go to college. Become a vet. And now . . ." She glared at me as though I'd done something wrong. "And now, just when I have a plan, I *see* something."

"I'm sorry?"

She swatted a hand at me. "Whatever."

"Do you want to tell me what you saw? Or do you think maybe it was a fluke. Want to give it another try?" I held out my hands.

Lily Grace considered this. "Yeah, maybe it was a fluke." But a minute after she took my hands again, she moaned like Rosalyn and I used to when we ate too many of Gran's turtle brownies. Her voice dropped an octave and took on a monotone. "Your future here is not what you planned."

Really? That was her big vision? It wasn't a secret to anyone in the village that I was here to fix up the house. And the badge pinned to my shirt hadn't been in the car on my drive up from Madison.

"I see," Lily Grace continued and then made a face, like she felt nauseated, and moved a hand to her belly. "I see beans."

"Beans?" I asked. "Beans as in zero, zilch, nothing? Or beans as in the vegetable?"

She considered this. "More like a legume." After another few seconds, she opened her eyes. "That's it."

"Glad I didn't pay for that."

"It doesn't mean anything to you?" Lily Grace asked hopefully. "It would be kind of cool if my first ever legitimate reading actually meant something." She gasped. "I wonder if this is going to happen all the time now. Geeze, just when I'd accepted my title as Queen of the Misfits. Now I'm just like every other freak in this village."

"What kind of beans? Did you actually see them? What did they look like?"

"I don't know." Lily Grace sighed, distracted by her own problems now. She put her fingers to her forehead as though trying to recall the image. "A pinto bean maybe?"

"I do like Mexican food," I joked then a thought struck me. "Did you by any chance hear that Shoppe Mystique had a break-in?"

"Nope. That sucks. Did anything get stolen?"

"Castor beans."

For a second, her eyes lit up excitedly. "Freaky."

"Indeed." I stood and brushed dirt off my butt. "Sorry for traumatizing you. Maybe your gift is a one-and-done and it will go away again?"

Lily Grace made a little snort of disgust. "I wish."

"I'm off to make the rounds and meet people. See you."

Meeka and I wandered in and out of the shops surrounding the pentacle gardens. Then down to the marina where we said hi to Oren and met his dad Gill, the marina owner. They were busy doing final checks on all their equipment in preparation for the summer season.

I'd never been a beat cop before. There wasn't a lot for me to do, since the tourist crowd was still fairly light, but I got a lot of steps in and learned where everything was. I met all of the shopkeepers, one or two gave me the kind of enthusiastic welcome Violet, Honey, and Sugar had. Most were neutral about me being in town, relative of The Original or not. They all loved Meeka, though. I'd never seen her eat so many biscuits. By the end of my first shift, I felt confident I'd be able to direct people anywhere they wanted to go . . . in the commons area, at least.

The path back to the sheriff's station took me past Quin's. I wanted to ask Donovan about the harlequin I found in Yasmine's tent so took a left into his shop.

"Ms. O'Shea, how nice to see you again," Donovan greeted in his cool, in-control way, but nowhere near as friendly as the first time I'd entered. His gaze traveled up and down my body. "In a deputy's uniform this time."

Had to admit it, the Glock strapped to my hip comforted me. "I'll be helping out Sheriff Brighton during the tourist season."

"I feel safer already." The words were genuine, but the turn of his mouth and roll of his eyes revealed a good dose of sarcasm. "Only during the season?"

"That's what we agreed to." I pulled out my phone and flipped to the picture of the doll in Yasmine's tent. "When I was here yesterday we talked about your harlequins."

"I recall."

I held the picture out to him. "Did you happen to make this one?"

His cheerful expression clouded over. "It looks like one of mine."

Not the response I expected. "You don't know?"

He sighed, as though he didn't have time for my questions. Then he glanced around the shop and checked the dressing rooms, presumably looking for customers. Finding no one, he returned to me.

"I don't like for the tourists to know this. It either makes them nervous or they treat me like one of the fortune tellers." If the crinkling of his nose meant anything, he didn't care for the fortune tellers any more than he did me. "I'm a psychic as well as a practicing Wiccan."

He held up his wrist with the Triple Moon Goddess tattoo as though it offered proof of some kind.

"Anyone can get a tattoo, Donovan."

"Anyone who lives in the village, however, knows that only coven members may wear the Triple Moon Goddess symbol, whether in tattoo form or jewelry or what have you."

"What happens if a non-coven member disobeys that directive? Tar and feathering? Sandwich boarding? Or maybe you put them in stocks next to the negativity well?"

He shook his head. "It simply isn't done."

"If the Triple Moon symbol is supposed to be your members-only gang tag, why is it on display all around the village like a logo?"

He glared at me. Didn't like me dissing their moons, apparently.

"The Triple Moon symbol," Donovan said, his voice tight, "acts to protect us and honor the Goddess."

More witchcraft mumbo-jumbo. I wiggled my phone at him. "What does that have to do with this harlequin?"

"May I ask, where did you find it?"

"Do you know a young woman named Yasmine Long?"

Understanding immediately showed on his face. "It was with her belongings."

"How do you know that?"

"I, most likely, put it there."

"Are you purposely trying to confuse me? You 'most likely' put it there? Care to explain that?"

He walked over to the shelf loaded with harlequin dolls beside his checkout stand and held a hand out to them like a *Price is Right* model. "I told you that these were for sale."

"You did. And that you give away others."

He nodded at my phone. "The doll in that photograph is one of the latter."

I glanced at the image of the empty eye sockets and dehydrated appearance. "Because it's so creepy-looking you wouldn't be able to sell it?"

He stood tall and pushed his wide shoulders back. "My gift is that I know when death is coming. When the visions come to me, I go into a trance state."

Sounded like an excuse for trying to get away with murder to me. "That's a gift?"

"A gift is not always a positive or pleasant thing, Deputy O'Shea. 'Psychic' is a loose term for me. I can't foretell events, as our clairvoyant friends in The Triangle can. I can't bring on my visions, they just happen. When they do, I know who will die but not exactly when. Usually, it's within a few days. When the vision comes, I go into the trance and end up in my art studio where I create a doll. Then I deliver the doll to the person."

"This doll," I held up the picture, "it gives the appearance of dehydration and illness."

"Correct. Once complete, the doll will resemble the person in death. As I understand, Miss Long died from poisoning."

Poisoning. Not food poisoning.

"Where did you hear that?"

He turned his attention to tidying a rack of men's shirts. "Around."

Did the whispering trees share that tidbit? Couldn't imagine Sheriff Brighton had, especially since he didn't seem to believe Yasmine had been poisoned. Who else knew? Keko and her gang. Tripp. Deputy Reed? The medical examiner?

"You're telling me," I began, "that you create dolls that resemble the victim's death and then deliver them all while in some sort of trance?"

"That is what I'm telling you." He gestured at the village in general. "Ask anyone who lives here. It's common knowledge."

"Will an impending natural death also put you into one of these *trances*? Or does it only happen when a person is murdered?"

"Miss Long was murdered?" His surprise felt forced.

"I have reason to believe it's a possibility."

He was silent for a minute, but rather than offering a respectful moment for the deceased he appeared to be analyzing this information.

"To my knowledge," Donovan said, "there's never been a murder in Whispering Pines. It's rather unsettling to think one has happened."

"It is. How long have you been here? Your whole life?"

"No, I'm not one of the fortunate souls born here. I moved to the village about six months ago."

Not that it mattered, but how extensive could his knowledge of Whispering Pines' history be after only six months?

He crossed to the accessories table to untangle some necklaces. "Was there anything else, Deputy? I have no knowledge of what happened to the young woman. Only that she died. I have no idea who did it."

To me, he sounded like suspect number one. But if the entire village would back him up, and I was sure they would, there was no reason to keep him on my list. At least I knew where the doll came from.

"That's all I came in for," I said, "to find out about the doll's origins. Whether it was purchased or a present."

"Not sure anyone would consider my dolls to be a gift. Except for old Mrs. Kaczynski. She was one-hundred and six and beyond ready to meet her maker. The day she received my doll, she invited everyone to her home for a pot luck. Died peacefully in her sleep that night." Donovan smiled. "It was lovely."

Whispering Pines was such a weird place.

"Thanks for answering my questions."

"Of course. Stop back next Sunday. I'll be putting all remaining spring clothing on sale."

"I'll keep that in mind." I walked to the door, then stopped and turned back. "My credit card."

"What about it?" Donovan asked.

"That's how you knew my name that day."

"That confirmed it," he admitted and let that slow smile turn his lips. "But I do see a lot of Lucy in you."

I held his gaze while fighting off a shiver—the guy creeped me out—then gave a nod and left the shop.

Officially done with our shift, Meeka and I returned to my vehicle. I thought of Lily Grace's vision as I got into the Cherokee.

"Did she see pinto beans or could they have been castor beans?"

I didn't believe in any of this mumbo-jumbo. But the villagers did. Someone steals Morgan's beans and then Lily

Grace's gift turns on so she can give me a message about beans? Somehow, it was all connected. It had to be. I sure hoped the internet guy came today, because I had a lot of research to do.

Chapter 22

BACK AT THE HOUSE, I found a dusty, sweaty Tripp in the front yard hauling a wheelbarrow full of debris out to the container.

"How's it going?" I asked from the driver's seat of the Cherokee.

"I should have the dining room and living room cleared out by the end of the day. I'm setting aside anything unbroken or fixable. How was your first day on the job?"

"Compared to Madison? This is like a day at the lake." I gave him a big cheesy grin and pointed to the lake. "Get it?"

Tripp groaned and turned his back on me.

"Do you know if the internet guy came yet?" I asked.

"Yep, he finished about an hour ago. He left his card on your table and said you should call if there are any problems."

"Perfect. Can I interest you in barbecued chicken for dinner?"

"If you insist," Tripp deadpanned.

Sappy as it sounded, I was really grateful that I'd met him. I didn't believe in the witchcraft woo-woo around here, but I was pretty sure that sometimes in life you got exactly what you needed. I didn't know what that meant regarding

Tripp, but I was glad to have him around.

Meeka, happy to be off her leash after four hours, raced around the backyard then ran to the front where she barked, playfully, presumably at Tripp.

Inside, I pulled off my uniform shirt and hung it on the portable clothes rack. The boathouse was plenty big enough for me and Meeka. I didn't have a lot of possessions, even back in Madison I lived light, so the sleeping area, kitchenette, and living area provided more than enough space. The hanging rack, though, wasn't very big. Maybe there was an armoire in the main house I could move over here. Or, Tripp could install some cabinets.

I pulled on my favorite ratty T-shirt—with Harry, Hermione, and Ron on the front—and then glanced at the clothes I bought at Quin's yesterday. To me, the tunics were fancy. Mom and Rosalyn would have pulled on any one of them just to run to the grocery store.

It was a shame to let them hang there. What the heck. Tripp was coming for dinner. Wouldn't hurt to look a little more like a girl now and then. I'd just need to be careful to not get barbecue sauce all over it while I made the chicken. I pulled off the T-shirt and my hiking boots and slipped on the light blue tunic with fluttery sleeves and the flipflops with the multicolored crystal butterfly at the toe that Rosalyn gave me. She called them my dress up shoes. Had to admit, I instantly felt swanky.

The internet guy had left all the router info on the table with his card. While my five-year-old laptop powered up, I grabbed a Spotted Cow from the mini-fridge and a couple of minutes later, I was reading emails. One from Mom explaining that she had set up a line of credit for repairs to the house. A box with a checkbook, credit card, and salon supplies should arrive via UPS tomorrow. One from Dr. Maddox wondering how things were going up here. And one from Jonah.

I hadn't spoken to him since the morning I moved out of

our apartment.

Hey Jay,

Jay. His shortened version of my name stopped me cold and brought a flood of memories. Years of holidays and birthdays. Great weekends spent with friends. His insistence that I didn't have to work if I didn't want to, especially as a cop. The phony people he started hanging around with because they could 'catapult' his political career to the next level. The phony significant others of the catapultiers he wanted me to hang around with, because government was a tight-knit group.

Our excitement over planning our future. It really had looked bright. Jonah was brilliant.

The surprise trip to Paris four months ago; his way of helping me get past the shooting. It had been a perfect trip, I'd loved every minute of it. Until the last night when, at the top of the Eiffel Tower, he pulled out a ring. As I stared at the spectacular diamond encrusted band, all I could think was that I'd been making very bad decisions lately. I had loved him fiercely for years. My mother did, too. Especially the fact that, "He comes from such a good family!" As time ticked on, and he refused to support the career I was passionate about, my love started to fade. I couldn't imagine not being a cop any more than I could imagine being a politician's wife. So, I said no.

Hey Jay,
I'm going down to Chicago with some of the guys this weekend. I'm looking for my Cubs hat. You know the one? I got it that time we went down for the weekend and stayed at The Ritz-Carlton off Michigan Avenue. That was the best weekend, wasn't it? Anyway, do you have any idea where that hat might be?

What a jackass. Trying to butter me up with a good

times memory. Going 'with some of the guys'? Right. He was probably going with that gorgeous new accountant in finance. I hit reply.

Sorry. No clue.

"Find your own damn hat!" I yelled at the screen.

I added that he should look in the old trunk in the storage locker, deleted the words, and was about to hit send when a realization struck. I broke his heart. He didn't do anything to me. He proposed to me, and I said no. The devastation on his face . . . I'd remember it forever.

Hey Jonah,
Sorry, I'm not sure where your hat is. Did you check in that old trunk in the storage locker? Have a good time in Chi-town.
Jay

I pushed away from the laptop, grabbed a package of chocolate cookies from the cupboard, and stomped out onto the sundeck. I had devoured six cookies in ninety seconds before I caught myself. If I'd learned one thing in the last six months, it was that self-medicating with food would not take away the pain of Jonah. Or Frisky. Not permanently, at least. The instant gratification was always obliterated by crushing guilt and shame afterwards.

Glints of sun sparkled off the soft ripples on the water. A breeze blew up and rustled through the pines. With my eyes closed, I breathed in the smell of the lake. I listened to the tree branches rustle together.

A few deep breaths later, I was back to normal. Well, normal for me. This — listening to nature, feeling the breeze on my face, and breathing it into my lungs — was a much better way of dealing with stress. By the water, far away from all the pressures in my life, was exactly where I needed to be. Or did I specifically need to be in Whispering Pines?

As in not just for a month or the summer, but permanently.

Another gust of wind rushed through, and I shivered, but not from cold. The temperature was perfect today.

A scolding bark from below made my eyes snap open. Meeka was on the pier below, looking up at me.

"Yes, I know. I'm supposed to be researching."

After one more restorative breath, I went back inside. I shoved the package of cookies to the back of the top shelf of the cupboard and returned to the laptop. After first deleting Jonah's email, I closed the program and opened a browser.

"Castor beans," I mumbled as I typed.

Five minutes later, I knew that the castor plant was a distinctive, slightly tropical-looking reddish plant that produced puffy red flowers. Castor oil, expressed from the seeds, had numerous medical and cosmetic uses. The seeds themselves produced . . . Whoa. I sat up and paid closer attention. The seeds produced ricin, a highly toxic poison.

The waste left behind after expressing the oil contained the toxin, which could be dehydrated, crushed into a powder, and then mixed into food or dissolved in a beverage. Chewing and swallowing a whole bean would also release the toxin. A single bean could kill a person in as little as two days.

I got to my feet and paced around the apartment, out onto the sundeck, and back inside. I tugged a small stack of papers from the ream in the box on the couch and taped twelve of them together in three rows of four pages. At the top I wrote, *Yasmine poisoned?* Below that and to the right I wrote, *Morgan stolen castor beans >> castor beans = ricin >> ricin = poison.* To the side in red ink I wrote *ONE BEAN CAN KILL* and circled it multiple times. Next, on the center page, *Signs of Ricin Poisoning.*

I returned to my laptop and typed those same words, signs of ricin poisoning, into the browser. The results were virtual echoes of the symptoms Keko Shen and Duane Crawford said Yasmine had: nausea, vomiting, abdominal pain, diarrhea, dehydration, possible seizures.

"Initial symptoms occur in less than twelve hours," I read aloud, "progressing rapidly over the next twelve to twenty-four hours. Death can occur within thirty-six to seventy-two hours depending on method of exposure and amount of dose."

After writing all of that on the wall, I did a search for Yasmine Long. A number of hits for that name appeared, but it took me approximately three seconds to find the woman who had been laying at the edge of my property. Yasmine had been a true beauty with long platinum-blonde waves, brilliant white teeth, and a body perfectly adorned by the black-and-white striped bikini she wore in the picture. The woman I had found was a shriveled shell compared to the vibrant Yasmine in the picture, surrounded by friends and smiling big.

I couldn't help but note that Frisky had looked more like the Yasmine I'd found outside than the one in the picture on the internet. My heart ached for both of them as I clicked print. I needed an image of Yasmine for my suspect wall. She'd go at the very top, like the apex of a pyramid. I also copied the image to a file in my computer I titled simply, 'Yasmine Long'.

On the left side of my suspect wall at the top I wrote, *Suspects*. My list included: Keko Shen, Martin Reed, and Donovan. Even though the village would likely back Donovan's trance excuse, that didn't mean he didn't do it.

Finally, I clicked the 'Images' tab on my browser and typed in 'castor beans.' I covered my eyes with my hands before the result appeared, not sure I wanted to see the image I knew would be there. Slowly, I peeked through my fingers. There on the screen was a collection of oval beans, light brown in color with random brown streaks.

They looked very much like pinto beans.

Chapter 23

TOXIC CASTOR BEANS RESEMBLED PINTO beans. I think I knew the method used to poison Yasmine. Someone gave her castor beans, and it was a safe bet that they came from the shelves hidden behind the rack of wreaths at Shoppe Mystique. The one filled with jars of 'dangerous' plants. I added *Morgan Barlow?* to my suspect wall. Was she somehow involved with Yasmine's murder? If so, why? And why did she even stock poisonous plants?

I had to talk to her. And I needed to let Lily Grace know that it looked like the reading she did for me had meant something.

I glanced at the time on the laptop—nearly five-thirty. Was Shoppe Mystique still open? I grabbed my keys and rushed out the door just as Tripp was coming up the stairs.

"Hey," he said with a smile. "I was at a good stopping point so . . . what's wrong?"

"Pinto beans look like castor beans." I shook my head at his confused expression. "I've been doing some research. I'll explain later. I've got to talk to Morgan." I dropped my head back and groaned. "Damn. I forgot to put the chicken on the grill."

Tripp took my hands and said nothing until I looked

him in the eye. "Calm down first. You're too agitated to get behind the wheel."

He was right. It's not like this was an emergency. Worst case scenario, I'd talk to Morgan in the morning. "Okay. I'm good."

"You look nice, by the way." Tripp flipped the hem of my tunic. "I like this. Where's the chicken? I'll have it ready when you get back."

And he cooks, too? Was this guy for real? Now I needed to calm down for an entirely different reason.

"Thank you," I said. "The chicken is in the fridge. I shouldn't be gone that long."

Tripp and Meeka seemed happy with each other's company, so I left them together. Ten minutes later, I was climbing the steps of Shoppe Mystique.

Morgan looked up from a ledger and what looked like receipts spread out in front of her. "Jayne. Blessed be."

I always felt like I was supposed to place my hands together and bow or cross myself when she said that. Instead, I just nodded.

"What's wrong?" Morgan asked. "You look frantic."

"Why do you stock dangerous plants?" I strode over to the shelf hidden behind the rack of wreaths.

"Various reasons." Morgan took a jar from the shelf. "Morning Glory is not only an adorable flower, placing the seeds beneath your pillow will stop nightmares. The flower petals won't harm you, but the seeds contain an LSD-like chemical." She returned the jar and took another. "Consumed, daffodil can cause nausea and vomiting, but the symptoms should dissipate after a few hours. It is, ironically, quite effective in love spells, and in the bedroom, it increases fertility." She gave me a suggestive wink. "Add Bearberry to a sachet to increase your psychic powers, but do not consume it if you have liver disease." She took another. "One of my personal favorites is Blue Flag. It can cause abdominal issues, but used in the proper dosage it's beneficial for healing. I keep a bit of the root in my cash register to increase business."

These jars were identical to the ones on the shelves across the store. The only difference was that while the safe plants had old-fashioned tea-stained labels, these had tea-stained labels with black backgrounds and a skull-and-crossbones at the top.

I glanced at the jar labeled "Castor Beans." It was empty.

"What about castor beans? Why do you carry those?"

If Morgan heard the accusatory tone in my voice, she didn't acknowledge it.

"Castor beans serve numerous purposes," Morgan explained. "As you already know, the oil is used as a laxative. It can also soothe sore muscles, hemorrhoids, and arthritis pain. It can help with hair growth and preventing split ends. It heals scratches and acne. It will also repel moles in the garden. I use the beans in witch balls as they absorb evil and are, therefore, excellent protection against negativity."

Mumbo. Jumbo. "What about as a food?"

"The oil is perfectly safe," Morgan said.

"And the beans?"

"Oh no. The beans must never be consumed as they are highly toxic." Morgan tilted her head to the side. "But you already know that. What's going on?"

"I think Yasmine Long was poisoned."

She didn't miss a beat. "And not only do you believe that my beans were used, you think I'm responsible. Correct?"

"I'll have to see the results of the autopsy," I said, "but from the information I've gathered, her symptoms are the same as those in ricin poisoning."

She stared at me for so long I started to worry she was placing a hex of some kind on me. The clock on the mantel in the reading room softly struck six. Morgan glided to the front door and turned the hand carved wood sign from "Open" to "Closed."

"The last time we talked, Jayne, I told you that one of the prime rules of Wicca, if not the only rule, is to do no harm. I respect life, in all of its forms, far too much to ever consider taking one. I didn't know Yasmine; I had no reason to harm her. I'd never even met the poor girl until she arrived in Whispering Pines."

I wandered to the table of amulets and talismans. "The coven . . . council . . . whatever. They didn't approve of her, did they?"

"Many in the council did not approve of Yasmine." A small smile turned Morgan's mouth. "I had to give her points for ingenuity, however. The girl needed to earn money and no one would hire her—"

"Despite the fact that her aunt lives in Whispering Pines?" I couldn't find a single Triple Moon anything on the "Amulets and Talismans" table. I didn't see the symbol anywhere in the shop except for the one hanging around Morgan's neck.

"Normally, having a relative who lives here helps," Morgan said. "I know Flavia quite well, but I don't know what happened between her and her niece. I do know there was a falling out. Perhaps it had something to do with the car washing."

"Is Flavia a member of the council?"

"One of our longest sitting members." An expression that was part amusement, part annoyance crossed her face.

"What was that look for?" I asked.

"Flavia is one of the oldest Originals in the village. She has taken it upon herself to act as our mayor."

"Does the village need a mayor?"

She smiled again, this time sadly. "Your grandmother was the village elder. We looked to her for decisions."

That seemed fair, since she owned the land and all.

"We let Flavia think she's running things," Morgan

whispered and gave a little wink. "No real harm and it keeps the peace."

"Keeps the peace?"

"She has a bit of a short temper."

"What do you mean by that? Is it possible she became so upset with her niece's behavior that she — "

"Do no harm doesn't apply to just me," Morgan interrupted sternly. "Wicca is a way of life we all abide by. We cherish life as a gift given by the Goddess. Taking a life is an unconscionable act."

"It is possible, though." I looked over my shoulder at her. "Right?"

After a great deal of obvious internal debate, Morgan relented. "Yes. I suppose it is possible that Flavia harmed her niece."

I crossed the aisle from amulets to "Oils and Incense," contemplating her claim. I believed Morgan and mentally crossed her off my suspect wall. There was nothing in her behavior, nothing in her responses, that made me think she was lying. In fact, she looked devastated by the possibility that Flavia had 'caused harm' to another.

"Yasmine was poisoned," I said. "I'm sure of it. There is a very high probability that she was poisoned with your castor beans."

Morgan shook her head and blinked repeatedly. "That any of my plants were used to do this . . ."

"Do you think that Sheriff Brighton is really searching for the thief?"

Morgan spun toward me, a tinge of anger mixing with shock. "What are you saying?"

I backed down. "Nothing."

"He seems fairly certain it was a tourist, and I agree. We know the people in this village. I can't imagine any of them either stealing from me or poisoning another person."

"A tourist," I said thoughtfully.

"You have someone in mind?"

I met Morgan's gaze. "You told me that Keko Shen was here often. She wanted to learn negative magic, right?"

Morgan's face brightened, but with understanding, not pleasure. "Keko? She definitely wants to learn magic, both negative and positive. She said once that she wanted to learn to cast a love spell, but sadly, a spell to repel seemed far more important to her."

"Repel what?"

Morgan shook her head. "She didn't say. Honestly, I didn't encourage the desire. All I told her was that if she wanted to learn a spell to harm or repel a person, she needed to find a better way to deal with the situation. She didn't argue, so I think she did want to repel a person."

"You're saying Keko wanted to attract someone with a love spell while also repelling someone else?"

The scorned cheerleader look on Keko's face popped into my mind. Did Keko want to repel Yasmine? Even though they'd just met, maybe Yasmine reminded her of someone she used to know. Someone who had embarrassed or one-upped her? Maybe Yasmine had hooked up with a guy Keko was interested in. Petty reason to murder someone, but people were killed for petty reasons every single day.

"Is Keko a suspect?" Morgan asked.

"I'm not making any accusations at this point. She is a person of interest, though. I need to know the results of the autopsy first. It's possible it was simply food poisoning that Yasmine couldn't recover from. Then again, Keko had answers for a lot of my questions even though she claimed to not know Yasmine well. There's also her interest in dark magic." I gave Morgan a hopeful look, like maybe she could supply a conclusion. "When I put all the pieces together, a lot of things point to her."

"Sheriff Brighton hired you to patrol the village, correct?"

I hung my head. "I know. It's not my job."

"But you can't stop yourself," Morgan concluded.

"I can't. I'm trying. It's just not possible for me to shut this off."

Morgan studied me for a few moments and then held up a finger, indicating I should give her a moment. She took a silver tray and a small purple muslin bag, about the size of a deck of playing cards, from a basket beneath the large wooden table by the front door. Then she floated around the store, placing items on the tray.

From the herb corner, "Basil and bay. Cedar and thistle. Lavender and, of course, pine."

From the charms and amulets table, "A golden pentacle."

From the crystals and stones corner, "Quartz and black tourmaline. Now, come with me."

I laughed, internally, because it looked like she was getting ready to cast a spell. Didn't she need eye of newt? A hair from a unicorn? Dragon's blood?

She scowled at me, like she was reading my mind.

I silenced the bratty thoughts in my head as I followed her into the reading room. There, she pulled on one of the bookcase sections, and it slid opened to reveal a small hidden room. A circle extending almost to the walls looked like it had been burned into the wood floor. At the center of the circle was a small rectangular table covered with a purple cloth. Morgan set the silver tray on the table. From an antique cupboard in the corner, she retrieved one white and one black candle.

The déjà vu feeling I got in Gran's office returned. There was something about this whole set up . . . the table, the cloth covering it, the candles. It all seemed so familiar.

"I want you to think of only two things," Morgan instructed as she laid out the table. No, not a table, an altar. "Two things and nothing more. Can you do that?"

"I think so," I answered, confused. "What two things?"

"Love and protective energy."

"What are you doing, Morgan?"

She held up the small purple bag. "I understand why you can't step away from this, and I won't ask you to, but I fear that you are wandering into potential danger. I'm creating a spell bag for you."

I was about to protest, I didn't need magical help, but I knew she wouldn't listen and that things worked differently in Whispering Pines. There was one rule that applied to being new to or when visiting an area: listen to the locals.

After lighting the candles, she held a bundle of herbs tied together with a purple string to one of the flames. She came to me, took my hand, and pulled me into the circle drawn on the floor. Her lips moved but she didn't speak out loud as she wafted the smoke from the bundle around me, front and back, head to toe.

"Stand right here," she said when she was done. Then she prompted, "Love and protective energy."

I played along and started chanting the words over and over in my head as Morgan stepped behind the table. She closed her eyes, as though in meditation, and held her hands over the items on the tray, a look of serenity on her face. Taking one item at a time, she placed everything from the tray into the little bag and tied the bag shut. She began chanting silently again and held the bag near, but not in, the flame of each of the candles. Finally, she extinguished the flames with a candle snuffer and pressed the bag into my hands.

"Carry this with you at all times," Morgan instructed. "Keep it in a pocket or tuck it into your bra if you have no pockets. Sleep with it under your pillow. It will protect you from whatever is going on in this village."

Whatever is going on in this village? Murder? Some other kind of danger? I turned the bag over and over. It was just a bag full of herbs and rocks. But to Morgan, it was a bag full of love and protective energy. I thanked her for it.

"Be careful, Jayne. Nothing like this has ever happened

in Whispering Pines. We are a peaceful, loving community that accepts everyone as they are."

"Unless you're an outsider," I added. "Like Yasmine was." Or Tripp. What about me?

Morgan frowned. "I still can't imagine any of us harming her. The tourists however . . . I can't speak for them."

"I know it's not my job, and that I should let this go, but I feel like no one else cares about what happened to Yasmine. Not even Sheriff Brighton. That's not right."

"It's *not* right. I think it's very noble of you to step up. I do care, and I'll do what I can to help you figure this out."

Her confidence and support, far more than the little purple bag of trinkets, comforted me.

"Are you going home now?" Morgan asked as she returned to the ledger she'd been working on when I got there.

I should, the chicken should be getting good and crispy. "Soon. I have one quick stop to make before that."

~~~

As I hoped, the sheriff's station was empty at six-thirty at night, Sheriff Brighton's phone number posted on the door in case of emergencies. I signed on to Deputy Reed's computer, not too difficult since he had taped a sticky note with his username and password to the bottom of his keyboard, and went straight to his email program. Reed had been copied on many of Sheriff Brighton's emails, including those from the medical examiner. The latest arrived late this morning and had "Preliminary Autopsy – Y. Long" in the subject line. Not even forty-eight hours after I had found her body. It was sobering to think how much things could change in such a short amount of time.

The first thing that caught my attention was Yasmine's age. She had turned twenty in April, a little more than a month ago. Her adult life had barely begun. Approximate time of death was listed as Saturday, the day I arrived, sometime between one and three in the morning. Her weight, only ninety-three pounds. There were no external injuries discovered, except an abrasion on her right cheek. The internal exam showed severe dehydration. As expected, there was no cause of death listed. Final autopsy results, in uncomplicated cases, generally took weeks. Add in things like toxicology reports, as we had done, and it could take months.

Dr. Brody included a photo of an unusual tattoo over Yasmine's heart. It looked like a lower case "y" with an extra-long straight tail, a horizontal line crossed the tail near the bottom. Directly below the line to the right of the tail was what looked like a lower case "m." Beneath it all, a lower case "w." Weird. Wonder what it stood for? Weirder still, Dr. Brody reported that the mark wasn't a tattoo. In his opinion, it had been drawn on with magic marker, possibly within hours of her death.

Within hours of her death Yasmine had been too sick to do anything but puke. Someone had come to her tent and, for all intents and purposes, branded her? Had Yasmine known her killer?

I continued reading, searching for any mention of pending tests. The tox panel had been ordered, hadn't it? I read the report again. Nothing. I closed the email and looked for another from the medical examiner's office. Maybe correspondence regarding the tests came separately. Nothing. In fact, other than the preliminary report, there hadn't been any email contact between Sheriff Brighton and Dr. Brody in the past week. None that Deputy Reed had been copied on, at least.

When I first mentioned the possibility of poisoning, I hadn't taken into consideration that if the sheriff requested a standard toxicology workup, the medical examiner would only check for standard substances like amphetamines, cocaine, marijuana, and opioids. To find ricin in Yasmine's system, they would need to test specifically for ricin. And unless the sheriff knew something he wasn't sharing with me, he wouldn't have known to request that.

I was about to reply to Dr. Brody's email with a follow-up request when Tripp's and Morgan's pleas for me to be careful echoed in my ears. My first thought was to dismiss it, they were just protecting me. Very sweet. But Morgan had lived here her entire life. She knew how the locals watched out for each other. Was the sheriff protecting someone? Was that why after two weeks, he had nothing to offer Morgan in terms of a suspect for her break-in? Was that why he wasn't really investigating Yasmine's death? The two crimes had to be connected. Was he protecting the killer?

I couldn't even guess the number of times I had been told, since my first day as a rookie cop, that I needed to trust my gut. My gut was whispering 'cover-up.' I hit reply on the email from the ME. Maybe the sheriff had ordered the tox panel, and Dr. Brody simply hadn't mention it because there were no results yet. Or maybe the sheriff simply forgot. He did have a lot going on. There didn't seem to be any harm in sending a follow-up reminder. With a note that he should also check for ricin.

Chapter 24

TRIPP'S CHICKEN WAS QUITE POSSIBLY the best I ever tasted. Perfectly seasoned, juicy, and crispy. He also added the two or three vegetables in my mini-fridge and a few spices from Gran's kitchen to rice and made a savory pilaf.

"Why have I been cooking when you can come up with a meal like this?" I asked, enjoying every mouthful.

"You offered," he said. "I enjoy eating other people's food."

"Where did you learn to cook like this?"

"One of the many jobs I had since leaving California was as a cook at a diner. All they served was simple, home-style food."

"You learned well. This is really good. I vote that you take over making dinner every night." I looked up from my plate to find him smirking at me. "What?"

"It's cute how you assume we'll be eating together every night."

My face heated with embarrassment. "I didn't . . . I meant—"

"I'm teasing you, Jayne. I like spending time with you. And having dinner together is certainly nicer than eating by myself."

I stared out at the lake, into the fire pit, anywhere but at Tripp. I hadn't felt so awkward since the night I met Jonah. I had spun away from the bar at a nightclub, full drink in hand, and directly into him. He had insisted the beer wouldn't ruin his sweater and said if I danced with him all would be forgiven.

"Better now?" Tripp teased when I finally looked at him again.

I nodded.

He told me about the progress on the house — "Tomorrow I'll start on the kitchen and great room clean up." — and asked about my wall.

"When I went in to get the chicken, I couldn't help but notice the papers taped all over it. What's that about?"

"Suspect wall," I said and took a swig of milk. Couldn't remember the last time I had milk without cookies to dunk in it. It paired well with chicken and pilaf. "I had to organize my thoughts. That's how we do it . . . did it at the police station."

"Morgan and Keko are on it."

"I just talked to Morgan." I laid my hand on top of the spell bag in my pocket. "I'm crossing her off the list. I need to ask Keko a few more questions. I'll stop on my way to the village in the morning."

Tripp shook his head. "I'm not even going to say it this time."

"Morgan told me that Keko has a definite interest in casting negative magic."

"Are you accepting witchcraft now?"

"There's nothing magical about a bean being poisonous. If Keko knows about the ricin in castor beans, and since she wants to be a green witch or whatever it's likely she does, she's a prime suspect. She had more access to Yasmine than anyone."

Tripp stared at me, silently admonishing my inability to

stop investigating.

"Look," I began then blew out a calming breath. "Sheriff Brighton is all but ignoring Yasmine's death. I can't let a possible murder fade into the background because it wasn't assigned to me. I'm doing my snooping off the clock."

"Okay." Tripp raised his hands in surrender. "I appreciate your intensity. Really. I'm just worried about your safety. If you're right and there is some kind of cover-up going on, you don't want to get caught in the middle of it."

~~~

The sheriff decided he wanted me to patrol during the afternoon. Not much happened in the morning, usually just older people and families wandering the village. If trouble was going to happen, it would be later in the day. Deputy Reed pouted so much about me coming on board that Sheriff Brighton put him on call during the nighttime hours. That worked for me. Reed could deal with the drunks.

Still, I popped out of bed at seven the next morning, my mind spinning. There was no breathtaking sunrise like there had been the other days. Today was gloomy, not raining but gray and overcast. Still, starting my day here, sitting on the deck with a big mug of coffee and a scone from the assortment I'd picked up at Treat Me Sweetly, was something I'd already become used to. I thought of walking up to the campground to talk to Keko, but this early in the morning would be rude.

After I finished my coffee and got dressed, I returned to my suspect wall. I'd already filled the twelve sheets of paper I'd taped there with thoughts and research details, so I grabbed a few more pieces from the pack. The envelope with the coffee ring stains, the one that fell out of the cabinet in Gran's office, had somehow gotten stuck in the ream of paper.

"I put you back in the cupboard," I scolded the envelope. It must have fallen out again and gotten mixed up with the other things I'd taken.

I inspected the envelope more closely this time, and noticed my name printed very faintly beneath the coffee rings on the front. It looked like Gran had written it in pencil and then erased it. The envelope was sealed tight and when I held it up to the light, I could see something inside. Tearing off one edge, I found a sheet of printer paper inside. A single word was written at the top in Gran's distinctive, curly but shaky cursive: Flavia.

Maybe she planned to write Flavia a letter and had only gotten as far as the greeting? No way to know the answer to that. As far as I could tell, Gran had been sharp right up to the end. Although, every now and then she came up with some head-shakers. Like the lake having moods.

"Jayne!"

From out on the sundeck, I saw Tripp standing by the garage.

"I need to show you something," he called, waving me over.

I slipped on my flip flops and as I crossed the lawn, I made a mental note to go talk with Flavia. Off the clock. Not only was I curious about her relationship with Gran, no one in the village should be able to tell me more about Yasmine than Flavia. Maybe she knew of someone who had a beef with her niece.

"What's going on?" I asked Tripp.

"I thought you might find this interesting."

He led me through the garage to a stairway at the far side. I'd never been into the loft. Gramps' workshop was up there, and our mother told Rosalyn and I to stay out because of the dangerous tools. But as Tripp and I climbed those stairs, that sense of déjà vu struck again with full force.

"I told you there were lots of things in the house that didn't get broken or damaged," Tripp said, interrupting the vision trying to form in my mind. "I figured I'd put it all somewhere while I'm working to keep it safe from construction debris. I started in the attic in the house, but it's full of furniture."

"Not surprising. My grandparents were world travelers. Gran had a weakness for antiques."

"It's great old stuff."

I knew what he was thinking, that it would work well in a bed-and-breakfast. Couldn't argue with that.

"Anyway," he continued, "basements tend to be damp, so I checked here over the garage. I thought you'd want to see this."

He stepped further into the loft and held out a hand for me to come in. This was not a workshop. At the far end, by a large picture window that overlooked the lake, there was a table. A Triple Moon Goddess symbol was burned into the front edge of the six-inch thick table top. It reminded me a lot of the one in Morgan's hidden room. As we stepped closer, the items on top of the four-foot high table became clear. A blue cloth with a silver pentagram embroidered in the center covered the top. One purple and one silver taper candle stood in simple silver holders at the back, a white pillar candle and a silver goblet between them. Scattered around the pentacle were a small black cauldron like the one I found in Gran's office, a stick that resembled a magic wand, a dagger, and an incense burner. This wasn't a table. It was an altar.

At that moment, the déjà vu memory that had been playing at the edge of my mind for two days struck me like a gust of wind off the lake.

Rosalyn and I are climbing the stairs to Gramps' workshop. There has to be something really good up there. Why else would Mom tell us so many times to stay out? About half way up I see shadows flickering on the walls. It must be moonlight bouncing off the lake. The moon is full and super-bright tonight.

At the top of the stairs, I see Gran standing by a big window. Must be the one I see when I'm in the backyard. The flickering shadows are coming from three burning candles. Gran has on a cloak. It's the same color blue as the lake on a sunny day. One of those sun, moon, and stars symbols, like on that big welcome sign by the road, is on the back by her neck right below the hood. The cloak is so pretty. I want one.

Gran turns and sees us standing there. I'm sure she's going to be angry, but instead she smiles and tells us to come closer.

"What are you doing?" Rosalyn asks.

"I'm honoring Hecate," Gran answers.

"Who's Hecate?" I ask.

"She's a moon goddess." Gran sounds excited, like my friends when they talk about a cute movie star boy. I wonder if a goddess is the same thing as a princess.

Gran shows us a big circle drawn on the floor and places us on a spot just inside the circle. She tells us to stand right there and to be very quiet. She pours something from a bottle into a small bowl and holds it up into the light from the full moon. She says, "Bless this oil," but I don't know who she's talking to. The moon? The princess in the moon? Gran says more words that I can't hear and then comes over to Rosalyn and me. I want to reach out and touch her cloak, but she dips her thumb into the little bowl and places a tiny bit of the oil on our foreheads.

"Hecate, I ask that you bless my granddaughters."

We stand and watch while Gran goes back to the table and says more words we can't hear. I feel special to be blessed by a moon princess. When Gran is all done, she makes us promise to keep what we'd seen a secret.

"What you saw tonight is very special. For your eyes only."

"I promise," we say at the same time.

But the next morning, Rosalyn tells Mom everything. Mom gets really mad and stomps upstairs. She packs all of our things, and we barely have time to finish our breakfast before we leave Gran's and Gramps' house.

"It looks to me like this has been here for a while." Tripp's words yanked me from the memory.

That was the day the feud between my parents and grandparents started. Because Rosalyn and I saw Gran performing a ritual? My dad seemed to have shrugged it off. As far as I knew, he didn't follow Wicca, but that would explain why he accepted the religion so easily. Mom, though, so concerned about appearances and fitting in with 'normal' society, would never accept such a thing. No wonder she hated Whispering Pines so much. No wonder she had such issues with Gran. She must have thought Gran was trying to convert us. Or sacrifice us. Or who knew what.

I looked at Tripp and blinked. "Sorry, what did you say?"

"Were either of your grandparents Wiccan?"

"My grandmother was." I told him everything I had just remembered. "I don't know if she was before she invited Morgan's family and others to live here. Morgan told me that Wiccans tend to keep their beliefs to themselves to avoid ridicule." I thought again of our family feud, the one that would never be resolved now that Gran was gone. "I think that's what caused the problems for my family."

"You know nothing breaks up a party faster than politics and religion."

"Indeed. Thanks for showing me this. Maybe Morgan can tell me more."

"Do you care if I bring stuff up here?" Tripp shoved his hands in his pockets. "I mean, this isn't like a shrine or a temple or someplace we're not supposed to enter, is it?"

"I don't think so," I said with a shrug. Was there a protocol for someplace like this? "Go ahead and haul stuff up. Just, you know, be respectful."

Right now, I needed to get over to the campground before my shift started and talk to Keko about her own intentions with witchcraft.

Chapter 25

I FOUND KEKO SITTING ON a log outside her tent, staring at the dying embers of a campfire.

"Keko?"

"You're back," she said like she was glad to see me.

It took about two seconds to realize she'd be happy to see anyone right then, even her own reflection. Her eyes were bloodshot and she was fidgety. She patted the log, inviting me to sit next to her. I did and could tell by the smell that whatever she'd swallowed, shot into her arm, or smoked had been chased by a lot of booze.

"I've got a few more questions about Yasmine," I said.

She dropped her head to her knees. "God, I miss her."

Really? Or was that just drunk talk?

"You told me before that you wanted to learn from Morgan Barlow."

Keko sat upright . . . kind of. "Totally. She knows everything there is to know about plants and spells and stuff."

"She told me you wanted to learn to cast a couple of specific spells. A love potion and a spell to repel."

Keko snorted and mimicked, "Spell to repel. That's funny."

"Is it true?"

"That I want to make spells and stuff? Yeah."

"You also said something about black magic."

She looked around, as though making sure no one could hear us, and then giddily nodded her head.

"You know that Morgan has a stash of dangerous plants?" I asked.

"Yep. Poisonous. Bad stuff. But how cool would it be to make a spell to repel?" She laughed again. Apparently, rhymes were hilarious in her current state.

"Did you also know that someone broke in to her shop and stole some of those plants?"

"No." Her eyes opened wide and she became very serious. "What did they take?"

"Keko, I think Yasmine was poisoned."

She nodded dramatically. "Food poisoning."

"No, I think whoever stole those plants used them on Yasmine."

She started to cry then. Agonized sobs that I'd only heard from people who had lost someone they were very close to. Not just a friend, but a loved one. Considering Keko's current state, leading questions weren't going to work. Blunt was the way to go.

"Keko, did you poison Yasmine?"

She sat straight and stared at me, shocked. "Did I what?"

"You know about Morgan's plants and said you want to become a green witch. You said you wanted to perform black magic."

"You think I killed her?" She hugged her arms tight against her chest and looked offended as well as shocked. "I loved her."

Over the years, I'd heard plenty of drunken or stoned *I love you, man* proclamations from partying college students, patrons stumbling out of the bars at close, and street junkies. This wasn't one of those. Keko sincerely cared about

Yasmine.

"Didn't you tell me you barely knew her?"

"Did I?" She considered this then lifted a shoulder. "I didn't know her well, but I loved what I knew. For sure, I wanted to know her better."

"What about the spells you wanted to cast?"

"I wanted to make a spell to repel the men. It killed me to see her with them. I wanted to be the one with her."

"Wait." I held up a hand for her to be silent while my brain caught up. "When you say you loved her, you mean you were *in love* with her?"

"I wanted Yasmine to be my girlfriend, not my girl friend. The love potion was to attract her to me."

"Why didn't you tell me that before?"

"Because she's a fruitcake," came a voice, probably Duane's, from inside the army green tent. "She doesn't know what she feels about anything. She falls in love with anyone who talks to her for more than five minutes."

"That's not true," Keko said.

"I recommend that you leave soon, Deputy," Duane cautioned. "She'll be casting love spells on you next."

Should I have seen this coming? What had I missed? I mentally scanned through everything Keko had told me. Nothing I could remember led to Keko being in love with Yasmine. I had been positive it was a case of jealousy over Yasmine getting so much attention. The ousted cheerleader wanting revenge on the head cheerleader.

"I loved Yasmine," Keko repeated, more to herself than me. "I can't believe someone would kill that beautiful woman."

"Thanks for talking with me. You too, Duane."

"No problem," he called from the tent. "Can you cuff her and lock her up for being a whack job?"

"Sorry."

"Figured. Thought I'd try. Sucks about Yasmine."

"If either of you think of anything that might help, any

little thing, let me know."

Meeka and I returned to the Cherokee. She gave my hand a quick lick as I put her in her crate in the back.

"Thought I had it, Meeks." I pulled her in and hugged her. "I was so sure Keko was the killer."

Maybe my captain in Madison had been wrong. Maybe I wasn't qualified to be a detective.

~~~

A few more tourists had arrived in Whispering Pines. Beating the traffic, they told me as I patrolled, and trying to get a few hours of peace in the quaint village before the mobs came. They were mostly older couples and a handful of families with preschoolers or kids they'd pulled out of school a day early. Other than introducing myself to them, letting them know the sheriff and his deputies were available should they need us, and chatting with the village shopkeepers, it was a slow, still-overcast day.

I found Lily Grace sitting beneath the same tree as the other day.

"This your designated spot?" I asked.

She looked up from the extra-thick novel she was reading, *A Woman of Substance*. "Yep. It's out of the sun, not that that's a problem today, and I can see the marina from here. Which means I can see my boyfriend, Oren."

"I didn't know Oren was your guy." I could picture them together. Cute couple. I gestured at the paperback in her lap. "Good book?"

"It's really old, found it on my grandma's bookshelf, but yeah, it's good. It's about this servant girl who's determined to make her mark in the world."

Sounded like she was quoting the back cover. "Does she?"

She held up the book to me, her finger marking her place at about the two-thirds spot. "I wanted to finish before the season started, but that's not gonna happen. It's like nine hundred pages long and I'm on five-eighty-six."

I had a sudden yearning to go home and pull out the books I brought.

"I thought you might want to know," I said, "your reading the other day did end up having meaning for me."

For a moment, she looked excited but quickly rearranged her face into something more nonchalant. "Yeah? What?"

"Remember the break-in I told you Morgan Barlow had at her shop a few weeks ago."

"Yeah."

"And that the thief took castor beans?"

"Right."

"Turns out that castor beans closely resemble pinto beans."

Again, for the briefest of moments, Lily Grace looked proud. "But you don't know what that means?"

"Not entirely. What I do know is that castor beans are poisonous."

"And Yasmine Long was poisoned?"

"I can't prove that yet. Not until the autopsy results come in."

Lily Grace inserted a pine needle into the book to mark her page, set the book down, and held her hands up. Sheepishly she asked, "Can I try again?"

"To do a reading?"

She shrugged and dropped her hands to her lap. "It's cool if you don't want to."

"No, it's not that. I'm surprised you want to."

"I'm curious now. Don't know if it's my *gift* turning on, or whatever, or if it's something about you."

I sat next to her while Meeka sniffed around the tree, searching for her own evidence of some kind. With my hands resting on hers, Lily Grace closed her eyes and went into a trance, like she had the other day. Her body shuddered slightly, responding to unseen stimulus, but she didn't pull away. A minute later, she said, "I see an altar."

The one in Gran's attic? It bothered me that I didn't remember that Gran was Wiccan. Even though I didn't understand what she was doing at the time, a woman in a beautiful cloak praying to a moon princess sounded like something a ten-year-old girl would reenact many times. Was I somehow projecting that to Lily Grace?

"I see a lady in the water." Lily Grace made a face and paused, as though waiting for another message. "There's black stuff on her." She inhaled deeply and her eyes snapped open. "What did I say?"

"You don't remember?"

She shook her head, anxious for my response.

"You could be tuning into me." I told her about the altar in Gran's attic and the rest of what she had said. "Maybe a lady is going to get tangled in the weeds and drown in the lake this summer? I hope you're wrong about that one."

"Me, too," Lily Grace agreed.

I thanked her for the reading, then made my way across the village to Shoppe Mystique.

Morgan was outside, tending her gardens and humming to herself. Or, more likely, humming to the plants. She gave me her blessing and immediately asked what was troubling me. Someone else who could tap into my emotions. How come none of my family members could do that?

I told her about the memory of my grandmother at the altar.

Morgan smiled. "Are you doing anything this evening?"

"Tonight? No." As though I was booked every other night but my schedule happened to be free this evening.

"Directly north of here you'll find two bridges. The first crosses the road that cuts through the village, the second crosses the creek. On the other side of the creek to the right is my house. I'll expect you there around eleven."

"Eleven? Kind of late, isn't it?"

Before she could respond I reminded myself, for the hundredth time in five days, that this was Whispering Pines. Nothing, except murder, was strange here.

"I'll explain everything tonight, Jayne. See you at eleven. Blessed be."

A dismissal if ever I'd heard one. What would she tell me then that she couldn't tell me now?

Chapter 26

AT TEN FORTY-FIVE, I PARKED the Cherokee in the lot by the creek. Once I'd turned the headlights off, I couldn't see a thing. My immediate reaction was to open the flashlight app on my phone. No one else around here needed a flashlight, I could handle the dark. Truthfully, I would have felt better with Meeka at my side. It was going to take more than five days in the Northwoods to convert me into a country girl.

The full benefit to limited street lights became obvious once my eyes adjusted. There wasn't even the tiniest sliver of a moon in the sky, which allowed the stars to appear in full force. I never saw that many stars in Madison. If it wasn't for all the crime and traffic accidents that would surely result under a cloak of darkness, I wished all towns could turn out the lights like this.

I followed the path north to the first bridge. The road was only two lanes wide, I could just cross, but as I placed a foot onto the pavement, a car raced around the blind corner. I understood the need for a bridge. There was little traffic now, but during the day, especially during tourist season, crossing could be treacherous.

On the other side, I walked the equivalent of probably

four city blocks—which felt more like a mile in the dark—past a cluster of cottages like those surrounding the pentacle garden. These were homes, though.

There were only a few lights on inside the cottages and no streetlights at all in this area. With my vision compromised, my hearing sharpened. Along with my own footsteps crunching on the gravel, I heard crickets and small critters scampering in the woods. The different perspective was liberating, and proved that I could rely on my other senses if necessary.

The sound of running water told me I was close to the creek. I crossed the second bridge and after another hundred yards, spotted a cottage light in the distance. Morgan was waiting on the front steps, dressed in denim cutoffs and a green tank top. Guess the witchy wardrobe was more of a uniform for Shoppe Mystique than a standard outfit.

"Before you ask," she said, "I promise I will answer all of your questions. About your grandmother, about the village, about the villagers . . . anything. First, however, we must prepare."

"Prepare?"

"Tonight," she spread her arms and looked to the black sky, "is the new moon. A time of new beginnings. A time to decide upon and set your intentions for the coming cycle, and then tell the Goddess of them."

Oh, God. Or perhaps I should say, oh, Goddess. More witchcraft.

"I've prepared a bath for you," Morgan said.

"You . . . a bath?" Now I wished I'd brought Tripp with me. Not for a bath, although that could be interesting, but as a bodyguard.

She took my hand and led me through her house, which was surprisingly bare compared to the abundance of Shoppe Mystique. Dream catchers adorned a few windows, small plant bundles hung on doors, clear glass jars filled with various items sat on the floor in corners. Morgan led me to the end of a hallway and a bathroom lit by a dozen or more candles. The claw foot tub was indeed filled and waiting.

"Scrub your entire body with the loofa in the little silver basket on the edge of the tub. This will free you of negativity. While you do that, think of what you want to attract to your life. Nothing is off limits so don't be afraid to dream big."

"Morgan, I'm cool with meditating on what I want to achieve, but I'm not taking a bath."

"Trust me. Remember, I do no harm."

"Yeah. Not getting naked in your house."

She frowned, disappointed, but had an alternate plan to offer. "Will you allow me to smudge you?"

"Excuse me?"

She led me back through the house to her backyard and produced a bundle of dried plants bound with string, like the one she used yesterday when she made the spell bag for me.

"Sage clears the space around us. It doesn't work as well as the purifying bath, but we'll make do."

She held up the bundle, eyebrows arched in question. When I agreed, she held it to the flame of a candle until it started to smoke. The sage smell was delicious and reminded me of Thanksgiving dinner. Embarrassingly, my stomach rumbled. She waved the smoking bundle first around herself, then me, and finally around a small wooden table and chair. On the table lay a pen that resembled an old-fashioned quill and a sheet of beautiful handmade paper with bits of plants and flowers visible on the rough surface.

Morgan extinguished the smoldering bundle and faced me.

"As I said, dream big. What would you like to attract to your life over the next moon cycle? Write those things on the paper as positive declarations, starting each with a statement like 'I will' or 'I am' or 'I have.'"

Morgan went inside the cottage, leaving me to my task

with only the light from an oil lantern. Out of the corner of my eye, I saw a small shadow scuttle past and prayed it was Pitch, the black rooster.

Writing down goals sounded like a good idea. I closed my eyes and thought about what I wanted in my life. That was easy, I'd thought of little else lately: I wanted to get back to work serving and protecting in whatever way I was best suited. To do that, I needed to forgive myself for my part in Frisky's death. I wanted to get back the confidence I had before Frisky was killed. I wanted to move past my heartache over breaking up with Jonah. I wanted to live my own life without my family scrutinizing my decisions.

I opened my eyes and started writing. As I did, I realized all of these things had to do with me starting over, like the moon starting a fresh cycle. And just that fast, I understood a tiny bit more about Wicca. After I'd written down my goals, using positive declarative statements, I read through the list. Two of the items surprised me, mostly because I didn't remember writing them. *I will fix my grandparents' house and turn it into a bed and breakfast. I will stay in Whispering Pines.* Was that really what I wanted?

Morgan appeared a minute later. She had changed out of her shorts and tank and was now wearing a floor-length, raven-black dress. The corseted bodice revealed a lot of cleavage and the long sleeves fluttered every time she moved her arms. A silver headband encircled her head, a small Triple Moon Goddess charm dangling like a third eye at the center of her forehead. Beneath the black makeup around her eyes and deep blood-red stain coloring her lips, her pale skin glowed like the moon in the sky. A black velvet cloak, like Gran's beautiful blue one, topped everything.

"That's quite a list." Morgan nodded at the paper in front of me.

I blinked, mesmerized by her appearance, then look down at my list. Had I made it too long? She hadn't told me how many items to include. Unsure of what to do next, I held it out to her.

"Keep it. You'll offer it to the Goddess later. Remember, as with any desire, not all will come true. At least not right away. The Goddess doesn't perform magic, but she will help those who help themselves, so focus your energy. Are you ready?"

"For what?" My head felt a little foggy.

"You may borrow this for tonight." She held out another hooded cloak she had draped over her arm. This one was made of deep, midnight-blue velvet. It clasped in front to completely cover my jeans and tunic.

With my scrolled list in hand, I followed her along the same path I'd taken earlier, continuing along the creek instead of turning onto the bridge. After a couple hundred yards, I saw an orange glow through the trees ahead and heard people chanting. A little further and we came upon a group of cloaked figures gathered in a clearing around a large fire.

"This is the Meditation Circle," Morgan explained in a soft voice.

Deputy Reed had mentioned this place to me. That shooting range should be a little north of here.

"Tonight is an extra special night for us," Morgan said, stopping inside the tree line a few yards from the clearing. "It's the new moon before the tourist season begins. We look at this night as the start of our year to come."

"Wiccans run on a fiscal year?" I joked.

"Wiccans run on a thirteen-month Celtic calendar, which begins on Samhain or Halloween," Morgan said. "Whispering Pines runs on a fiscal year. Tonight, we will first pray as a group for prosperity and peace for the village this year. Individually, we have each created our own lists, like yours, and we'll offer them to the Lady and Lord."

I counted the people standing around the fire ring. "Is this the coven?"

"It is."

"There are more than thirteen people."

"All Wiccans are welcome in the coven, we don't exclude anyone," Morgan explained in her comforting way. "They're waiting for me. I'll let them know you're here to observe. As you've already figured out, your grandmother did follow Wicca. Before you start asking questions, I wanted you to first have a better understanding of our religion. Stay right here for now. You're welcome to join us during the individual offerings if you choose. If you would prefer not to, I'll find you after and we'll talk."

While Morgan had been standing in the trees with me, I noticed over her shoulder that Flavia had gathered the group together. Everyone's attention was on her, until Morgan joined them and everyone's attention shifted. Morgan said something I couldn't hear. Must have been about me because they all turned to look my way. It was hard to tell through the heavy shadows and hooded cloaks, but I thought I recognized Donovan, Honey, and Sugar. I wasn't surprised to see scowls from Flavia and Donovan, but Sugar didn't seem happy to see me there either. She continued to stare at me after the others had returned to ritual business. When she finally turned back to the circle, I spotted one more person I knew in a hunter-green robe. Sheriff Brighton was Wiccan?

At the start of the ritual, Morgan spoke to the group. Again, I couldn't hear her words, but it reminded me of a preacher standing before her congregation. When she finished, they joined hands, raised them to the sky, and chanted as a group. Really, it wasn't any different than parishioners sitting in a church or temple singing and praying to a statue—Jesus, Buddha, Ganesha—except their 'statue' was the moon, or the lack thereof tonight.

By the time they started their individual offerings, I was getting tired and honestly, a little bored. I watched, stifling occasional yawns, as one by one the members offered their list for the new moon cycle. Some read their list aloud, others read to themselves, and then put their paper in the fire or dug a hole among the trees and buried it.

The final member to step forward was Flavia. She had kept her back to me up until then, so I'd only seen her outline in the firelight. Now, I could tell that her robe was blood red with embroidered silver symbols. Each symbol was different, but all were made of varying combinations of curved or straight lines and dots. I'd seen those symbols before. They looked very much like the graffiti painted on the walls in the house.

Like the others had, Flavia chanted or prayed, or whatever the proper term was, while holding her list before her. When done chanting, she placed her list in the fire. The paper must have been very thin because it floated in the air on a heat wave, hovered, and then burst into flames. As the burning bits raised into the air, Flavia looked at me with narrowed eyes, and suddenly the pieces flew straight at me.

I ducked and covered my head with my arms. When the heat died down, I pulled off Morgan's cloak to be sure none of the burning pieces had stuck. Once I was sure both it and I were okay, I turned to Flavia and locked eyes with her. She looked furious, held my gaze for a few seconds, then raised her narrow chin and turned away.

What the hell was that? If I hadn't known better, I'd swear she just tried to set me on fire. But that wasn't possible. Flavia couldn't control the wind. It had simply been a wave of heat off the fire that sent the paper at me.

I didn't know a thing about this woman. Only that Yasmine was her niece, she seemed perpetually crabby, and she clearly had an issue with me. After the look she just gave me, one of pleasure that I almost caught fire, the feeling was mutual. And, she just soared to the top of my Check Her Out list.

A few minutes later, the group dispersed, and Morgan returned to my side.

"Do you understand better now?" she asked.

"Some things." Tired from the long ritual, I didn't bother to disguise my yawn. Plus, I was a little cranky about having burning paper blown at me. "Those symbols on Flavia's robe, what are they?"

"They're sigils."

"What's a sigil?"

"They're symbols, like you said, but a true sigil is more than that. They have power attached to them and symbolize a phrase of intent. They're made by combining the letters from a declarative statement, like the ones you wrote on your list, into an image. For example, you combine the letters in the statement 'I am queen of the world' into a symbol like you saw on Flavia's robe. That symbol, or sigil, now has meaning for you. You will immediately remember your goal of being queen of the world when you see that image."

"Like a self-fulfilling prophesy. A mindset thing."

"You could look at it that way. Why the interest in sigils?"

I pulled out my phone and showed her the pictures I'd taken.

"These are on the walls in your home?" She seemed concerned. "May I come to see them?"

"Sure. Tomorrow night after work? You can take a look at the altar, too, if you'd like."

She hesitated. "That's the other thing I wanted to talk to you about. Your grandmother wasn't just a practicing Wiccan, she was our high priestess until the day she died."

Gran was the high priestess? That was like being queen of the Whispering Pines Wicca world. She had a whole life going on I knew nothing about.

"You're worried about something." I narrowed my eyes at her. "What's going on?"

"I don't want to draw any conclusions until I see the walls."

"But?"

"But these symbols," she pointed at my phone, "they're troubling. I'm concerned some may have negative intent."

Chapter 27

EVEN THOUGH I WAS DROP-DEAD exhausted by the time I got home, I sat cross-legged at the end of the pier with my list. I turned on the flashlight app on my phone and read what I had written. Morgan instructed me to offer it to the elements by burying it, burning it, letting the wind take it, or tearing it into tiny pieces and dropping them into the lake.

It was a good list, all things I sincerely wanted to happen. It made more sense to put it someplace I could see it and be reminded of what I was working toward. So, I taped it to the wall by my bed where I'd see it first thing and last each day.

I slept like the dead that night and woke the next morning starving. Maybe it was all the nighttime fresh air or all that energy surrounding the new moon ritual, or the fact that I had patrolled the village on foot for four hours. Or maybe I was just hungry. Whatever the reason, a scone wasn't going to do it. Maybe Gran had something more substantial in her pantry or freezer. I pulled a pair of sweats on over my sleep shorts and shuffled across the backyard with Meeka running circles around me. I opened the French doors and was engulfed by the most amazing smell. Normally, unexpected aromas would concern me, but this was bacon.

"Hey," Tripp greeted from behind the kitchen island. He filled a mug with coffee and handed it to me. "Want some breakfast? I had enough money to buy eggs and bacon. Hope it's okay that I dug through the cupboards. I wanted pancakes, too."

It was so nice having a cook on staff.

"That's a big yes to breakfast." I settled onto one of the barstools across from him and added a good shot of milk to the mug. "And if it means I get pancakes, you can dig through the cupboards all you want."

"How did it go last night?"

As he took the bacon off the frying pan and started ladling out the pancake batter, I told him about the ritual. I understood my grandmother's religion a little better now and could honestly say I had no problem with it. I didn't have a problem with anyone's religion, as long as they weren't hurting others in the name of it. For me, the world was too messed up to believe that there was a god or goddess or some dude with four arms and an elephant head out there watching over us. If there was, they needed to quit with this learn-your-lesson-the-hard-way thing and just take charge.

"Morgan is coming over tonight to look at that graffiti." I held out my mug when he offered a refill. "She thinks it might symbolize something negative."

"Don't touch the walls," Tripp said. "Got it."

While he finished the pancakes and moved on to eggs, I wandered into the front of the house to see the progress he'd made. The clean-up was done there—he was right, it looked significantly better already—but before he could start on the repair work, I needed to call for someone to come pick up the furniture that needed fixing, re-finishing, and recovering. I'd have to ask around for a good furniture place.

"Don't worry, Gran and Gramps," I whispered. "We'll

fix everything."

"Breakfast is ready," Tripp called from the kitchen.

"On my way."

Walking down the hallway toward the kitchen, I noticed a graffiti mark on the wall I was sure hadn't been there before.

"Tripp? Has this been here all along?"

He joined me in the hall and locked his hands behind his head as he studied the symbol. "Not sure. There are so many."

I flipped through the pictures on my phone. I'd been very thorough, snapping a shot of every image, individually and entire walls. Tripp stood so close, looking over my shoulder as I scrolled, that I could smell the bacon aroma wafting off him. When I got to the hallway shots he put one hand on my shoulder and pointed at the screen with the other.

"Look, that's this wall," he said. "The symbol must have been behind that picture."

"Do you remember any other marks hidden behind things?"

He pondered that and shook his head. "I don't remember any, but there could have been."

"What's so important about this tag that they hid—" I froze midsentence. I knew this symbol. "Someone drew that exact mark over Yasmine's heart."

"She had a tattoo of that?"

"No, drew it on her. Like with a marker."

Both graffiti tags and sigils stood for something. According to Morgan, a sigil was basically a positive visual affirmation for the creator. A graffiti tag could be pure vandalism, it could mark gang territory, or be a warning of possible violent activity in the area. What did these symbols on my walls mean? Something positive or a warning? Not sure anyone would break into my home to affirmatively vandalize it.

I snapped a picture of this new mark and by the time I got back to the kitchen, I was angry.

"What are you so deep in thought about?" Tripp asked, taking the stool next to me.

"Is moving to the village really such an offense that they'd resort to trying to run me out? I've done nothing wrong, so that's the only reason I can come up with for someone trashing the place."

"First, you're talking to the wrong person about moving to town."

"Sorry."

He shrugged off the apology. "Have you considered that maybe you did do something?"

I looked up from cutting my pancakes with the edge of my fork. "What do you mean?"

"I warned you about getting involved with small town politics. You've wormed your way deep into this Yasmine thing."

I stuffed my mouth with a too-big bite of pancakes so I couldn't respond right away. He was right, of course. He, Morgan, and Sheriff Brighton all told me to mind my own business.

"Yasmine was murdered, poisoned and left to die a painful death. No one was investigating it, not really. I couldn't just let that slide."

"I understand your reasons. Not sure they matter to the locals, though." He placed his sunny side up eggs on top of his pancake stack and let the yolk drizzle over the sides. "Wasn't the damage done before you got here?"

It was. What did that mean? No one knew I was coming, so the damage couldn't have been directed at me. Either it was random or directed at my family in general.

"If your theory is right," Tripp said, "that all of this is connected, who can you tie to these symbols?"

"Easy. Flavia. Everyone at the ritual last night wore robes. Hers had symbols all over it that looked a lot like the ones on the walls."

"Is there a chance that the two *aren't* connected?"

Unless I hadn't noticed and these symbols were a common thing in Whispering Pines, I wouldn't place a bet on it.

After breakfast, Meeka and I headed into the village well before the start of our scheduled shift and went straight to Morgan's shop. I needed to know something, anything about the images on my walls and couldn't wait for her to come over tonight. We entered to find someone new standing behind the counter table. Looked like Morgan had help for the tourist season. Good. Couldn't imagine her handling the crazy-busy shop all on her own.

Five foot nine, very thin, skin so pale it's almost white, coarse red hair to her waist.

"Merry meet," she said in an airy voice. "Welcome to Shoppe Mystique. I'm Willow, is there something I can help you find?"

"Merry . . . hi. I'm actually here to see Morgan." I glanced around and spotted her across the shop, helping customers.

The smile never left the woman's face as she took in my uniform. "I hope there isn't a problem."

"No problem, this is a personal matter."

"I remember you. You were at the Meditation Circle last night."

"Jayne O'Shea. My partner against crime here is Meeka. Thanks for letting me observe."

By the way her eyes narrowed and her smile tightened, she didn't like that I'd been at the gathering. "I hope it helped you with your research."

"No research. Again, it was a personal matter. I'll just wait for Morgan. Thanks."

I busied myself by looking at the amulets. One in particular caught my attention. It was a small glass vial on a silver chain, filled with tiny pieces of crystals and stones, and stoppered with a silver filigree cap at both ends. A small round apple-green stone dangled from the bottom.

"Blessed be."

I looked to find Morgan next to me. "I thought you were helping customers."

"I believe your uniform scared them off."

"Sorry."

"Not at all. If a sheriff's deputy causes customers to run, they were likely up to no good. What's troubling you this morning?"

"What makes you think–?"

"Jayne, tension is surrounding you like a fog."

I brought up the picture of the newly-discovered wall tag. "Do you know what this means?"

Her brow furrowed as she inspected the picture. "I'm familiar with it. This is on your wall?"

"Someone also drew it on Yasmine's chest. What does it mean?"

She crossed her arms. "It's a symbol from the Theban alphabet. Some call it the Witch's Alphabet because witches used to use it to disguise text. Most of us now are proud to announce our beliefs, so few can even identify it let alone write the language."

"It's a letter of the alphabet? Which one?"

"Actually, this is the symbol for a full stop or period."

"As in at the end of a sentence?"

She nodded, pondering.

"But it was by itself on the wall," I said. "What could that mean?"

"I don't know," she admitted. "If I had to guess, it's meant as a warning. Or a negative sigil."

"Period," I mumbled, understanding. "Full stop. Did I mention this image was drawn over Yasmine's heart?"

"Not at all telling." She pulled her lips into a thin line. "I'm becoming concerned."

"You're not the only one."

"I'll make a witch bottle for your house."

"A what?"

"A protection charm. Stop by to pick it up before you go home. I'll give you instructions on what to do."

"I don't need a charm," I objected. Although the only time I hadn't been in contact with the spell bag since she gave it to me was when I showered. I might not be a believer, but I saw no harm in taking help when offered.

"You do need protection. Never mind, I'll bring it over tonight. I want to see the other images on your walls."

No sense arguing with a determined witch.

"The shop is open until seven now that the season has officially started. I'll leave at six. Willow can handle the final hour alone." She took one of my hands in hers. "I can't help but notice you seem drawn to this amulet."

"Drawn? I guess." I'd forgotten I was holding it. I reached to put it back, but Morgan stopped me.

"I'm not surprised this one calls to you. It contains chips of amethyst, black tourmaline, quartz, and amber. This one hanging at the bottom is peridot. A truly powerful protective blend."

She opened the clasp, attached the chain around my neck, and dropped the vial beneath my shirt. With her hand pressed over the amulet, she closed her eyes and moved her mouth in a silent chant.

"Don't take this off," she ordered. "Not for any reason. I'll see you tonight."

Her concern for my safety was freaking me out a little. Time to do something about this apparent threat to me and/or my family.

"Do you happen to know where Flavia lives?"

Her shoulders sagged. "Don't go looking for trouble, Jayne."

I suspected that Flavia was involved with the vandalism. Morgan's response all but confirmed it. "Me? She tried to start me on fire last night."

It was a joke. I expected Morgan to argue, to say that was ridiculous, but she didn't. She also refused to tell me where Flavia lived, but Morgan wasn't the only one in town with knowledge of the locals.

"Sure, I know," Violet told me a few minutes later as she prepared my mocha. "The acreage between the road and the creek is where most of the Wiccans live. Follow the path all the way to the last left before the creek. Flavia's cottage is the third one in on the creek side. You can't miss it. It's three stories tall and creepy as hell." She slapped her hand over her mouth, looked around at the customers, and then lowered her voice to add, "Sorry, but it is."

I tipped her generously for the free coffee and information. After Meeka finished her biscuit, we went to find Flavia. It was time for a chat.

Chapter 28

WHEN I'D FOLLOWED THIS PATH last night, all I could see were the lights from inside a handful of homes. In the daylight, this section of Whispering Pines looked like any neighborhood in any town. Cottages were scattered about in no set pattern, seemingly wherever the builder thought best. Narrow brick-paved streets allowed only one-way traffic. The yards were dotted with children's toys and lawn ornaments—gnomes and fairies and lots of glass orbs. Perfectly normal. And then I came to Flavia's cottage.

'Creepy' didn't begin to describe it. Like the other structures original to the village, it was stained black-brown. It was indeed three stories tall, as Violet reported, and the perimeter led me to guess there were probably no more than two rooms per floor. Tall, thin, dark, imposing. Just like Flavia except she was tall, thin, pale, and imposing.

"Miss O'Shea?" Flavia appeared at the front door. "Is there something I can help you with?"

Neither the snip in her tone nor the sour look on her face said she was interested in helping me. I came here to figure out if she had anything to do with Yasmine's death or the vandalism at my house, but asking her flat out wouldn't work. I'd need to employ a subtle method for interrogating this woman.

"We haven't officially met." I went into confident cop mode and extended a hand to her. "Jayne O'Shea. You probably know that Sheriff Brighton hired me to help during the tourist season."

She took my hand, with only her fingertips, and gave it two tiny shakes.

"You're Yasmine Long's aunt, correct?" My heart was pounding suddenly. Why did this woman make me nervous?

Flavia's gaze skittered across the other homes—checking for nosey neighbors?—then she opened the door wider and stepped aside. "You clearly have questions. Come inside and we'll talk."

Flavia sucked in a breath, like a hiss, when Meeka followed me.

"She won't harm anything." I needed my K-9 by my side. Not only was she trained to sniff out drugs and cadavers, she had a sense about people and places that I'd come to trust without reservation. Besides, should the need arise, Meeka could protect me far better than Morgan's vial of stones. "She's not only a trained police dog, she's my partner."

"Of course." Flavia scowled but couldn't object.

Inside, the cottage was as stark and cold as its owner with unadorned, all white walls. Every piece of furniture was made from wood, had straight severe lines, and stained medium brown. She led me to a small rectangular dining table, the chairs' seats made from woven rush. The chairs, I had to admit, were surprisingly comfortable.

"May I offer you some tea?" she asked in a monotone, obviously more out of duty than hospitality.

Meeka sneezed. Even though there wasn't a speck of dust in the place, and despite my mouth being dry, I took the sneeze as a warning.

"No, but thank you," I replied.

Flavia poured a cup for herself from a utilitarian white tea pot, almost as if to prove that whatever I'd been worried about was misguided. Still, I stuck with my decision.

"You're wondering about the disagreement Yasmine and I had," Flavia offered.

"Yasmine had become friends with a group of people at the campground near my house. They say she wouldn't give much detail about the fight."

"That's because the girl was embarrassed." Flavia hissed again. "She arrived in the village with no warning and expected I would take her in." She narrowed her eyes at me. "Why are you so interested in my niece, Miss O'Shea?"

I was in uniform. The lack of use of my professional title was her attempt to control the conversation.

"You know that I'm working with Sheriff Brighton."

"As a temporary beat cop," Flavia said. "You were hired to patrol the village. Why are you here asking about Yasmine?"

Despite my pounding pulse, I looked her in the eye and didn't blink. "Because Sheriff Brighton doesn't seem very concerned about Yasmine's death, Flavia. Neither do you."

She pursed her lips and sniffed. "Her mother is my sister. I am appropriately concerned about the death of a family member I barely knew."

"Your sister doesn't live in the village. Did she ever?"

"She did as a child," Flavia said. "She lives in the Milwaukee area now."

By the way she clipped the end of her words as she spoke, it was clear Flavia had an issue with her sister. What was Flavia's story? Was she left alone to care for dying parents? Was she left to be abused by her parents? Was she simply jealous that her sister got to leave Whispering Pines?

"You're angry with her," I said. "Is this why you wouldn't welcome Yasmine?"

"The girl is impure."

"One of the girls at the campground used that word. I

don't understand what it means."

"You saw her." Flavia's face wrinkled, as though looking at something offensive. "I know you did because you found the body on your property. Everything about the girl was fake. From her processed hair to her chemically whitened teeth to her sprayed-on tan to those breasts." More hissing. "I'm sure you heard of how she paraded through the village, half naked, putting herself on display to everyone. Every bit of her, including her black soul, was unnatural."

Flavia and her niece had height and eye color in common. As I listened to her tear her niece apart, I noticed that Flavia also had faint freckles sprinkled across the bridge of her nose and her cheeks. That detail got to me. Millions of other people were five foot six with blue eyes, but the simple addition of freckles tied these two women together. Not enough, unfortunately, for the aunt to welcome the niece. Had any other familial traits passed through the bloodline?

"Why did she come here?" I asked. "Was she having problems of some kind?"

"Yes, she was having problems." Flavia held one bony-fingered hand in front of her breasts like a claw while the other gripped the tea cup. "She turned herself into a freak and then wondered why men made inappropriate advances on her."

"I have to respectfully disagree with you." My job was to help people, to save them sometimes. To me, saving a person from their own ignorance qualified. "A woman's appearance is never an excuse for giving unwanted attention. If she chose to walk around fully naked, that still wouldn't excuse a violation. Granted, she'd get arrested for indecent exposure—"

"Everything about her was indecent." Flavia slammed a hand down on the table, rattling the teacups. "I am not responsible for that girl. I wouldn't have anything so tarnished under my roof."

"Flavia, did you kill your niece?"

She inhaled sharply through her nose. "I did not."

Meeka pressed against my legs beneath the table. A warning or a plea to go? Either way, she was right. There wasn't anything more to learn here. Nothing about Yasmine's death, at least. Puritanical Flavia simply wouldn't allow her harlot of a niece to live in her home. A good deal of that choice was fueled by Yasmine's appearance, but I was reasonably certain the rest had something to do with her sister leaving the village.

"I have one other, unrelated question for you." I pulled out my phone and opened the pictures of the graffitied walls. I turned the phone so she could see and slowly flipped through the images. "You know that this is my grandparents' home?"

"I've been in there many times." If she had an emotional response to what she saw, she didn't show it.

When I got to the final image, the one of the full stop mark, I held it in front of her for a long while.

"Do you know what this symbol means?" I asked.

"I do."

She said no more, probably thinking she was being clever by not offering up the information. That, however, told me more than if she'd simply explained the mark.

"Thank you for talking with me, ma'am." I put my phone away and pushed back from the table that had been scrubbed as clean as Flavia's face. "Oh, I wanted to thank you for allowing me to observe the ritual last night."

"It's not done," Flavia muttered. "Morgan had no right."

I waited for her to say more, but again her lips sealed up tight.

"I couldn't help but admire your robe," I continued. "Not only is it a beautiful color, the embroidery is unusual."

This time, the Ice Goddess softened a little. She lifted her chin and looked down her sloped nose at me. "I assume

Morgan has been teaching you about Wicca."

I nodded, staying silent myself in the hopes that she'd keep talking.

"The majority of the images are sigils that I have created. You know about sigils?"

I nodded again.

"The others come from the Theban alphabet." She made a *tsk* sound and shook her head. "Shame that so few witches honor the old script anymore. Only a handful of us in the Whispering Pines coven even know what it is."

My blood froze in my veins. *So few . . . Only a handful . . .* Yet, Flavia could instantly identify the markings painted all over my house. Meeka must have sensed my discomfort because she squirmed and butted her head against my calf. Was Flavia my vandal? I couldn't tell from her tent-like dress, but she didn't appear to have the muscle to trash my house. It didn't take muscle to tag walls, though. Maybe she hired some thugs and gave them instructions. Plenty of gang members didn't fully understand the meaning behind the graffiti they drew.

Flavia released the death grip she'd had on her plain white tea cup and accompanied Meeka and me to the front door. Hanging on the wall, hidden earlier by the open windowless door, were the only items I could see that resembled decoration. Two framed photographs. One of Deputy Reed and the other of Deputy Reed with Sheriff Brighton. I paused, my hand on the knob, and examined them. In both, Reed was in uniform, beaming with pride. My guess, it was the day he was deputized.

"May I ask, why do you have pictures of Deputy Reed?"

"Martin is my son," Flavia stated.

Shock stole my ability to speak for a second. "I didn't realize you were married."

Flavia looked down at her hands clasped in front of her. "My husband died many years ago."

She supplied no more information.

"Sorry to hear that. Again, thank you for speaking with me."

As I walked away, I could feel Flavia's glare boring into me. She explained that Yasmine's indecency and black soul were the reasons she had to live at a campground. I was positive there was more to the story. More about the sister.

The further from the cottage we got, the less intense the laser beam between my shoulder blades felt. I looked down at my furry companion.

"Yasmine Long and Martin Reed were cousins. I wonder what other secrets are waiting to be revealed." I guess that wasn't really a secret. I simply hadn't known. "Let's go pay a visit to The Inn. I'd like to verify that Reed and Yasmine ate there together that night."

Chapter 29

MEEKA PROTESTED GOING INSIDE THE Inn. I couldn't blame her, it was packed. So was Grapes, Grains, and Grub, the pub a few cottages away. A hoard of tourists had arrived while I was questioning Flavia. And it seemed they all decided to have lunch at the same time. If Meeka was a bigger dog, crowds wouldn't bother her. Having had her paws and tail stepped on one too many times, however, and she had issues being around that many people. I commanded her to sit and stay in a corner of the front porch. She slid into a cluster of potted plants and looked content to stay right there.

There were only three servers on duty at The Inn's restaurant, and they were running their feet off taking and delivering orders. Those not in the building to eat were trying to check into their rooms. The only way I'd be able to ask a question, other than putting my name on the wait list and getting a table, was to interrupt one of the servers in the middle of helping diners.

Sylvie, the Wiccan-beer girl who waited on Tripp and me the previous night, was on duty. I tried to flag her down, and she held up a finger indicating she'd be with me shortly. After she passed me for the fourth time without stopping, I followed her to the drink station.

"I was in a few nights ago," I said.

"I remember you." She nodded at my uniform. "Looks like you'll be around for a while. What do you need?"

"I just have a couple of questions and then I'll leave you alone."

"Talk quick and I'll pour slow," she said, seeming grateful for the opportunity to stand still for a minute.

"You know both Martin Reed and Yasmine Long?"

"Of course, I know Martin. Yasmine was the bikini girl who died, right?"

"Right. Do you remember seeing them in here together for dinner maybe a week ago?"

"Absolutely," she said as she lined up pre-filled glasses of water like soldiers ready for battle. "I remember thinking that Martin scored big with that girl. She was nice enough, obviously gorgeous, but there was zero chemistry there."

"Any idea what was going on?"

"No clue. They acted super uncomfortable with each other, like neither of them wanted to be here. Sat in that back corner, same table you sat at. They were here for an hour, talking real quiet. Never stopped unless I got within ten feet of them."

"Last question, I promise. Do you have any idea what they were talking about?"

"Sylvie," another Wiccan-beer girl snapped and glared at me, "table six is ready to order."

"No clue," Sylvie answered while transferring filled water glasses to a round, rubber-lined serving tray. "Gotta get back to work."

"Thanks, Sylvie," I called as she headed into the cluster of tables.

On the porch, Meeka had attracted attention of her own. A man had crouched next to her to investigate the tag on her collar.

"Can I help you?" I asked. "Is my dog having a

problem?"

His bloodshot eyes went wide when he saw the uniform, but quickly claimed concern over Meeka's wellbeing. "You always leave her tied up outside in the heat?"

"First, she's not tied up. Second, she's in the shade, well protected from the elements. Third, it's not hot today."

"What if she suddenly bolted? She could get hit by a car."

Possible, but highly unlikely. I glanced at Meeka. Her ears were down and her tail was still. She didn't like this guy.

"Since you seem so interested in her, let me tell you a little about her background. She's very well trained and has never once run away from me. Also, she's a K-9, trained to detect weed and other illegal substances."

The man immediately stood, shoved his hands in his pockets, and backed away. "Okay. Well, good. Just making sure she's safe."

Right. The way his girlfriend was looking at my cute little Westie, he was about to dognap my Meeka.

"Enjoy your stay in Whispering Pines, sir. The sheriff and I are around should you need us." As the two of them hurried away, I bent to attach Meeka's leash. "Sorry, girl. I'm bringing you inside places with me from now on, even if I have to carry you."

We walked around the commons, greeting and welcoming the growing crowd of people. Meeka let most of the children pet her. She had a good sense of those who would pull her tail or ears, or otherwise be nasty to her. She stood close to my legs when kids like that reached for her, and I'd step in with, "Sorry, she's on duty right now."

"But that other girl just petted her," one particularly snarly boy complained.

"She did. But Meeka must sense trouble now." I gave him a purposeful stare. "See how she's standing so close to me?"

He glared at me. When I didn't give him his way, he turned and punched his little sister in the arm. Meeka and her senses, spot on again.

The main village, filled with tourists, was buzzing with activity. In the pentacle garden, the tuxedo man stood at the center and explained to the tourists what a negativity well was. He also explained that he wore the tux, "In case the Whispering Pines Circus ever need a fill-in ringmaster. That's my dream." The tinfoil hat lady helped direct folks to where they wanted to be. A man teased her that the hat must be to keep aliens away.

"That's exactly what it's for," she responded.

"Does it work?" the man asked, rolling his eyes at his friends.

"Do you see any?"

The line at Treat Me Sweetly was out the door. I thought of the look Sugar gave me at the ritual last night and wanted to stop in to find out if there was a problem or if it had been my imagination. Also, I wanted ice cream.

While Honey prepared my single serving of Coconut Almond Chocolate Chunk, I stepped across the aisle to Sugar.

"I know you're crazy-busy," I said, "I just need to be sure you're not upset with me."

"Upset with you?" Sugar asked while she filled a box with cookies and pastries for a customer. "Why would I be upset with you?"

I leaned in and quietly said, "Because of last night."

Her usually bright and cheery smile faltered. She finished tying the box, handed it to the waiting customer, and signaled for the next person in line to wait for a moment. She pulled me behind the counter and put her hands on my shoulders.

"My reaction wasn't directed at you personally, Jayne. We never allow non-Wiccans at our gatherings."

Instantly, I felt bad for telling Tripp about what I'd seen. I hadn't realized the gathering was private. "Morgan wanted—"

"She explained why she brought you." Sugar held my gaze and then let out a resigned sigh. "Honey and I and many of the locals see how involved you've become with the death of that girl. We love that you care so much, and your grandmother would be very proud of you. It's just . . . be wary of digging too deeply into the goings on around here."

Not a threat, but another warning. How far was too far to dig? And if I kept going, what would I uncover?

"Here you are." Honey handed me a single serving cup so loaded with Coconut Almond Chocolate Chunk, I was sure I'd lose some of the teetering tower.

"You're too good to me," I said. "Seriously, I'll never lose weight."

Honey patted her own belly and swatted an oh-go-on hand at me.

I nodded my thanks to Sugar then found a shady spot beneath a tree to eat my ice cream and give Meeka some water. We'd just settled in when Sheriff Brighton and Deputy Reed appeared between Treat Me Sweetly and Shoppe Mystique. They were deep in conversation, the sheriff gesturing wildly, clearly angry. Reed tried to interject a few times but was shut down. He cast his eyes at the ground and said nothing as the sheriff ranted. What had Reed done to upset the sheriff? Or was Sheriff Brighton taking out frustration on his nephew? A murder and two break-ins in a tourist town days before the season began couldn't be good for business. Frustration was understandable. The sheriff taking that frustration out on his deputy, especially in public, was not. A minute later, they went their separate ways, leaving me wondering once again what was going on.

Finished with my ice cream, I returned to patrolling and immediately spotted Keko Shen going into Shoppe

Mystique. Meeka and I waited outside for her, chatting with tourists and giving directions. A woman, over six feet tall with red hair that hung to her knees, and a little boy, about five years old and missing his right arm, came out of Treat Me Sweetly. They were quite a pair, sharing licks of their ice cream cones with each other. The boy ended up with nearly as much around his mouth as in it.

Keko emerged from Shoppe Mystique, and I waved her over.

"You're still in town," I said. "I thought you'd be gone by now."

"Changed my mind. I was asking Morgan if she needed help for the summer. It's crazy busy in there. She said I should come by half an hour before opening tomorrow and we'll talk." Keko held up a hand before I could respond. "I know what you're thinking. I'm kind of a screw up, I know that. But part of the reason I came to Whispering Pines was to get myself straight. All I do is smoke a little weed now and then."

I raised an eyebrow.

"Fine. Sometimes harder stuff, too." She put a hand in the air. "I swear I don't drink much. Don't really like the taste. Anyway, I already know a lot about her shop and what she sells. I kinda like it here, too. If Morgan will take a chance on me . . ."

She seemed sober right now, and I believed that she wanted to get on track. If I knew Morgan half as well as I thought I did, there was a potion or a spell bag in Keko's future to help her get there. Maybe a job, but that would surprise me.

"Good luck," I said sincerely. "I have a quick question for you. Did you know that Yasmine and Martin Reed were cousins?"

Her eyes went wide and then she laughed. "They weren't cousins."

"Sure they were. Yasmine's aunt told me earlier today

that they were."

"Then she's lying."

"Why do you think so?"

"Yasmine told me Martin Reed was her brother." Keko paused, analyzing her own statement, then shook her head. "Whoa. That would mean her aunt is really her mother."

Chapter 30

KEKO'S BOMBSHELL MADE MY HEAD spin. She was right, I absolutely believed her. Yasmine and Flavia were mother and daughter. It was the freckles. Those damn freckles. Then why did everyone think they were aunt and niece? I also believed that Flavia told me the truth about why she wouldn't let Yasmine stay at the house. Her disgust for Yasmine's 'impurity' was genuine. But what did impure mean? And was she disgusted enough to kill her own daughter?

"O'Shea."

I spun, startled, to find Sheriff Brighton standing by the backdoor of the sheriff's station. He did not look happy.

"Yes, sir?"

"My office. Now."

It was a cool day and the Cherokee was parked in the shade, but I still took a minute to lower all the windows for Meeka.

"Stay," I commanded. "I'll be right back."

She lay down in her crate and rolled to her side. Meeting so many people had tired her out. She'd be asleep within a minute.

Inside, Reed was at his desk as usual, but he didn't say a

word to me. Instead, he looked up and smirked, like he knew something I didn't.

"I'm glad to catch you," I said, entering Sheriff Brighton's office. "I've been wanting to ask if you had any leads on the break-in at my house yet."

He looked at me like I was dense, which told me he hadn't done a thing. He paced his office and demanded, "What have I told you again and again?"

"Sir?"

"I hired you to patrol the village. Not stick your nose into the Yasmine Long investigation. In fact, I specifically ordered you to stay out of it."

Dressed down, I stared at my feet.

"But what do I hear? You've been asking questions about her all around the damn village. Today you showed up at Flavia Reed's house to harass her about the case."

"I didn't harass her. She invited me in and freely answered my questions."

"You admit that you were there, interrogating her about a case you have no business even thinking about. Why, O'Shea? Why did you go there?"

"I was exploring the village. You told me to wander around and get to know—"

He held up a hand. "Stop. Why can't you leave this alone?"

Leave it alone? Why did he so desperately want me to? My instincts were screaming coverup.

"Because a girl was murdered, Sheriff Brighton."

He stared at me, his chest heaving. In a tight, clipped voice he asked, "Did you also log into Martin's email and order a toxicology report?"

"I was reviewing the autopsy—"

"Which is also none of your business!" He threw his hands in the air. "Damn it!"

"I didn't see anywhere that the test had been ordered. I didn't know if you asked and he forgot, or if it never got ordered at all. I was just sending a reminder."

"Which is not your job." His face pinched with pain as his hand went to his hip. He dropped into his desk chair. "If you had a concern of any kind regarding this investigation, you should have come to me."

"I'm sorry, Sheriff. It's just with so much going on around here, I thought you may have forgotten to order it. I figured I'd help you out." I was treading so close to insubordination I could taste it. Why couldn't I stop myself? I couldn't even stop defending my reasons for disobeying direct orders. "I was just following up and helping out. Since I work for the department—"

"Not anymore."

"Sir?"

"You seem to feel that rules don't apply to you, O'Shea." His voice was eerily calm now. "I should have suspected this wouldn't work. When you told me the details that led up to your coworker shooting an unarmed civilian, I should have known hiring you was a bad idea. You felt you could handle the problem with your partner, didn't you?"

"I—"

"You thought if you just talked to him long enough, if you kept browbeating him with your opinions, you'd be able to convince him to get help. Or did you think you were as qualified as the precinct shrink and would be able to help him yourself?"

"No, sir, not at all."

"Whatever you thought, you broke protocol and a woman died."

I had to literally bite back a laugh. The sheriff of Whispering Pines was lecturing me on protocol? Regarding my past behavior, I couldn't argue with him. In many ways, I had been the most by-the-book cop on our squad. But yes, I had a habit of going rogue. If there was a wrong in need of being righted, I had to dig in. That was my fatal flaw. The reason my entire life was such a mess.

"Hand over your badge and belt, Ms. O'Shea. You can return your uniform shirts to me tomorrow."

He wouldn't look at me. No, more like he *couldn't* look at me.

I placed my belt and badge on his desk. "I just wanted to help."

Now what would I do? I was so close to figuring out what had happened to Yasmine. And now I was more convinced than ever that Sheriff Brighton was covering something up. That he was protecting someone. If I was able to prove it, who should I tell?

Chapter 31

I CRACKED OPEN A THIRD beer and slumped into the lounge chair on the sundeck, feeling buzzed and sorry for myself. Once again, I'd ruined a good thing in my life. I'd been telling Tripp about the drama of my day—what I'd learned about Yasmine and the news that I'd been fired—when a small black Fiat appeared in the driveway, and Morgan got out. Thank god. I couldn't seem to stop myself from yammering. In about two minutes, Tripp would reach full capacity on hearing about me and my woes, and he'd walk out of my life, too.

"Be right there, Morgan," I called and reminded Tripp that she was there to look at the graffiti. "Wanna come?"

"Sure. How often do you get the chance to see a witch at work?"

Meeka had already raced over to greet her, but Morgan was all business.

"This day flew by," she said. "If it was any indicator of what's to come, this is going to be a very prosperous season. Thank the Goddess I've got Willow to help me."

"Keko tells me you might hire her," I said.

Morgan dismissed that thought with a crisp shake of her head and moved on to why she was here. "I've felt very uneasy about these symbols in your house."

"Let's go take a look." I led her to the great room, the room that had received the most ink.

She stood with her hand covering her mouth, shocked by the sight.

"What do they mean?" I asked, my beer-buzz wearing off as quickly as Morgan's astonishment rose.

"At the ritual last night, I gave you a very basic explanation of how sigils are made," Morgan said. "Let me explain more. You write down a statement of intent that has powerful meaning for you."

"You used 'I am queen of the world' at the ritual," I said. "What would you do with that?"

She scribbled on a piece of paper. "First, we would disregard all of the vowels and any repeated letters. This would leave us with M, Q, N, F, T, H, W, R, L, and D. You then arrange those letters into an image. It's okay to twist and turn, stretch and pull, and overlap them as necessary to make them fit together. When you're done, you have an image and only you know the phrase behind it.

"Then you cast the sigil. There are various ways to do this. One would be to take the paper you've drawn the sigil on and light it on fire, holding the paper until it will burn you if you hold it any longer. Then, you do all you can to make the statement come true. In this case, you start taking steps to become queen of the world."

"Do you have any idea what any of these mean?" Tripp asked.

"I don't," Morgan said, "and I can't tell you who created them either. Many in our coven use sigils. Just the process of putting one together is a powerful exercise that helps you focus on your goal."

"I know who created these," I said. "Flavia. She has it in for me. She's got these same symbols on her robe. And she tried to burn me."

"I know your instincts are telling you something about

her," Morgan said. "I advise you to be wary. Don't accuse unless you have proof."

She wandered around the house, looking at the different images, and focused on two in particular. One looked like an upside-down capital letter "Y," except the main trunk extended so it was even with the shorter lines. It resembled an upside-down tree. Or maybe a pitchfork? The other looked like an "S" lying on its side, a dot at the center of each curve.

"These two are bothering you," I said. "Why?"

"This one." She set her hand next to the upside-down Y. "If it were turned the other way, it would mean life or beginning. Upside down, it means the opposite."

"So, death and end?" Tripp said.

"Exactly." Morgan touched the wall near the S-shaped symbol. "This means water."

Tripp glanced at me. "Those two symbols, drawn next to each other like they are here, are in almost every room. In some they're large and painted on the walls. In others, they're small and scratched onto furniture or the floor."

"I'm going to get the protection jars I made for you. They're in my car." Morgan left without another word.

"Is it just me," I asked, "or does she seem freaked out?"

"Protection jars?" Tripp asked.

I shrugged. "She insists they'll protect me from the baddies."

"You don't believe they'll work?"

I kept my eyes on the doors and lowered my voice so Morgan wouldn't hear me. "I believe that she, and the other witches in Whispering Pines, believe in their magic. The right mindset can have a huge impact toward a positive outcome. Morgan's herbs and oils, sure those have medicinal benefits, but that's not witchcraft. It's pharmacy."

"Even though your grandmother seems to have been a follower?"

I considered that before answering. "What I saw at the

ritual last night was a congregation honoring their god, or goddess in this case, just as faithfully as parishioners in any other church. This particular church just happens to be the forest, and their goddess is connected to the moon. Or *is* the moon. I'm not clear on that yet. I have no issues with my grandmother having been Wiccan."

Morgan stormed back into the house carrying two round bright green jars, about the size of tennis balls. Each held sharp objects — rusty razorblades, pins, pieces of barbed wire — and strands of red string. Something that looked like coarse salt was in there, too.

"I made one for the boathouse as well, since that's where you're staying." She handed me a paper cup. "I need your urine."

"I'm sorry?"

"Consecrated wine also works, but it's not as powerful." She looked me in the eye. "I'm quite worried about you, Jayne. You have your ways of protecting, this is what I know to do."

Tripp gave me a little shrug. "Mindset."

Fine. After three beers, I had to go anyway.

By the time I returned with the near-full cup, Morgan had spread an altar cloth on the kitchen bar and lit a black candle. She poured half of the contents of the cup into each jar and then stoppered them with a piece of cork. While chanting quietly, she let the wax from the candle drip over the stopper until it was completely covered. After the second jar was also sealed, she extinguished the candle and waited for the wax to harden. When it had, she stood on a chair from the dining room and placed one jar on the top shelf in the entryway coat closet.

"The bright color will attract any negative energy that enters this home," Morgan explained. "The sharp objects will deflect the energy and send it back to whomever is sending it to you. The salt purifies. The red string provides protection." She looked over her shoulder at me. "The urine identifies this space as yours."

Whether it was Morgan's belief or that her jars of herbs and flowers and amulets really did have power, I felt a little more at ease. Although knowing there was a jar of my own pee in the front closet was a little disturbing.

"I'll place the other jar somewhere in the boathouse," Morgan stated. "I'm going to try and figure out what's going on, Jayne. It will take a while. Weeks, maybe. I have to be careful with my approach. There are some very powerful members of the coven. Angering them could make things much worse for you."

"And you, I assume," I said.

Morgan dismissed the comment with a shake of her head. "This is my calling. I protect others with the intent of doing no harm to anyone involved. My karma is pure."

We were a lot alike, Morgan and me.

"I hear what you're saying," I said, "and appreciate all that you're doing for me. Sheriff Brighton hasn't even tried, so if you can help me figure out who the vandal is —"

"This isn't just a case of vandalism," Morgan interrupted. "I know you don't believe it, but there is something darker going on here."

I hadn't even known Morgan for a week yet, but I could tell she truly was worried about whatever was going on in Whispering Pines. We were a lot alike in that way, too.

"You figure out who this dark witch is," I said, "and I'll make sure the law takes care of them."

Later that night, I tossed and turned and couldn't fall asleep. Meeka whined at all the noise I was making, so I got up and went out on the deck. No sense both of us being awake.

A little sliver of the moon hung among patchy clouds. I gazed at it and all I could think about was Yasmine. She and Reed were siblings. How long had they known that? Flavia didn't want anything to do with her own daughter, that was obvious. Did Yasmine want a relationship with her brother regardless? If so, he didn't seem receptive. Why else would he deny knowing her when I asked?

The most frustrating question of all was why Sheriff Brighton refused to investigate Yasmine's death. The only answer was that he was protecting someone. And if that was true, someone in the village was the killer. He wouldn't be working this hard to protect a tourist. Until Yasmine got here a few weeks ago, it was likely only two people here even knew she existed. Flavia and Martin Reed.

And then there were two. Which of them killed Yasmine?

Chapter 32

HAVING SLEPT VERY LITTLE, I was crabby the next morning. Or maybe it was because I was unemployed again. How . . . *why* did I keep messing up the perfect opportunities in my life? According to my mom, it started when I changed my college major from pre-law to criminal justice. I never, not for one minute, saw myself as a lawyer or politician. That was Mom's dream for me. But a blood splatter analyst? Sure. Until I found out how much science was required. Not my strongest subject. A crime scene investigator? You bet. FBI agent had also been high on my list; that required more rigorous training after college, though. I was already chomping at the bit to start my adult life. Instead, I applied to and was accepted by the Madison PD. Then the role of homicide detective caught my eye.

Now, I had so completely messed up my career in law enforcement, I'd never get a job in the field again. Of course, according to the sheriff, I seemed to feel rules didn't apply to me, so maybe I had no business being a cop anyway.

I lay in bed, staring out the sliding doors at the lake. The patchy clouds from last night had merged into a full gray blanket, and it looked like rain would come soon. Since I had no job to go to, maybe I'd crack open those watercolors today. I also needed to start packing up Gran's possessions. I was already in a bad mood. Why not add depressed to the mix?

Meeka whined and stood with her front paws on the bed next to me. She pushed at my hand with her nose, letting me know she wanted out.

"Okay, girl." I groaned as I rolled out of bed, wishing I could stay there all day. The black deputy shirts caught the corner of my eye as I crossed the apartment to let her out. I set them on the couch last night, folded and ready to go back to the sheriff. He was expecting me to return them today.

First, I stuck a pod in the coffee maker and then went out onto the deck with my full mug. I had no idea what time it was, but the day was cool and damp, it probably wouldn't warm up much. In fact, it looked like a storm might blow through. I closed my eyes, sipped my coffee, and listened to the sounds of boats and jet skis taking advantage of the lake before the rain came.

A gust of wind whipped through, strong enough that I needed to plant my feet. Then another even stronger and I had to grab the deck rail. The rain would be falling before I knew it. Might as well take care of returning those shirts and then hole up in my apartment for the rest of the day.

~~~

The village was packed with tourists. There was easily double the amount of yesterday's lunchtime crowd, and many of them were crossing the highway that led around Whispering Pines rather than taking the bridge. The village needed to erect a fence. I made a mental note to suggest that as I crept along at five miles per hour, tapping my fingers on the steering wheel and ready to stomp on the brakes if anyone darted out in front of me.

Reed's van was the only vehicle in the station lot. I lowered the back windows halfway for Meeka, grabbed the shirts, and entered the station through the backdoor. Reed was at his desk, working on the computer and nibbling his trail mix.

"You don't work here no more," he said. "You can come in the front door like everyone else. And you don't get to use the parking lot no more either."

"Will do," I answered. "Just returning my uniforms."

He tapped a pen on the corner of his desk. "Put them there."

I'd never paid much attention to Reed's appearance, his big attitude always got in the way. I took the time to now as I set the uniforms on the corner. There were freckles across the bridge of his nose. Time to dive in head first.

"What is it, O'Shea?"

"Flavia Reed is your mother."

"Yep."

"I also learned that Yasmine Long is your sister."

He jumped to his feet. "Who told you that?"

"Doesn't matter. You just confirmed the truth." He was sweating, but it wasn't hot, and I didn't think it was from my statement. Something was wrong. "You okay, Reed?"

He put both hands on his desk, as if he was dizzy and steadying himself. "Must be coming down with something. Started feeling sorta sick this morning."

He reached for his bag of trail mix. A bag with pink Valentine hearts on it. Pink hearts. Why was that detail important?

"Hang on." I yanked the bag away from him.

"What the hell, give me that."

He reached for it, and I pulled back.

"Give me one minute. I want to check something."

I pulled out my phone and flipped through the pictures I'd taken of the contents of Yasmine's tent. About twenty pictures through, I found what I was looking for. Among the takeout containers from various places around the village were two plastic zip-top bags with pink hearts on them.

"Cute bag," I said, trying to keep my heartrate steady.

Reed shrugged. "The sheriff says they're leftover from the Valentine celebration a few months ago."

Despite my efforts, my heart raced. "Sheriff Brighton gave you the trail mix?"

"Yeah, there were two bags sitting here on my desk last night." Reed put a hand to his stomach like it was upset. "We had a disagreement yesterday. Guess this is a peace offering or whatever. I ate one bag last night, kept one for today. You wanna give me that now?"

That must have been the discussion I witnessed when I saw them standing between Treat Me Sweetly and Shoppe Mystique yesterday. "What were you arguing about?"

Reed looked at me, clearly debating if he should tell me. He wiped the sweat from his forehead and gave in. "Two things. First, that I gave you access to the computers and you hacked my email."

"I didn't hack. You gave everyone the same password."

"Whatever."

"What was the other thing?" I asked.

"When Yasmine got here, Sheriff said I couldn't let anyone know she was my sister. He didn't even want me to talk to her."

"But you went to dinner with her at The Inn." I investigated the contents of the bag and froze.

"How do you know that?" Reed shook his head. "Never mind. Keko Shen. Yasmine told that freak Keko everything. Then Keko told you and who knows how many other people. Sheriff is pissed."

And I was getting way too close to the truth. "I need you to stay right here, Reed."

"I ain't going nowhere. Unlike some people, I got a job."

"This is serious, Martin. I think you've been poisoned."

His face went blank and a bead of sweat ran down from his temple.

I held the bag out. "I need to confirm something with

Morgan. Please, stay right there."

I sprinted to Morgan's shop and found it full of customers. Morgan was helping two teenage girls who were squealing over the amulets and talismans. This time, I couldn't wait patiently for her to finish with her customers. "I'm sorry to interrupt, this will just take a second." I pulled her off to the side and showed her the contents of the plastic bag, pointing out one ingredient in particular. "Is that what I think it is?"

Morgan's brow furrowed. "It's a castor bean. Where did you get that?"

"Martin Reed said the sheriff gave it to him."

"He ate them? They'll be quite bitter; didn't he wonder what they were?"

"How many does it take to poison someone?"

"Someone Martin size? Two or three is all it would take to bring on symptoms if not kill him."

"I've seen him eating different varieties of trail mix since I got here. He shovels it in by the handful. One or two beans in a full bag? He wouldn't even notice them." I glanced around us to make sure no one would hear. "I found two bags identical to this one in Yasmine's tent. I can't say for sure, but it's possible that the sheriff gave the same mix to Yasmine."

"You think the sheriff killed her?" Morgan asked, looking as shocked as I felt by this revelation.

"Maybe, I don't know. I need to get Martin to a doctor."

Chapter 33

THE HEALING CENTER IN WHISPERING Pines could deal with minor illnesses, sunburns, and bumps and bruises. They could even set a broken bone. They had no way, however, to deal with ricin poisoning. The nearest ambulance was an hour away. The nearest hospital of any decent size was also an hour away. Simple math told me to drive Reed myself. Morgan called ahead to let them know we were on the way.

I tapped the button on the voice recording app, clipped the phone into the holder in the vent between us, plugged in the charge, then sped for the hospital.

"I'm recording your statement," I said.

"Good," Reed croaked.

"Tell me the story. What was going on between you and Yasmine?"

"Nothing was going on between us. Like I told you, the sheriff and I argued because he thought I was telling people Yasmine was my sister. The sheriff and my mother said no one was supposed to know." Reed groaned. "Pull over. I'm gonna puke."

I did and when we were back on the road I said, "This is beyond family secrets now, Reed. Your sister is dead."

"Like I care."

The air left my lungs. Was he really that heartless?

"I didn't mean it like that," he said, leaning his head back against the headrest. "I barely knew her. I didn't even know Yasmine existed until she showed up here."

"Do you know the story? If you do, you should tell me." How should I say this without coming off coldblooded? "I think you'll be fine. But in all honesty —"

"I could die," he concluded, blinking rapidly. "I don't wanna die."

For the first time since meeting him, I felt a genuine connection to Martin Reed.

"I don't want you to die either. I also don't want the killer getting away with this. Tell me what you know."

He stared out the window for a few minutes. I said nothing, giving him time to think. Also, silence made people uncomfortable. If I waited long enough, he'd talk. Sure enough, after another minute, he rolled his head along the headrest to face me.

"It was almost a month ago. Mother and I were eating dinner and Yasmine showed up."

He got quiet again. This time I prompted. "You didn't know her?"

"Not a clue. She looked sorta like my mother, though. At the time, she was dressed in jeans, red Converse, and a Marquette University sweatshirt." He motioned with his hands at the back of his head. "Her hair was tied up in a knot, and she didn't have no makeup on. She didn't look nothing like the Yasmine that appeared a few days later."

"Did Flavia let her in the house?"

"Yeah. She came in, Mother offered her some tea, and they talked for a half hour or so."

"*They* talked," I echoed. "You didn't talk to her?"

"Not that night. They sat at the table and talked, while I cleaned up the dinner dishes. I never heard the words 'daughter' or 'sister.' Well, not in any way that made me think Yasmine was *my* sister. Mother asked about her own sister, my Aunt Reeva. That's where Yasmine lived, with Reeva. I knew I had a cousin, but I never met her. Or my aunt, for that matter. Mother and I have never left Whispering Pines. Reeva and Yasmine never visited."

I slowed for a deer crossing the road up ahead and then sped up again. Anxious to get Reed to the hospital, but equally anxious to give him time enough to tell his story. "What else did they talk about the night Yasmine arrived?"

He didn't answer me and when I looked over at him, his face was a grimace of pain.

"Reed? You all right?" I flipped on the windshield wipers as the expected rain started to fall.

He held up a finger for me to wait a minute. Finally, whatever pain he'd felt had passed.

"Yasmine said she was moving to the village because things weren't going so well for her in Milwaukee."

"Your mother told me that she was being sexually harassed because of her physical appearance," I said for the recording.

"Yeah," Reed agreed, his voice getting weaker.

As I'd told Flavia, Yasmine's appearance wasn't a justification for harassment, but at the same time I couldn't help but think that Yasmine had turned herself into this creature. If the stories of her car washing were true, and many people had corroborated them, she flaunted her pinup-girl sexuality. Oh, what a nasty circle she had created.

"She wanted to stay with us." Reed clutched his belly but kept talking. "Mother laughed and said not only did we not have room, Yasmine couldn't stay even if we did."

"That's when Yasmine went to the campground."

"Yeah. Aunt Reeva must've warned her that her plan might not work. She had camping stuff, the tent and sleeping bag, with her. She kept coming over every few days, trying to work her way onto Mother's good side."

I literally bit my tongue. I couldn't for one minute

imagine Flavia having a good side.

"Anyway," Reed started and then doubled over. "You better pull over again."

He threw up alongside the road as the rain, steady but not heavy, fell on him. I worried that the effect of the ricin was speeding up. Reed must have thought the same thing because he went right back to telling his story without a prompt from me.

"I saw Yasmine in the village one day." He barked out a little laugh. "She was washing someone's dog. She saw me coming her way and leaned in close, being all sexy for the men standing around watching her. She asked if her and I could get together and talk. I nodded and told her The Inn was quiet on Wednesday nights."

"That's how you ended up at The Inn together."

"Yeah. I wasn't even thinking about it being a public place. We could've met at the station or somewhere in the woods. Anyway, she said that for her twentieth birthday, Aunt Reeva told her the truth about who her parents were."

An icy tingle spread over my body. Whatever he was about to say, it was going to be big. I glanced at my phone to verify that it was still recording.

"You don't have the same parents?"

He blew out a breath, winced and moaned with pain, and shook his head.

"My parents are Flavia and Horace Reed. My father was the original sheriff. Constable Reed, the villagers used to call him. He died when I was three. Bear attack."

"I'm sorry," I said. "What a horrible way to die."

Reed frowned and nodded. "I don't remember him at all. Yasmine claimed, from what her mother told her, that after Father died, Karl . . . Sheriff Brighton would come over to check on us, help Mother with chores and such."

I had a sick feeling of where this was going.

"Karl's comforting got carried away one night and, well—"

"Sheriff Brighton is Yasmine's father?" Even though I knew that's what he was going to say, it was still a shock.

"That's what she claims." Reed stopped talking to fight off another wave of nausea.

"Hang in there, Martin. We've got about ten miles to go."

I depressed the accelerator as he nodded and spoke faster.

"I asked Mother if it was true. She didn't deny it but also wouldn't confirm it. I think it's sorta obvious though. All that talk about Yasmine being impure. She was born out of wedlock to a new widow and a married man."

"Who was Sheriff Brighton married to?"

"Reeva."

My mouth fell open. "Okay, let me get this straight. Flavia and Reeva are sisters. That's how Karl Brighton is your uncle."

"Right."

"Karl has an affair—"

"A one night thing," Reed corrected. "According to Yasmine."

"Karl and Flavia have a one night stand resulting in Yasmine. How long has Yasmine been living with Reeva?"

"Her whole life, I guess," Reed said. "I don't know the details, Yasmine wasn't too clear on them either, but she and Reeva ended up in a small town north of Milwaukee after Yasmine was born."

"Why didn't the sheriff go with them?"

"Couldn't tell you."

"Did Yasmine ever try to live with him?"

"Don't know. Nobody in town knew who Yasmine was."

"And when Yasmine came to town, looking to reunite with her parents, Flavia freaked out and poisoned her."

"No! Mother didn't do it. I told you, the sheriff gave me the trail mix. He must've given it to Yasmine, too."

If that was true, and assuming the sheriff knew the castor beans were in the mix, that would explain why he didn't investigate the break-in at Shoppe Mystique. If he stole the beans, he obviously wouldn't implicate himself, and even though it would have been believable that a local had done it, he wouldn't falsely accuse anyone. Easiest to blame it on a random tourist.

The hospital was just up the road; I could see it on the right.

"Sure hope they're ready with a treatment for you," I said, more to myself than Reed. "Morgan said she'd explain everything to them. She was going to call your mom, too."

Reed seemed to give in to the ricin then. He'd held it together long enough to make a statement. Thankfully, I was able to record the whole thing.

Two nurses were waiting at the ER doors for us. One with a gurney, the other with a clipboard and forms.

"Hang on," I said before they took Reed inside. "Martin, do you have any idea where Sheriff Brighton is now?"

"Haven't heard from him all day." His voice got weaker with each word. I had to lean in close to hear him. "Check his house. Or the shooting range. He likes to shoot when he's upset."

I gave him a few words of encouragement, and he thanked me. After I told the nurse with the clipboard everything I could about him, including the contact information for his mother, I headed back down the road to Whispering Pines to find the sheriff.

Chapter 34

SHERIFF BRIGHTON HAD TAKEN THE Glock and my tool belt from me yesterday. My personal Sig Sauer was in Madison. This meant I had no weapon. What I did have were Reed's keys. He gave them to me to lock his gun in the sheriff's credenza and to lock up the station before we went to the hospital. I had no intention of shooting Karl Brighton, and I didn't really even want to bring a weapon with me, but it would be irresponsible not to. There were tourists everywhere now. If the sheriff went off, I needed to protect them.

The rain had started falling harder, so I borrowed a raincoat from the back of the sheriff's office door. Before beginning the search for him, I stopped at Shoppe Mystique to give Morgan an update on Martin.

"Thank the Goddess you got him there in time," she said and then her smile faded. "You're distracted. What's going on?"

I hadn't planned to tell her yet, I didn't want her to worry, but someone should know where I was going. Just in case. I gave her a very quick recap of Reed's statement.

"I need to find Sheriff Brighton and bring him in."

Morgan sighed as though I'd just put the weight of the

world on her shoulders. "Jayne, you need to be careful. Take someone with you. What about Tripp? He'd surely help you look for him."

"Tripp is a civilian. I won't put him in danger. This isn't his fight."

"It's not yours either."

Her meaning came through loud and clear. In four words, she stopped me cold. "Because I'm an outsider."

"That's not at all what I meant." She looked as hurt by my words as I'd been by hers. "You've only been here a week and look at all you've gone through and done for the village. Everyone here loves you."

"Not everyone. Flavia clearly has issues with me. Donovan, too. A couple others were giving me the evil eye at the ritual Wednesday night." I shook my head. No time to go there right now. "Someone needs to track down the sheriff. I'm currently the most qualified."

"Do you have your spell bag?"

I patted my pocket. I may not believe, but it wasn't causing any harm to carry it around.

"And your amulet?"

I hooked my thumb beneath the chain around my neck to show her that the vial full of stone chips was still in place, too.

"Got anything else for me?" I was joking, but she plucked a necklace with a pewter pendant from the talisman collection. The pendant was about the size of a quarter, with a pentacle on one side and a "Y" with a trunk that went all the way to the top on the other.

"It's not a Y," Morgan said, reading my mind. "It's called Algiz. Not only does it symbolize beginnings, it's a powerful protection rune."

"As long as I don't wear it upside down, right?" Again, I was joking, but the look Morgan shot at me said she wasn't amused.

She held it in her palms, closed her eyes, and chanted

silently. Then, loud enough that I could hear, she said into her cupped hands, "Protect my precious Jayne from all who wish to do her harm."

As she slid the leather cord over my head and dropped it inside my T-shirt to join the amulet, I felt like I should say something. The only thing I came up with was, "Precious?"

With absolute sincerity, Morgan said, "Over this past week, I have come to care a great deal for you. Not only because of the bond between our grandmothers, but because you are a wonderful person. Our friendship has only just begun. There is much more for us to learn about each other." She blinked. "So, yes. Precious."

Not Jonah, my parents, my sister, or even my best friend had ever made me feel as loved and cared for as Morgan did at that moment.

"I'm not off to fight the Kraken, you know." I gave her a long hug. "I'm only going to track down an out of shape, fifty-something sheriff."

She fixed that look on me again. "Things work differently in Whispering Pines, you know that. Don't discount the sheriff because of physical appearance. And don't discount the danger here just because we're tucked into a quaint wooded hamlet instead of the streets of a big city."

Morgan Barlow may favor old-world ways, but she knew exactly what was going on in the real one.

After getting directions to the sheriff's house and promising to be careful, I gave Meeka the "Work" command, and we headed northeast to find Sheriff Brighton's place. The simple barn-red Cape Cod was surrounded by a grove of trees, a tall hedge, and really lovely gardens. Seemed the sheriff had a bit of green witch in him, too. Never would have guessed it. Thankfully, all that foliage provided great cover because a woman with a gun, peeking in all the sheriff's windows would probably make the neighbors nervous. After knocking on first the front and then the back doors, I decided he wasn't there. As we walked around the house on the fieldstone walkway, Meeka became interested in something tucked into the bushes by the front stoop.

I crouched down and found a harlequin doll dressed in pants and a tunic covered in a black-and-white diamond pattern. The traditional white china face had a strange, rosy-pink tint. The eyes were closed and the doll was positioned on its side with one hand to its chest.

Donovan claimed to only know who would die but not when. He claimed that he couldn't bring on his *visions*. What if he was lying about foretelling death? What if he was causing it? As quickly as Martin Reed had fallen off my suspects list, Donovan soared to the top of it.

That harlequin gave me reason enough to suspect that Sheriff Brighton was in danger. I clicked a couple of pictures of the doll, and then using a stone from the landscaping, I broke one of the small panes of glass on the front door and let myself in.

Chapter 35

"SHERIFF BRIGHTON? IT'S JAYNE. ARE you here, sir?"

I closed my eyes and strained my ears to hear any little moan, groan, or whimper. Not hearing a thing, I proceeded to search the sheriff's house, praying I wouldn't find another body.

The kitchen was spotless and empty, only a coffee cup in the dish drainer next to the sink. An outdoor sportsman magazine on the floor next to an easy chair was the only thing out of place in the living room. The sheriff wasn't in the bathroom or any of the three small bedrooms upstairs. He wasn't in the basement. The detached garage was empty except for his Tahoe, flat bottom aluminum fishing boat, and fishing gear. A nice-sized garden shed contained an abundance of gardening tools but, thankfully, no body. A check of the gardens surrounding the property also revealed nothing. The sheriff wasn't here.

Reed had also suggested the shooting range. I knew it was north of the Meditation Circle and that we were currently east of that.

Meeka and I followed the dirt path along the creek, and after a few minutes we came to Morgan's home. The house had looked dark, black or brown, at night. In the daylight, I saw that the two-story cottage was made from tan and brown fieldstones. A log fence surrounded the yard, every inch of which seemed to be filled with plants. A rooster crowed from somewhere within the garden. Very charming. I'd have to come back and explore the place more closely, but for now I had to find Sheriff Brighton.

The Meditation Circle also looked different in the daylight. Of course, the lack of witches in hooded robes gathered around a fire made a big difference.

"Something's wrong with that guy." A middle-aged man pointed into the Meditation Circle with one hand while holding a large umbrella above himself and the woman at his side with the other. "He's just sitting there. He won't talk or indicate if there's anything wrong."

I glanced through the trees to see Sheriff Brighton sitting on one of the many wood-plank benches surrounding the fire pit. His hands in his lap, his head bowed.

"I know him," I told the man. "I think I know what's wrong. Would you two do something for me?"

The man looked at the woman and they nodded uncertainly.

"Would you stand on the path over there?" I gestured toward a spot twenty yards away. "I just need you to guide people away from the area until I've talked to him."

The man nodded at the star emblem on my raincoat. "Are you a cop?"

"I am." All things considered, the fib was minor. I was a cop, just a currently unemployed one. "Everything's okay, but I need time to speak with him."

"How long?" The woman seemed hesitant to help.

"I'm not sure," I said. "That man is Sheriff Brighton. His daughter died last week, and one of our deputies was just taken to the hospital. He's having a hard time."

The woman placed her hand over her heart. "The poor man. We'll make sure you have the time you need."

As I walked with Meeka down the narrow path through the trees into the clearing, I stretched my neck side-to-side. I shook out my arms and blew out a long, slow breath. *You've got this, O'Shea. You're a good cop.* My furry partner looked up at me, her tail wagging as though encouraging me. I reached down to scratch her ears, thanking her for the encouragement.

"Sheriff Brighton?" I called quietly so as not to startle him. I took my phone out, and like I did with Reed's car ride testimony, started the recording app to capture whatever he said.

"I figured you'd find me here." He didn't move a muscle. "You're a topnotch detective, O'Shea."

"Just so you know," I said, holding my phone out to him, "I'm recording this conversation."

"Of course you are." He laughed softly and shook his head. "You had to get right in there, didn't you? Couldn't just stay out of trouble taking care of your grandparents' house. That's why I gave you the job, you know. To keep you busy so you wouldn't go sticking your nose into things that were none of your damn concern."

He'd underestimated me. My initial reaction to the sheriff was right: he was a sexist. And an ageist. Never expected that a twenty-six-year-old *girl* could expose everyone's secrets. I mentally scolded myself. This wasn't about me. *Stay on task, Jayne.*

"In a couple of weeks, Yasmine's death would have faded away. Everyone would have forgotten and she'd be a distant memory, that girl who died on the O'Shea property."

"She was your daughter." I maintained a safe distance and stayed on guard in case he attacked.

"She was my daughter." His voice broke. "And Flavia wouldn't let me claim her."

"Flavia? Why not?" I moved a step closer and held my phone toward him. I had to make sure every word was captured.

"She isn't the puritanical creature she appears to be. Everything she does or says must first be analyzed to see how it will come across to the coven. Because if the coven doesn't approve it . . ."

He let his words fade, and Flavia's words from yesterday sounded in my ears: *I wouldn't have anything so tarnished under my roof.*

"Yasmine wasn't approved," I said.

"I'll never know for sure since no one knew about her, but a child conceived the way Yasmine was? Our actions, mine and Flavia's, hurt my wife."

"And the one rule of Wicca, is to do no harm."

He nodded. "Flavia was sure breaking that rule would doom her chances at becoming the high priestess. Above all, Flavia Reed is an ambitious woman and would never put those ambitions in jeopardy because of a one-time mistake."

A one-time mistake? That's how he thought of his daughter? Poor Yasmine. My heart went out to her even more.

"Then why even have the baby? I mean, why not put her up for adoption. You could have claimed someone left her at the sheriff's station. You could have surrendered her to a hospital. Any number of things."

"Because her sister," his voice and face turned soft and gentle, "my sweet Reeva, is the most decent woman you could ever have the privilege to meet."

"She raised Yasmine."

"As if the girl was her own child."

"Why did they leave Whispering Pines?"

"Because of the scandal, of course." Sheriff Brighton looked down again. "I confessed to her what I'd done that very night. Flavia's husband, Horace, had been my best friend. If we'd been brothers by blood we wouldn't have been closer."

"Martin told me he died from a bear attack."

The sheriff sagged forward, his elbows resting on his

knees.

"That was my fault. Flavia had been in one of her moods that entire week. Horace wanted to go for a hike, lose himself in nature for a little while. I was supposed to go with him but at the last minute I told him I didn't want to go. I'd hadn't slept well the night before." Sheriff Brighton laughed, a sound laced with agony. "Because I wanted to take a nap, I wasn't there to save my best friend's life. If I had gone, the attack never would have happened. We would have been laughing and talking and making enough noise that the bear would have gotten scared off."

"You couldn't have known, Sheriff."

"No, I suppose not. I also couldn't know how deeply I would mourn his loss."

"That's how the night with Flavia happened?"

He nodded slowly. "We were comforting each other."

"Why did Reeva leave with the baby?" I repeated, we'd gotten off track.

"Like I said, I confessed to Reeva that same night. She needed a few days to meditate on what I'd done, and in the end, she forgave me." A single sob burst from him. "She said she loved me more than she hated what I'd done. The woman was . . . is a goddess. She also knew her sister. She knew Flavia was a driven woman and would never let a baby hold her back."

"Reeva decided immediately to raise Yasmine?"

"Immediately," he agreed, his head in his hands. "She said the child was mine and her sister's, which made the baby practically her own. In no time, word about what Flavia and I had done spread through the village. To this day, I have no idea who started it. I suppose either Reeva or Flavia could have confided to someone and they let it slip.

"No one knew about the pregnancy. Flavia was able to hide it for six months, but despite the shapeless dresses she wore, she couldn't hide it forever. We decided that Reeva would announce that she'd tried but couldn't stay married to me after what I'd done. The two of them left together, Flavia making sure everyone understood that she was going to help her sister get settled in a new home and that she'd be back."

The acid in his voice made it clear, 'we decided' translated directly to 'Flavia told us.' What had she held over her sister's head to make Reeva leave her husband?

"Flavia stayed away until the baby was born," I said. "Why didn't you leave, too?"

"To maintain the secret. Flavia insisted I stay. She wanted me to absorb the scrutiny and deflect it off her, she said. If I had left with Reeva, the villagers would constantly ask her about her sister and me. She said she couldn't keep reliving it."

"You let her bully you." What a witch. And not in the Wiccan sense. "You stayed away from your wife and your daughter for twenty years because Flavia couldn't admit her sin?"

He held his hands out, palms up. "She made it clear, she'd accuse me of rape. She said she'd tell a story so damning, I'd go to prison for years. Neither Reeva nor I doubted that."

"You accepted Flavia's prison instead." I almost felt bad for him. "What about Reeva? If she was willing to go along with this, she must have loved you a great deal. She had to live all those years without her husband."

"Life doesn't always turn out the way you plan."

They could have been together. All three of them. He and Reeva could have disappeared with the baby and no one would have been the wiser. Pointing that out to him now would be cruel and futile, he could only see the one option.

"All right," I said and took another step closer, "let's fast forward to a few weeks ago. Yasmine returns to the village looking to connect with her mother and brother."

"Beautiful girl, wasn't she?"

"She was," I said slowly, noting the hairline crack in his thick armor. The sheriff had loved his daughter. "Flavia turned her away, and because there's this secret to maintain, you turned her away as well."

"I'm not proud of it, Jayne. She's my daughter."

"She *was* your daughter." No more nice-cop. I was pushing for a confession now. "You killed your daughter."

"I did. I murdered Yasmine Long. I gave her trail mix with castor beans in it. Just like I gave to Martin." He looked to me. "Did you get to him in time?"

I'd expected him to argue, to deny, to put up some kind of a fight for his innocence. Not only did he confess immediately, he said it so loudly and clearly, the couple guarding the entrance probably heard him.

The rain started again. I pulled up the hood on the raincoat as Meeka huddled close to me, her little body shivering. "Martin is at the hospital. Hopefully they can help him."

"Good." He bobbed his head up and down. "Good."

"Why kill her? You could have sent her away. You could have simply given her enough money to start a new life somewhere."

He turned to me then, his bloodshot eyes stared right through me. "Reeva and I were so happy. Funny, isn't it, the damage a couple of stupid choices can create."

He was preaching to the choir on that one. His bad decisions resulted in his best friend's death, a baby, and a broken marriage. Little too close for comfort there.

"The method you chose, ricin poisoning, it wasn't a guarantee of death. Martin will likely be fine."

He nodded again but said nothing.

"You didn't want to do it, did you, Sheriff? For whatever reason, you decided that killing Yasmine was the answer, but you weren't committed to it. You wanted to give her a chance." I waited, but he didn't reply. "Did Flavia have anything to do with Yasmine's death? Is she the one who, once again, made the decision regarding her?"

"No," he responded too quickly.

I've never seen such sloppy work, Flavia had said that first morning I saw her.

Don't worry. I'm taking care of things, the sheriff had replied

That's how you take care of things? Flavia responded.

For the recording I restated, "You're telling me that Flavia Reed is one hundred percent innocent of the death of Yasmine Long?"

"Flavia had no idea I was going to give her the beans."

Maybe she didn't know castor beans would be the method, but Flavia was not innocent of Yasmine's death. Sheriff Brighton was a broken man, anyone could see that, and Flavia was the puppeteer manipulating his strings.

"You need to be careful, Jayne. You don't understand the power and control Flavia has."

A shiver wracked my body, and I pressed my fingers to the amulet and pendant beneath my shirt. That was almost verbatim the warning Sugar had given me. Then something else the sheriff had said hit home.

"What did you mean when you said Flavia is a driven woman?"

He reached into his jacket pocket. In a blink, I switched my phone to my left hand and unsnapped the strap over the gun with my right. Meeka whined and hid behind my legs.

"All she wants is to become high priestess," he said. "Reeva would invite her and Horace over for dinner and that's all we'd hear. 'I'm destined to be high priestess. The coven needs me. The village needs me.' No wonder Horace went on so many hikes. Problem was, the position was filled."

My blood chilled in my veins. "Who was high priestess, Sheriff?"

"At the time, Dulcie Barlow. She was your grandmother's best friend, Morgan's grandmother. I was a child, but I remember her well." He smiled fondly. "She used to slip bits of mugwort into my shoes, claiming it would make my legs stronger."

"What happened to Dulcie?"

The sheriff gave me a sad smile. "She died in her sleep. That was a shock for the entire village. Dulcie was never sick, not a thing wrong with her."

My instincts tingled. More herbal foul play?

"After Dulcie passed, Morgan's mother Briar became our high priestess. She guided us for the next twenty years. Everyone loves Briar."

"Loves? She's still alive?"

"She is, but she suffered a stroke. She can get around but not easily, and she has a hard time speaking. She spends her days at the cottage." He pointed east. "Lives with Morgan. Stays busy tending the gardens and making the wreaths Morgan sells in her shop."

My hand went to the handle of the Glock as the sheriff withdrew something from his pocket. From where I stood, eight feet away, it looked like a small amber-colored vial about the size of a double-A battery. Herbs of some kind?

"What's that in your hand, Sheriff?"

"Because of her condition," he continued, ignoring my question, "Briar stepped down as high priestess, and your dear grandmother stepped up."

"When was that?"

"About six months ago. Lucy was a faithful follower of Wicca, but that's all she wanted to be. A follower. Briar begged her and when the rest of the coven heard, we agreed Lucy was the perfect one to lead us."

And three months later, Gran was dead.

"Sheriff, what are you telling me? Did Flavia kill Dulcie and attempt to kill Briar? Did she murder my grandmother?"

Morgan was high priestess now. Was she next on the hit list?

"I've never been able to gather any proof that she did."
He opened the little vial and poured two capsules into his
hand.

I froze. "What are those, sir?"

"Maybe I didn't try hard enough."

"There were a lot of years between Dulcie's death and
Briar's stroke six months ago." I couldn't take my eyes off
those capsules. "Did something significant happen six
months ago, Sheriff?"

"I'm not a strong person, Jayne." He looked straight into
my eyes, his own heavy with grief. "Dig into this, not that
you'll be able to stop yourself. The proof is out there; I just
could never build a strong enough case. Be careful. Let
Morgan and Briar protect you."

These sounded a little too much like last words.

"Sheriff, please. Give me those pills." I stepped closer to
him, my hand outstretched.

"Most in the coven are good. You'll need to be wary of a
few." He shook the pills in his palm as though preparing to
take them. "If anyone can catch her, you can."

I dropped my phone and lurched forward, desperate to
strip the capsules from him, but I was a heartbeat too late.
He popped the pills in his mouth and bit down.

With his hands covering his face he mumbled, "I'm so
sorry, Yasmine. I wish I could've been a real father for you."
He looked at me. "Tell Reeva I've never stopped loving her."

Then he clutched at his chest and fell to the ground.

Chapter 36

I DROPPED TO SHERIFF BRIGHTON'S side and felt for a pulse. It was there but faint. The distinct aroma of almonds wafted from him. The capsules must have contained cyanide.

The man and woman were, thankfully, still at their post along the path.

"Is he okay now?" the woman asked as I ran up to them.

"No, he just collapsed," I said. "I don't want to leave him and there's no cell service here. Would you hurry to the village and call for help? Go to Ye Olde Bean Grinder, the coffee shop. Violet will help you. Ask her to contact the state police."

I did my best to make this sound urgent, but the sheriff was gone the second the cyanide hit his system. There was nothing that would have saved him out there in the middle of the woods, an hour away from serious medical care. The couple agreed and took off right away.

I returned to his side, thoughts of what I could have done differently swirling in my mind. I'd been standing right at his side. I should have taken the vial the second he pulled it from his pocket. A man was dead, ultimately because I couldn't keep my nose out of things.

That might not be the truth, though. Yasmine's death had been eating him up, I could see that. Uncovering her murder had been the right thing for Yasmine and the village . . . and myself.

Sitting on one of the nearby benches, I couldn't help but notice the position of the sheriff's body. On his side, one hand to his chest, his skin cherry-pink. Just like the harlequin.

Donovan was off my list again. Sheriff Brighton had committed suicide in front of me; Donovan had nothing to do with it. Still, these visions he claimed to have, his ability to foretell a person's death, didn't sit well with me. Whispering Pines was a great tourist destination. I'm sure that for many years it was even a great place to live. No, it was still a great place to live, but like anywhere it had a dark underbelly. Donovan, Flavia, and who knew how many others were a part of that darkness.

"I'm right, aren't I?" I asked . . . no one. Guess I was talking to the trees surrounding the meditation circle. "There's some cleaning up to do in this village, isn't there?"

An hour later, the state police arrived. Dr. Bundy and an ambulance shortly after that. The ME pronounced Sheriff Brighton dead and took his body away after the police had collected all that they needed from the scene. I led one of the officers to the sheriff's station where I gave him a full statement. Then I played the recordings of Martin Reed's statement and Karl Brighton's confession.

"Good work, Ms. O'Shea," the officer said. "Not many would think to record the conversations. Everything else looks clean. You'll be in Whispering Pines for a while?"

I didn't have the deputy assignment taking up my time now, so I could get started on packing up the house. Still, "I'll be here for at least a month. Maybe longer. Not sure yet."

He took down my contact information and promised

that since Whispering Pines no longer had a sheriff or deputy on duty, he and his fellow officers would wander through to check on us until someone was hired.

~~~

Tripp and I sat on the sundeck, sipping beer and munching takeout from the Grapes, Grains, and Grub Pub. Well, Tripp munched. I didn't have much of an appetite. Meeka lay next to me on the lounge chair. I rested a hand on her chest, letting her steady breathing soothe me as I told Tripp what had happened with Martin Reed and the sheriff.

"Wasn't that kind of dangerous for you?" he asked while investigating a chicken wing for more meat.

"I appreciate your concern," I said, "but in the realm of dangerous situations, this was maybe a three. The sheriff wasn't going to hurt me."

Tripp frowned and slowly grew angry. I tensed, preparing for the kind of lecture Jonah used to give me about finding a safer job.

"Why . . ." he began and paused. "How could he leave his wife and daughter that way?"

Once again, the abandoned twelve-year-old was before me.

"As an officer of the law," I said, "Karl Brighton swore to protect and serve. I think that meant more to him than I gave him credit for. Something bad is going on around here, has been for a while. I think he knew Reeva and Yasmine were safe, probably safer in Milwaukee than here, so he chose to stay and protect the villagers from Flavia."

At least I assumed he meant Flavia. Even at the end, he wouldn't implicate her.

"Maybe he saw his family more than we think," Tripp said, his expression hopeful. "Maybe he visited them on holidays or went to see Yasmine in school plays?"

"Maybe." My heart ached for Tripp. "You really want to

find out what happened to your mom, don't you?"

"I do."

"Do you ever think about looking for your dad? I mean, you moved a lot, right? Maybe he's been looking for you."

"I agree that someone needs to protect the village." Tripp slumped into his chair, ignoring my comment about his dad. "Something feels . . . off around here."

He was right about that, and it wasn't just the people. The lake had turned a deep, moody blue and the trees swayed slowly, as though trying to soothe themselves. I understood now why Gran said the lake had a personality. The trees did, too.

"It's probably because in the last week two people died by unnatural causes," I said.

Of course, after talking with the sheriff at the Meditation Circle, death by unnatural causes might be more common around here than the good villagers of Whispering Pines realized.

Headlights appeared from around the curve of the driveway, and Morgan's little black Fiat pulled up between the Cherokee and Tripp's old red Ford. She must've seen the fire burning in the pit on the sundeck because she headed straight for us.

"What's she doing here?" Tripp asked.

"No clue." I'd stopped by her shop after the state police left to tell her about the sheriff. Even though I was fine, she insisted on consecrating me with gardenia oil, claiming it would not only protect but bring me peace and harmony. It smelled pretty. That made me feel peaceful.

"I just came from a council gathering," Morgan announced when she was halfway up the stairs.

"I thought you did rituals at midnight," I said.

She shook back her long raven-black hair, her earrings jangling. "Not a coven gathering. This was an emergency council meeting. We had something urgent to discuss and vote on."

I shifted positions, Meeka, limp like a ragdoll, moved along with me. She hadn't left my side since Sheriff Brighton dropped to the ground. She was used to finding cadavers, not watching people become them.

"What thing?" I asked.

"With the passing of Karl Brighton," Morgan began, "there are only twelve on the council. We need an odd number and would like you to join us."

"Me?" I asked. "There must be a better option, someone who's more familiar with the village and the locals."

"That's exactly why we want you," Morgan said. "We feel that someone with fresh ideas, who isn't so ingrained with the inner-workings of the village, would be the best fit for Whispering Pines' future. You haven't been here in more than fifteen years, yet look how much you care about what happens here."

"She's just nosey," Tripp teased.

"That's true," Morgan agreed and grinned. "Seriously, you and I both know that there have been some negative things going on. The villagers feel that energy, too, and they don't like it."

"I feel it," Tripp scooted to the edge of his chair. "There's been a strange vibe."

"When do you think it started," Morgan asked.

He considered the question but not for long. "When Yasmine came to town."

Morgan nodded and looked at me. "If you hadn't been here to figure this out, who knows what else would be brewing right now. The council needs you, and I want you there."

She didn't need to work so hard to convince me. I tended to screw things up, but it seemed like this time my choices worked out well.

"Just curious," I said, "was the vote unanimous?"

Morgan shook her head. "You know there are some here who aren't in favor of your presence. If it helps, some members whom you haven't even met voted yes immediately. The fortune tellers, Cybil and Effie, as well as Creed and Janessa, two of the carnies."

I hadn't met any of the circus people, yet. A lot had happened this week, but there was a lot more about Whispering Pines I didn't know.

"Something else you'll enjoy," Morgan said. "The vote was in your favor even though Flavia got two votes."

"Why did she get two?" Tripp asked.

"The council has thirteen members," she said, "both for wide representation of villager interests and to insure there is never a tie. Years ago, Flavia decided someone should hold special privilege in case of special circumstances."

"Let me guess," I said. "She said she should hold that privilege? Being that she thinks she's mayor and all."

"She what?" Tripp asked.

"Tell you later," I said.

"We never thought the day would come." Morgan shook her head and then flashed a dazzling grin at me. "Well? What do you think?"

Tripp gave me a wink and a nod.

"Okay," I said, "you've got a new council member."

Morgan placed her palms together and clapped her fingers, then leaned down to give me a hug. When she pulled back, she asked, "You're still wearing the amulet and talisman, right?"

My smile faltered. "I am."

She nodded. "Keep them on."

I watched as the taillights of the Fiat disappeared down the driveway, wondering what I had just agreed to.

"Village council, hey?" Tripp said. "That's kinda cool."

"I guess." Sheriff Brighton's and Sugar's warning about digging too deep sounded in my ears. "Hope it's the right decision."

"Stop doubting yourself." He got quiet and stared into the fire as he finished his plastic cup of potato salad.

"What are you so deep in thought about?"

He hesitated before admitting, "Turning the house into a bed and breakfast. I know I shouldn't be thinking about it because it's none of my business, but you know how perfect it would be. Seven bedrooms, room for eighteen. It's perfect for couples or small families. We could also rent out the whole place to larger groups."

"We?" I laughed. "Maybe you forgot, but I don't know anything about running a B&B. I could probably handle making reservations. I could clean the rooms and bathrooms. I could—"

"Hire me," Tripp said. "You could hire me, and I'll take care of everything."

His request took me by surprise, and I responded with my best Southern belle, "Why, Mr. Bennett, is that a proposal?"

Instantly, he flushed bright red. Was Tripp Bennett actually embarrassed? I hadn't seen him unsure of a single thing in the past week. He really was serious about this.

"No one else here will give me a job." He jumped to his feet and paced around the sundeck. "I'm a really organized person; I know I can run a B&B. I can repair just about anything. I can cook."

"You can definitely cook," I agreed.

"I was thinking," he continued as though it was a done deal, "I could turn the attic into living quarters for me. Or I'll stay in my popup. That's fine, too."

"You clearly haven't experienced a northern Wisconsin winter yet."

"The attic it is, then."

"Tripp—"

"I'm sorry. I've crossed way over the line."

I stood, placed a hand on each of his arms, and guided him to a chair. "Sit. Stay."

Meeka lifted her head and dropped it again when she realized I wasn't talking to her. I went inside and came back out with the landline phone.

"Who are you calling?" Tripp asked, confused.

"Hi, Mom," I said into the phone.

"What's wrong?" she asked. "It's something with the house, isn't it?"

"Nothing's wrong, but I am calling about the house." I spent the next five minutes proposing the possibility of turning Gran's house into a B&B while also trying to ignore the fact that Tripp's gaze was locked on me.

"No," she said.

"Will you at least think about it?" She had given me five minutes. If she really hated the idea she would have said no four minutes and forty-five seconds ago.

"You know your father wants to be done with that house and that town."

"Neither of you would have to come here," I reiterated, for the third time. I looked at Tripp and winked. "The guy I hired to do repairs is really interested in running it."

"And you'll do what?" Mom asked. "Float around on the lake all day like a lady of leisure?"

"Of course not." I'd momentarily forgotten that I didn't have a job. I'd let Yasmine Long's murder occupy so much of my time, it had felt like I was still working. "How about I put some numbers together on what we could get in a sale versus how much we could get by renting the place out? If I do that, will you talk to Dad and give it serious consideration? Because I'm seriously proposing this."

She hummed for a few seconds and then blew out a deep exhale. "Fine. Put your numbers together. I've got to get back to work."

I hung up and Tripp jumped to his feet.

"What did she say?"

"She agreed to talk to Dad if the numbers look good. That's all I can do for now."

He pulled me into a hug then released me and stepped back.

"Sorry. I just . . . I really don't want to leave here."

"I know." I glanced out at the lake, dead calm after the day's earlier rain. "I'm starting to think I'd like to stay here, too."

"Or you," he blurted.

"What?"

"I don't want to leave you either."

I prayed I was misinterpreting that statement. I had enjoyed every moment with him over the last week, but I couldn't handle anything more than friendship right now. The pain of Jonah was still too fresh, my life a little too unsteady.

"I don't want you to leave either." I agreed and then pointedly added, "Good friends are hard to find."

He held my gaze for a little too long then nodded. "Yes, they are."

"I'll start putting together that plan for a B&B tomorrow. I'm going to need really good numbers if I have any shot at convincing my parents."

"You say 'I' like you're in this alone." Tripp handed me my beer. "I intend to be right here with you every step of the way."

One week ago, I drove into Whispering Pines with the goal of relaxing and trying to figure out how to get my life back on track. A week later, I hadn't done either of those things. I was still here, though, and would be for a while, so I still had time. For the first time in quite a while, I felt a thrill of excitement for my life and my future.

Acknowledgments

I had the best time researching and writing FAMILY SECRETS, but I'll be honest, I stressed over this one. This is my first novel-length work in a genre that I have fallen in love with, and I worried that I wouldn't get it right. I can't tell you what a relief it was when early feedback came in with glowing results. That praise has taken me from stressed to over-the-top excited to share this new world with you!

Because books never come together on their own, I have numerous people to thank. First, to a friend so dear she's practically a sister, Rachael Dahl. For patiently listening to my thoughts, reading attempts along the way, and for always being honest when I need to hear the truth. Thank you, girl!

My always awesome critique partners: Amy Laundrie, Susan Berk Koch, Donna O'Keefe, and Deborah Lynn Jacobs. Your advice continues to make me a better writer. I'm so grateful for you all.

To Erin Finigan, BJ Thompson, Teresa Kovach, and Rika Terblanche for hunting down those nasty typos for me. Thank you so much!

Troy Leibfried, for answering my many cop questions. Thanks for helping me bring Jayne to life.

For my fans, I *love* hearing from you and learning that my characters mean as much to you as they do to me. Don't ever hesitate to drop me a line.

And as always, to Paul. This time, because you never once worried when I started talking about ways to kill people. I love you with all my heart!

Dear Reader,

Thank you for reading FAMILY SECRETS, book one in the Whispering Pines series. I hope you had a good time and will come back to visit Jayne in the rest of the series. Word of mouth is the very best promotion. Please consider leaving an honest review with your favorite vendor or on Goodreads. It doesn't have to be long, a sentence or two is great! Not only will you help other readers find my work, you'll help me to be able to continue writing more books!

To connect with me, go to my website www.Shawn-McGuire.com to find all my social links including how to sign up for my newsletter and be the first to know about new releases.

Peace and love,
Shawn

Made in the USA
Columbia, SC
20 June 2020